PRINCE OF VEILS

Lawrence Anderson

Copyright © 2019 by Lawrence Anderson

Scheherazade Publishers supports the right to free expression and the value of copyright. The purpose of copyright is to encourage writers and artists to produce the creative works that enrich our culture.

The scanning, uploading, and distribution of this book without the express written consent is a theft of the author's intellectual property. If you would like permission to use material from the book (other than for review purposes), please contact ScheherazadePublishers@gmail.com. Thank you for your support of the author's rights.

First North American Edition: June 2019

Originally published in United States by Scheherazade Publishers.

The publisher is not responsible for websites (or their content) that are not owned by the publisher. This includes all social media sites maintained by the author.

ISBN 978-0-578-22559-3

Printed in the United States of America

CHAPTER ONE

Step one in robbing a bank was to scope out the location. This was that first step.

The heat and humidity of the summer day made Daniel miserable as he waited on a park bench. Even with the shade of the trees surrounding his seat, he was suffocating. He fanned his shirt and glared at strangers that passed by.

Daniel hadn't sleep very well. His mind had continued to jump between different scenarios of bank robberies. He dreamed of situations where him and Junior both died, and the Death cards presided over his funeral, each cloaked member taking a turn throwing dirt onto his casket as it was lowered into the ground.

Every hour, Daniel awoke with a sense of dread and a shimmer of sweat, only to fall asleep and experience a different dream with the same outcome. So when he opened his eyes the final time and refused to go back to sleep, he was groggy and tired.

The morning was uneventful. The first few weeks after being laid off, Daniel had spent the time he would have normally been at work to fill out job applications or contact job placement agencies. But his optimism had declined, and there were days when he completed one application while muttering about hopelessness. Today was such a day. He noticed job search sites usually contained the same dead-end options that he wasn't qualified for or had already applied, so he was in a period of waiting for a callback. Sometime before noon, Junior texted him and said they should meet at a local park north of downtown in the Design District. Daniel had questions in response, but Junior was being evasive, so three bus transfers and a train ride later, Daniel sat at the park waiting on Junior.

Twenty minutes after arriving at the park, he saw Junior approaching in jeans, a long sleeve white shirt and neon colored work vest. Even with all those layers of clothes, Junior didn't seem to be bothered by the heat. Having to work in the elements daily had given him an uncanny immunity to all the inclement weather conditions and that irritated Daniel even further. But the annoyance faded when he noticed Junior carrying two bottles of water.

"I knew you would be hot," Junior said.

"Why are we meeting here?"

"We need to start *casing* the joint?"

"Isn't this a little obvious? Coming so close to the place?" Daniel's eyes darted to the bank across the street from the park. He had failed to notice he had chosen the perfect seat to watch the bank. It wasn't directly in front of the bank but at an angle, and the foot traffic often obscured the view.

"In the movies," Junior said. "They always start off the planning by watching the bank. Seeing the activity and routines."

"We're really going through with this?"

"Of course. You saw what the tarot cards said. We do this, or the world ends."

"That's not-"

"We gotta save the world. My kids need a world to live in."

"Junior, I think last night it might have been the alcohol talking. I was thinking maybe we could have a more rational discussion once you sobered up."

"Well, I'm not any more sober now than I was last night."

"Wait... You drink on the job?"

"You don't?"

Daniel chuckled and shook his head. "I had nightmares about ways this could go wrong. My *spider senses* are telling me that this is going to end tragically."

"Or... your mind is showing you ways to avoid getting caught. Your voodoo is helping us be successful. *Use* that. Gotta look at the glass as half full."

"Junior, this is stupid. We're not thieves."

"Look, Daniel. I'm not sure what you saw in those cards last night, but you gotta stop fighting this. The only way we're going to achieve success in this is to go in wholeheartedly. If we half-ass this or if we're timid, then we're going to fail. Even your mind knows that you need to be fully committed."

"How can I be fully committed when I don't want to do this?"

"Hell if I know, but you need to figure it out." The tone in Junior's voice was beginning to slide from slightly irritated to tinted with anger. "You're worried about getting caught but doubting and trying to talk me out of this is what's going to blow this up."

Daniel crossed his arms and stared ahead, refusing to look in his friend's direction. Junior lowered his voice.

"I need full dedication on both of our parts for us to get this done. If you're showing doubt then that's going to make me feel like I can't rely on you. And that's going to increase my chances of failing, and it's just an avalanche of failure at that point. I need you bulldozing this shit with me."

"It's so hard. I'm not a criminal, and everything in me is fighting against this."

"No, it's not. Everything in you is fighting to win. Think about it. Your voodoo is showing you how to avoid getting caught. It knows what we need to do."

"Right now, I feel the need to talk you out of this."

"What else do you feel?"

"What?"

"Tell me what else is there. I know you have to be a clusterfuck of emotions because I'm a clumberfuck of emotions. Besides fear, what else do you feel?"

Daniel took a moment to reflect, the silence between the two unnoticed as the park's crowd attended to their activities. A female jogger ran past with her dog, and Junior became distracted as he watched her.

"I feel like we need to be here."

"What do you mean?" Junior was still staring at the woman.

"I mean, I don't think it's coincidence that I chose this spot that is perfect for *casing the joint*. Maybe my voodoo is helping us."

"It would be helpful if you could use your voodoo intuition to help us…" He trailed off.

"So you're right. If I'm going to do this, I need to be all the way in. Maybe that's what my intuition is trying to tell me. We will have a better chance at succeeding because I have my voodoo and you have that *thing* that you do."

"Puppetmaster."

"Yeah, *that*. So we can make this happen. One of the things I learned in my business class is that 98% of new businesses fail due to improperly planning. So we need to plan— Junior, really? That woman cannot be that damn beautiful for you to be this distracted by her."

Junior shook his head. "No, I'm looking at that woman that just came out the bank. The one crossing the street in the black and tan business suit. I think I know her."

"Know her from where?"

"A long time ago. I think she's coming this way."

"She's wearing a name tag. Fuck! Does she work at the bank? We should probably leave before she sees us."

"Fatima!" Junior said.

"Or call her over. Whichever seems best."

"Junior, is that you?"

"Hey, how are you doing? I haven't seen you in forever."

Junior and the woman embraced and passers-by flowed around them as if they were an obstruction in a river.

"What have you been up to?" she asked.

"Nothing much. Working and paying bills. Same shit, different day. This is crazy because I don't ever come to this side of town. I'm just here meeting with my buddy. Have you met Daniel?"

Fatima allowed Daniel a brief acknowledgment of salutation before returning her gaze back to Junior. Daniel was used to becoming background noise around his friend. Junior was visually appealing to women, and this always seemed to overshadow the mundane averageness of Daniel's facial features. But at this moment, he was grateful for the indifference. The less she remembered about his appearance, the better.

"Well," she said. "You're still looking good, I see."

"Not as good as you. I was just asking Danny who that beautiful young lady was crossing the street. I couldn't take my eyes off of you. Then I saw it was you. What are the chances?"

This isn't a coincidence, Daniel thought to himself.

"I see you still lay it on thick. You don't have to flatter me with compliments."

"I can't help it. You were always the one that got away. I have to take a chance and shoot my shot now that I have you here."

"Oh? You're trying to score some points?"

"I'm trying to do more than that. I'm trying to be your trophy husband."

Fatima laughed.

"You working at the bank, making big money as the — what does your badge say? *Bank manager!* I'm sure you need a fine gentlemen on your arm to take care of."

"I can't believe this. Handsome, charming and still a borderline narcissist. It's sad that I can't tell if you're joking or not."

"I'm as serious as a heart attack."

A moment followed where Junior locked eyes with her, and she couldn't look away. Daniel had seen this theatrical performance before. It was Junior's closure. Women would fall into his hazel eyes and start to see what could be. It was always at this moment that the women Junior preyed on would start considering their chances of being hurt by pursuing anything with him and would that hurt be worth it. Junior's body language and demeanor said he wasn't one to settle down. Fatima definitely had to know what this was. Since they already knew each other, Daniel was sure that she had ridden this roller coaster before.

Daniel had very little experience with reading auras. But he could see her opinion of Junior teetering on a tipping scale.

She rolled her eyes, decision made. "Sure you are, Junior. I know how serious you can be."

"Fatima, I really am serious. I really do consider you to be the one. I think about you almost every day if not twice a day. My mom used to tell me that I would know when I found the one. I think I knew, but I didn't know how to handle it."

"Really, Junior? This is what you want to feed me?" Fatima chuckled and turned to walk away.

Junior grabbed her arm and stepped around her. They faced each other.

"What do you want me to say? I'm trying to set things right."

"You don't have to say anything. We dated, and it didn't work out. I don't have time to pick up what you're trying to put down."

"I'm not trying to play games. I liked you. We had fun together, right?"

"It was entertaining."

"It was more than entertaining for me. I genuinely enjoyed being around you. I'll admit that what I was saying earlier was bullshit, but that's because I miss you. I want to get back what we had. Even if it's not serious."

"What did we have? Because if I remember-"

"We had fun. A lot of fucking fun. Am I right?"

"Yes, it was fun."

"Are you single? Are you seeing anybody?"

"I'm in between husbands right now."

Junior smiled. "So let's have fun until… until it's not fun anymore."

Fatima paused and stared Junior in his eyes, waiting for him to look away. Daniel wasn't sure what questions she was asking herself, but he could see the internal dialogue dancing across her facial expressions. He could also see when she reached a decision.

"That's all it's going to be is fun," she said. "When I say it's over, it's over."

"That's all I'm asking for."

After taking another moment, Fatima gave him her phone number and told him to text her later. A look of accomplishment sparked across Junior's face as he watched her walk away.

"Well," Daniel said. "We definitely won't be going for *that* bank."

"Yes, we will."

"What? We can't rob…" Daniel looked around to make sure nobody was listening and lowered his voice. "We can't rob that bank. You *know* her. That's gonna get us caught."

"This is perfect. We were here to get information about the bank. What better way to get information than an inside employee? A bank manager, at that."

"Are you crazy? It's one thing for me to join you in this stupidity, but you think you have enough charisma to convert that lady from honest woman to criminal?"

"I don't need to convert her. I just need information from her. I think we can get that from her without her knowing the reason."

"So you're using her?"

"Nah, I don't use people."

"You are intentionally pursuing her and giving her hopes of a reunion in order to get something from her that improves your personal standing. That's the definition of using."

"You act like she's not getting something out of it too. You heard her agree to have fun with me. Why are you attacking me about this?"

"I'm not attacking you. Junior, listen." Daniel took a breath to calm down. "This entire idea is ludicrous enough. Have you even thought about the fact that we are planning a crime?"

"I know exactly what we're doing."

"Well, I don't. This whole scenario is just a snowball rolling down a hill."

"We just talked about you doubting this."

"I can't help it. It's in my nature. I'm going to critique and second guess and foreshadow every chance that I get."

"That's going to get annoying as shit, bro."

Daniel shrugged, and they stared at each other. Junior looked away and watched the crowd rush past, individuals pushing forward to get back to their mundane lives. A woman in a black skirt and green blouse gazing up from her cell phone to avoid running into other people before returning her eyes back downward. A man in khakis and a white polo shirt glanced down at his watch with a sense of urgency and cussed at nobody in particular. A young woman pushed a stroller and tried to corral two other children so they could cross the busy street. All the individuals Junior saw were hurried or stressed. And that's the life he wanted to escape. He wanted to not have to worry about making an appointment or how he was going to have to organize his overdue notices to avoid disconnection. Robbing a bank was his way to happiness.

"I'm going back to work. We can talk later. Maybe figure out how we can make these abilities work in our favor."

The mention of voodoo reminded Daniel of something he wanted to bring up with Junior.

"Hey, that shop where you got the tarot cards," Daniel said. "Where is it?"

"Over off Kline by the rec center. Why?"

"I'm interested in getting more information on the cards."

•   •   •   •   •

Daniel had been visiting *The Grey* for as long as he could remember. Even before he even knew what it was called. As a child, his visits usually occurred while he was asleep. He assumed he had drifted off if it happened while he was awake. But *The Grey* wasn't a dream. It was a separate reality from the real world that only he and others like him could access. It was what the voodoo community referred to as 'blood of voodoo' or 'voodoo's essence'.

If anybody were to ask Daniel to describe *The Grey*, he would tell them that it was a shadow of the living world where everything was muted. Colors weren't as bright. Sounds weren't as rich. And smells weren't as delicious. Everything was… grey.

Even the layout in *The Grey* was different than the real world. The streets were familiar and the houses well known, but they didn't mirror the real world. But when Daniel entered *The Grey* it was always from the same house; a structure that grew in size as he grew in age. As a child, the house had resembled his childhood home. Over time, it had morphed into something greater, collecting various parts from other places he had lived. The other dull toned houses on the street had changed but not as gradually. Each visit, a new house evolved into a different style. Some maintained an old rustic stature that reminded Daniel of homes from the Victorian era. Others were more modern and fit the image of what he was used to in the real world.

In the beginning, the only activity Daniel remembered from *The Grey* was wandering around. He had roamed around exploring but never looking for anything and never seeking anybody. Just being curious. There wasn't an end goal to the dream or a feeling that anything needed to be accomplished. It had been mindless drifting.

Daniel was in middle school when he learned *The Grey* was more than a dream. He encountered another person in the environment. It wasn't uncommon to see other people roaming the streets. They were apparitions of people come and gone; transparent images flickering in an action sequence that would last for a few moments before vanishing in a puff of smoke. Some places in *The Grey* had areas where the size of the crowd was overwhelming. It was hard to see where you were going because the images were so dense that they overlapped. He became immune to these ghosts and stopped noticing them. Then one day, he witnessed a solitary man walking down the street. The man's solid appearance immediately drew Daniel's attention. He watched the man with interest as he approached, not knowing what to do or what to say. When the unfamiliar man reached him, the stranger said, "So our paths cross again, huh?"

That was the day Daniel learned he had the power of voodoo. The stranger, who Daniel later found was named Javier, became his teacher regarding anything about *The Grey* and its power.

Daniel came to depend on Javier for more than just teaching. He relied on him for advice. He sought him when he needed to vent about problems in life. Javier wasn't quite a father figure, but he was more than a friend. He was a therapist, a companion and a mentor.

So on the day that Daniel decided he wouldn't be able to talk Junior out of robbing a bank, he entered *The Grey* seeking Javier's advice. Javier might not be able to help with the interpretation of the tarot cards, but he could also be a moral compass.

"Well, look who it is." Javier clapped his hands. "Me and Veronica were starting to think you were dead. I guess there goes our inheritance."

"Yeah. Sorry about that." Daniel said. "My life is kind of upside down right now. I've been trying to get everything back in order."

"Don't try too hard. Life is a bitch. She's not somebody you can make do what you want."

"Hey, Veronica, how are you doing?"

Veronica, another friend of the group that Javier had recruited, was seated next to him; her legs crossed, back straight, eyes forward. When Daniel first met Veronica, he had assumed she was a model. She had the build, the walk and the arrogance of women that you would see on Paris runways and magazine covers. But to his surprise, she was an artist. She painted. She played the piano. She danced. If you asked her, she would never admit to being talented though. Veronica would tell you that she was a creator.

She afforded Daniel a brief nod without taking her attention from the couple.

With an electric intensity, she studied the ghostly performance of a man and woman as they waltzed to and fro across a ballroom floor. Their image fading out after each twirl, leaving a trail of colored smoke that invoked a cosmic symphony of beauty that any audience would find captivating whether they were a fan of theater or not.

Daniel lowered himself into the seat next to Javier, taking a moment to admire the beauty of the performance hall then allowing himself to be caught in the aura of the performance.

"So?" Javier asked.

"So what?"

"I know when you have something on your mind. Plus, I know you're not a fan of the waltz. Tell me what's going on."

Daniel sighed. "I'm trapped between a rock and a hard place. I feel like I'm a cow being herded to the slaughter house. And even though I know what's coming, there's nothing I can do. I can't turn around. I can't... "

"Does it have something to do with why you've been gone so long?"

"Kinda sorta but not really."

"I get the feeling you want to talk about it, but you don't want to give us many details. Which is fine. I'm not going to push."

"I don't know if this is something I want to get y'all involve in." Daniel scratched his beard and shook his head. "I had a reading last night. It's been a while since I picked up a tarot deck."

"And?"

"The cards included my own fate into the reading. I've never had that happen before."

"Tarot card reading is a silly practice you should have never tried to learn. If you're here to get help with interpretation, I can't help you."

"It's not so much help with interpretation. When I performed the reading again, I got a different result."

"Hmm… So you're a deciding factor in the fate of whomever you were reading. I'm assuming it was a friend? I can't see you picking this aspect back up for a stranger."

"I'm not finished. There were five Death cards in the deck."

Veronica turned her head from the performance, suddenly attuned to the conversation. A pair of dancers stopped on the dance floor and posed for dramatic effect before turning to move in the opposite direction.

"That's definitely not good," Javier said. "Odd."

Veronica nodded her head in agreement.

"The deck was new," Daniel said. "But it was authentic. I could hear it sing to me. Is there a chance that it could have been flawed or tampered with?"

"Anything is possible. It might do you some good to speak with the shop owner that sold you the deck."

Daniel refused to tell them someone else had purchased the cards. Best to avoid their disappointment.

"Can I ask," Veronica said, "what was the question the cards were answering?"

Daniel looked down into his palms and didn't answer.

"So you can't tell us?"

"Where do we draw the line with good and bad with using our voodoo?" Daniel asked.

"Oh, this is an ethics question?" Javier laughed. "If we're talking morals, I don't believe anybody is completely good or completely bad. We're all in that *grey* area. I might be one shade of grey and Veronica could be 50 shades of grey."

"Funny."

"So I'm understanding that you are going to have to do something bad with your power that you've never had to do before? And this will prevent you from experiencing whatever the Death cards predicted for you?"

Daniel touched his nose with the tip of his forefinger.

"How bad are we talking?" Javier asked. "Kicking a puppy? Murder? Where are we on the morality scale?"

"What's the worst thing you've ever done with voodoo? Have you ever cursed somebody or let them die?"

"We let people die all the time. Who wants to know when they're going to die? Most people get their future read in order to procure the winning lottery numbers or to find out if Brad will ever fall in love with them. They don't want truth."

"I didn't want truth either, but here I am. How do I accept it?"

"To answer that, we need to revisit the scale. Are we taking the waiter's pen because it writes really well or are we setting a nursing home on fire?"

"Somewhere in the middle of that."

"You know, everybody is going to die eventually. We have decisions that create forks in the road. Each branch leads to a longer life or a shorter life. As selfish as it sounds, I suggest you choose the fork that will lead *you* to the longest life."

"I just wish I felt it was more my decision than the decision of a deck of cards."

"Don't let the tarot control you. They are the tool, not you. Let me tell you a story." Javier crossed his legs and leaned back, looking up at the exquisite ballroom ceiling. "When I was in high school, I lived with my aunt and uncle. I was going through typical teenage stuff. Thought I knew everything. Nobody could relate. Woe is me. You remember. You were like that a few months ago."

Daniel rolled his eyes.

"So one night I got home late, and my uncle was in a rage. I had forgotten to do some chore out of the millions of other chores I had, not to mention, keeping up with school and a social life. We argued, and I stormed out. I just needed to get away and breathe. While I was breathing, I stopped at a convenience store that just happened to be getting robbed."

Daniel blinked at the mention of robbery but tried to keep his face neutral.

"I was fully aware of my voodoo abilities at the time. I could've stopped it. But I was angry at the world and saw this as my way of getting revenge. So I did nothing. I said, 'This isn't my battle. I have other demons to fight.'

"Well, the robber left the store and at some point in his escape, he encountered a man and killed him. Do you know who this man was, Daniel?"

"Your Uncle Ben?"

"Oh, I've told you this story before?"

"I think at this point everybody knows the origins of Spiderman."

"But did I tell you why I was living with my aunt and uncle? When I was ten, my parents and I were leaving a Broadway play and they were killed in an alley which invoked my fear of bats."

"You're not helping."

"*Mira*. The point is, no matter what I tell you, it is in your nature to survive. The cards showed you what you need to do. So it boils down to a decision of can you live with the guilt of having done what you needed to do *or* are you okay if you die upon your mountain of good morals."

"I don't want to be a bad person." Daniel's said, letting his eyes trail back to the dance floor.

Veronica cleared her throat and patted Javier's knee. "I think I know what might help. Daniel, sometimes we have to do things we don't like in order to survive. Other times we use our voodoo as a show of strength. This is not a lifestyle that you can maintain and be weak. Let me tell you a better story than what Javier has to offer."

Javier smirked and cut his eyes at her.

"When I was younger, I met my soulmate. We married in our early twenties after a short courtship. It seemed fast, but I loved every minute of it. Gerald wasn't perfect. I wasn't perfect. But we were perfect for each other. Early in the marriage, I was teaching dance at a studio. Ballet. Gerald had just graduated law school.

"I remember always having this doubt in the back of my mind that Gerald was too good for me. It's funny because in high school I would have never given somebody like him a second glance. I was Miss Popularity. I was involved in cheerleading and theater. Everybody knew me because I was there to be seen. But Gerald was the studious nerd who was expected to excel in life. He didn't peak in high school like the rest of the popular crowd. But even with his degrees and good job, he wanted *me*: a ballet dancer turned instructor. And I gave him all of me. I became everything that I thought he wanted me to be.

"Personally, I never wanted kids, and we had discussed this before we married. But Gerald brought it up occasionally, and I began to think that if I gave him a child, it would prove my worth. It would show that I could bring something to the table, too. So we conceived. And I could tell he was genuinely happy.

"Looking back, I had absolutely no reason to be insecure." Veronica shrugged. "None. Gerald never gave me a reason to doubt his love or for me to feel inadequate. I've heard people say that they felt complete with their spouse, but I don't think I ever felt that way. So logically, my next step was to have a child. I was searching for purpose, and what gives your life more meaning than a child?"

Veronica paused and watched a pair of dancers leave the floor. A flash of applauding hands surrounded the trio momentarily then vanished. Daniel snuck a quick glance at Veronica to try to read the emotion on her face. Her voice was naturally dry, so it was difficult to hear the soberness.

The silence lasted long enough for Daniel to wonder if he should ask her to continue. But he didn't have to.

"I was young, "she said. "I conceived. It was amazing. Gerald was so happy. I was happy, too. I loved my son before I had even met him. Gerald would fantasize about who he would grow up to be. But my mind would wonder what kind of personality he would have. What would he be like as a toddler, a teenager, an adult? The one thing that scared me was thinking what would happen if my child turned out to be a horrible individual. I would think about how the world would judge not only my child but the parents who raised him. How much of my son's actions would I be accountable for?

"But it didn't matter. In my second trimester, there were complications and…"

Daniel did not need to look at Veronica to know she was crying. Her voice cracked and trailed off.

"Veronica, I'm so sorry," Daniel said.

Javier held up his hand and shook his head, telling Daniel to wait. There was more.

"So anyway," she continued, "I woke up in the hospital and was told not only had I lost my son, I also had lost my ability to have children. Everything that I had wanted to give… I couldn't… I didn't know how to go on. I had never felt so empty before in my life. Gerald was there, and he comforted me and said everything that a husband should say to a wife. Everything that one parent who lost a child can say to the other parent. Through my tears, he assured me that everything would be okay."

Daniel turned away from Veronica and watched a large number of dancers walked onto the floor for a group dance.

"I was still tired and loaded on medication. The hospital said they would need to hold me for a couple of days, maybe a week. So Gerald said he was going to go grab some of my things to make me more comfortable during my stay. I didn't want to be alone, but I think he needed some time to process. I felt selfish because I was unloading my grief and I hadn't seen him shed a single tear. My mind said let him go home and scream and get out any frustration that he might have. And so I was alone in the that sterile, unfamiliar room.

"A few minutes after he left, I received a text from him. It said 'I miss you. I need to see you'."

The ballroom performers braced against each other in a dramatic pose waiting for the music to start. It was as if they felt the shock of the statement and were astonished. Javier stared into his hands and rolled his thumbs, a frown on his face. Daniel's mouth dropped.

"It took me so long to process what I was reading. My first thought was 'he just left. Why does he miss me already?' I didn't know. Maybe it was the drugs slowing down my mind. Maybe it was the fact this was not something that happens right after you lose a child. Either way, my mind eventually got there, and I realized he was having an affair. And not only was he cheating, but he decided he needed this woman on the day we both lost our son. It was the most unbelievable…"

Veronica ran her hands down her jeans, composing herself. At some point she had begun to slump, so she straightened her back and lined up her shoulders, becoming once again Veronica, the dancer.

"Of course, he realized his mistake and immediately came back to the hospital. I can't even remember what excuse he tried to give or how he tried to explain it. Hell, he might have even been trying to apologize. I don't know. I didn't hear a word. At some point, he stopped speaking and was waiting for me to respond. I remember looking into his eyes... and seeing fear. I don't think he knew the extent of my power until that moment. He wanted to run. It was too late. I was in control of my senses. I had made my decision regarding his fate. Gerald had pissed me off. And so I tore his soul from his body, gathering every part of his essence and every part of him that makes him unique and surrendered him to *The Vale*."

"*The Vale?*" Daniel asked.

"It's like *The Grey*... but different."

"*The Vale* is..." Javier said. "Some people say it's the opposite of *The Grey*, but it's more like the reciprocal. In the real world, you can take parts out of *The Grey* and use it to shape someone's reality. As opposed to *The Vale* where you take parts of someone and offer them in *The Vale*."

"I used it to place Gerald in my own personal prison," Veronica said. "A popular phrase amongst religious individuals is 'You don't have a heaven or hell to place me in.' But guess what? I have one of those.

"Gerald was such a charismatic and social person. He had a constant need to be the center of attention. He was always attending parties and happy hours. He loved the attention he probably didn't get in high school. I might have been popular in my youth, but he was popular in adulthood. And one thing I learned as a teenage girl is that the best way to hurt a social butterfly is to clip their wings. Not to mention that humans need social interaction to survive. So I placed him in an environment where he will never have social interaction as long as I live."

"What do you mean?" Daniel asked.

"I mean, he is trapped in *The Vale* ... *alone*. He has nobody to talk to."

Daniel didn't know what to say.

"I'm not sure what will happen to him when I die. He may be trapped there forever or he may be released. I don't care."

"Vee," Javier said. "Have you considered that by holding him prisoner that maybe he is holding you prisoner, too? You need to forgive and let this go or else…"

"Don't." She warned.

They stared at each other. Daniel looked away.

"Guilt can be a heavy load to carry, Daniel." Veronica said. "I have killed. And it wasn't life or death or personal gain. It was extreme selfishness on my part. But I do *not* regret it. If you are forced to do something that is life or death, don't look at yourself any differently. You are surviving. Does this make you look at me any different?"

"I understand."

"Voodoo requires strength. It will weed out the lessers. We are not weak."

Daniel stood up. The idea of *The Vale* made him uncomfortable, and he wanted to get back to the real world as soon as he could. But first, he had one question.

"So what happened to Gerald's body since it doesn't have a soul?"

"It slipped into a coma. And as his wife, I was the person authorized to make the decision as to whether or not to continue life support."

•   •   •   •   •

One day, years ago, while traveling in *The Grey* with Javier, Daniel had noticed a group of individuals pouring into a cathedral. It was the largest group of people he had ever seen in *The Grey*. A quick estimate put the number at 50 to 100. He was mesmerized by not only their quantity but their attire.

They were adorned in robes of green and white. The colors of their clothing didn't seem to dim like everything else in *The Grey*. Especially the robe of one member. It was pale blue with a white sash.

"Who are they?" Daniel asked.

"The followers of La Marieé des Espirits. It's best you avoid them." Javier said.

"Why?"

The woman in blue had her attention on Daniel and matched his gaze. From this distance, he couldn't see her facial expression, but he could tell she was a stern woman.

"I've always had a bad feeling about that group. They don't practice the same voodoo that we do. Their art is more spiritual."

Daniel had felt something. He had assumed it was his sense of curiosity but now that it had been pointed out, he knew it was something else. He wasn't sure if it was a desire to join them, though.

Javier shook his head and turned to leave, not looking back to see if Daniel followed. "It's like those plants that use a sweet smell to attract flies then eat them. She's trying to pull you in."

"Are they dangerous? I'm interested."

"Yes, and they use the lure of that danger to pull you into their cult and don't let you leave. Avoid them at all costs."

But Daniel learned that there were differing opinions of the cult. Later, during another visit to *The Grey*, Daniel mentioned the encounter to Veronica.

"They are completely harmless." Veronica said. "It's a very traditional style of voodoo. La Marieé des Espirits is a very powerful priestess, and I've always gotten the impression that Javier is envious of her legacy."

"Yeah, he pretty much told me they would take me hostage."

She laughed. "You shouldn't take everything Javier says as scripture. They don't have a dungeon to hold you in. Personally, and this is just my opinion, I think they have the most power out of any aspect of voodoo you might encounter."

"And who doesn't want power? I can see why Javier feels threatened."

"Javier's sect is a non-threat to the spiritualists. Although I'm sure they won't allow you to be members of both their group and Javier's. If you join them then you'll have to renounce Javier."

"This was more information than I was expecting. How do you know so much?"

Veronica smiled slyly.

Daniel couldn't shake his intrigue. He continued to ask around.

Keith, an older member that Daniel rarely saw in *The Grey,* provided better advice.

"I'm a firm believer in the gathering of knowledge. My sister used to say never stop your education."

"Your sister sounds wise," Daniel said.

"She should be. She's lived quite a few lifetimes by now. Actually, she recently became my niece."

Daniel frowned.

"Our family is cursed. It's one of the reasons why I started learning voodoo. She tasked me with learning if there was a way to break the curse. I thought at first it was because she was ready to die but now…" He sighed. "It's a long, complicated story."

"But how is she your niece?"

"Devourer of souls. Body snatcher. Shape shifter. I really don't know the specifics."

"That doesn't sound like a curse."

"Blessing to some, I guess. But either way, I do not think a conversation with Katrine would hurt. That's her name, by the way. When you first meet her, I would suggest you address her as Madame Comtois. She leads the order of spiritualists."

"You know her personally?"

"I wasn't strong enough for her to even acknowledge me, but I trained with them for a little bit. If I wanted to learn all aspects of voodoo, then I needed to speak with the masters all over. It's like I told my kids when they left for college. Explore as many majors as you can before making a decision.

There's no harm in learning. Unfortunately, one of my children decided to make college into a professional career. I'm assuming he's trying to avoid entering adulthood."

"What exactly does she teach you that Javier can't?"

"Magic as a whole is like transportation. There are trains, planes and automobiles. Voodoo is one aspect of the whole system. Voodoo is a car maker. Madame Comtois is a specific model of the Voodoo brand. We can all get to the same destination, regardless of the car, but her car is flashier. Different."

"Who doesn't love a garage full of cars?"

"Probably the person that gave you the first car. Keep in mind that when Javier finds out – and he definitely will – he won't be too happy about you seeking them out."

"Veronica already warned me that he might feel some type of way about me approaching them."

"He sees in them what he wants to be but never will."

Daniel had marinated on Veronica and Keith's advice for a few days before making his decision. Although, he knew from the moment Madame Comtois had locked eyes with him that would they would meet. It wasn't any siren song or intense curiosity. It was destiny.

The day Daniel made his decision, he entered *The Grey* with the intent on finding Katrine. He wasn't sure how he was going to find her, but he knew a great starting place was the location where he had seen her.

As luck would have it, she was there. Her robes, this time a medium hued purple, waved in a non-existent wind. Straight, jet black hair framed her face, and Daniel was enraptured with her exotic features.

They stared at each other for a moment before she beckoned him to follow her inside.

Daniel entered the cathedral and was enthralled with the beauty of the décor. From the stain glass windows to the painted ceilings, his eyes roamed the interior with a whirlwind of excitement. With the information that Keith provided, Daniel was able to discern that the colored window panels told the story of Marie Laveaux. He was familiar with the story, but he still followed each remarkable chapter in the order portrayed. He felt it would be blasphemy if he didn't.

The beginning of her life as a free woman during America's slavery era, progressing through the deaths of her children with only two surviving daughters. Three windows dedicated to her rise of power in the Catholic Church, the spy network she infused in her hair salon and the brothel she maintained in French Quarter of New Orleans. The final glass depicted her solo figure wearing a crown to signify her undisputed claim as the Queen of Voodoo. Daniel searched for any mention of her death, which he would assume would be the final window but couldn't find it.

"I expected you a lot sooner."

Madame Comtois' voice was thick with a French accent that made Daniel have to listen carefully to catch each word.

"I needed time to think."

"Think about what?"

"I was divided on whether this would be a good idea or not. My curiosity eventually got the better of me."

Madame Comtois took a seat in the pew and invited Daniel to join her. He sat beside her and resisted the urge to let his eyes roam around the cathedral again.

"It is not curiosity that pushed you. It is the internal desire to nurture the essence of voodoo that resides with in."

"Is that what calls everybody to seek you out?"

"No. Everybody is different. *Mais je te connais.* I knew you before you knew you."

"Yeah, I've gotten that a lot."

"You do not think you came to nurture what you have? You do not believe me. Then tell me why you think you have come to this place. Why you have come to speak with me?"

"I want to know more about what y'all do. I want to learn. Keith told me to explore all aspects of knowledge."

"Ahh, Keith, *le fils prodigue.*"

"The prodigal son?"

"*Oui.* He spent time learning. He is – how do you say? – a hoarder of lessons. He speaks that his goal is to lift his family curse but even with the solution in front of him, he is blind to see. So he seeks. But he will return when he is ready. Octave's descendants always return. But they never succeed."

"What can I learn?"

She rose from the pew and glided down the aisle. Daniel followed.

"One of the basic avenues of voodoo is communication with spirits. There are many types of spirits. We do not say they are good or evil. Some might have malevolent intentions, some good intentions. Some are so powerful that they could kill. And some are so minor they couldn't stir a breeze to cool your soup. But they always want one thing."

"What's that?"

"To feed. They have a hunger that they require us to help them satiate."

"And you're going to teach me how to control them?"

Katrine came to an abrupt stop and turned to look Daniel in the eye.

"We cannot control spirits. That is not within the power of voodoo. We communicate. We request. We bargain."

"I understand."

"Do you? Spirits can be dangerous. Thinking you have dominion over them can push you to be careless. You must always be on alert with them. They are tricksters. You do not understand now but you will. Every one that practices the spiritualistic side of voodoo will be tested."

Daniel paused, not knowing what response she expected.

"You have so much power in you for such a child. You should join us. There is so much we can do with that power."

"I'm happy with Javier."

"Are you? With my training you could be a king. *The King of Voodoo.* You will not obtain that under Javier."

"I'm not leaving him. I only came-"

"So much waste. But you are young. I will see you again. You will also be *un fils prodigue.*"

Daniel smiled awkwardly.

As they approached the front of the chapel, Daniel's gaze wandered to two stone figures that framed both sides of the altar. Two onyx stone statues hunched down with overbearing facial features that gave him the impression they were in pain. Leathery wings adorned the back of one while feathered wings cloaked the other. Animalistic faces on human bodies, Daniel's first thought was the most obvious.

"Gargoyles?" He asked.

Daniel reached out his hand to touch the stone. Katrine gently pushed it back to his side, shaking her head.

"If a gargoyle were present, he would be offended that you would call this grotesque creature such. No, this is not a gargoyle. They only feature it shares with a true gargoyle is its stone heart. This… is a spirit. A not so minor spirit. It is best not to touch them or else you awaken them from their slumber."

He watched, waiting for any movement that would rebuke his sense that this was an inanimate object. There was none.

"So they are sleep?"

"They are… in a state of indecision."

"What are they trying to decide on?"

Katrine did not answer.

Daniel turned his attention away from the stone figures to find Madame Comtois' arms embracing a scarlet tome, the leather binder held firm to her bosom. Two men in matching black robes exited from the side of the altar and approached the pair.

"Open your heart to the lesson we have to give you," Madame Comtois said. "There are minor spirits called the *voleur.* Any member of the voodoo practice can communicate with the *voleur.* Today, we will grant you one of the many to communicate with as you will. It will… help you to assimilate how spirits react with your voodoo practice."

A feeling of discomfort and nervousness fluttered inside Daniel's stomach and he became unsure of his decision to seek out an audience with Katrine. He was new to his power and if he needed to defend himself, he was more than sure the purple robed woman could overpower him. That was a certainty now that there were three members opposite him.

He watched as they removed her robe from her shoulders, at least one of her hands remaining on the book during the process. Daniel didn't look away as she casually shrugged into a new robe, this one black and longer than the first. The tail of the robe put Daniel in the mind of a wedding dress train as it dragged down the steps from the altar to the aisle.

"This," she raised the book, "Is *Le Livre Des Esprits*. The lesson we give you today, Sebastian LeBleu, is the gift of the *voleur*."

Daniel's eyebrows rose at the mention of his voodoo name and wondered how she had come to know that name.

"Our sect holds more knowledge about spirits and voodoo than any individual person or book could ever teach you. Let it be known, if you were to join us, this book and all its knowledge would be yours. You only need to pledge your life to the following of La Marieé des Espirits."

He shook his head and the priests stepped back, disappointed in his decision.

"A drop of blood, a lifetime of knowledge."

Daniel could feel the heat in his ears as his temperature rose. The dark red book seemed to pulse with the thundering of his heartbeat in his ears. But the mention of giving blood brought him out of his reverie and reality compressed his awareness.

"No, I do not accept."

"So much power." Daniel wasn't sure if Katrine spoke of him or the book.

Her eyes rolled back into her head to the point that only the whites showed. Daniel felt a prickling rush along his skin. He shivered as a chill ran down his back. The feeling of

26

being watched made him look around the cathedral. The pews that had been empty were now littered with robed men and women. He was startled by not only the fact he hadn't noticed anybody enter the sanctuary, but that they were all entranced with something at the top of the cathedral. All the members were staring upward forcing Daniel to do the same.

Staring back at him were a thousand eyes enveloped in darkness. He couldn't tell if the ceiling had lost any residual light from *The Grey* or if there were so many creatures braced above him that they obscured the ceiling.

He realized he was in over his head.

"What are those? What is happening?" He asked.

"Those are the *voleur*. They have come to pay respect to their new prince?"

"I'm not a prince. I only wanted to learn."

"And they only want to serve."

Daniel swallowed his fear and squinted his eyes in an attempt to focus on one individual set of eyes in the legion of a thousand. The eyes roamed across the top of the ceiling as if they were ants. Once his eyes pinned one pair, it would be replaced by another. And the grating sound of their voices caused him to cringe. Daniel wanted to leave and never return.

"Which one is mine? Which one will I be able to communicate with?" His words contradicted his feelings and surprised him.

Katrine's laugh bounced across the walls and stain glass of the cathedral. The priest to her left smirked.

"So much power and at so young age." She closed the book and slid her had across the cover. "*Mon fils prodigue…* all of them are yours."

●　●　●　●　●

"We've never had a full discussion on the limits to our powers," Junior said.

Daniel focused on lining up his shot as he leaned over the pool table. The smoky atmosphere of the bar caused his vision to blur as he ignored Junior's attempt to distract him. He swallowed the response that popped into his head and slid the stick back and forth across his knuckles.

"I think that if we're going to be partners in this," Junior continued, "then we should at least know what each other can do."

Daniel thrust the pool cue, sending the white ball careening across the table. It slapped into the ball he was aiming for but didn't knock it into the pocket.

"Okay. So you first," Daniel said. "Tell me what you can and cannot do."

"I can control people. Make them move how I want and say what I want. It's like there are strings attached to the wires in their brain. I play them like a harp."

"Just people?"

"And animals. I can't control objects though. I'm not an X-Man. I don't have telekinesis. Is that what it's called? Probably a good thing I don't have that. I'd scare the shit outta people making them think their house was possessed. Oh, and I can't control dead people."

"Please tell me how you know you can't control the dead?"

"Because I tried."

"You were *destined* to be a supervillain."

Junior choked on his beer with laughter. "Why do you say that?"

"Because you're using your ability to try to make zombies."

"I was *not* trying to make zombies. I was experimenting with my gift."

"Everything about your power just screams comic book villain. What good could you do with the power to

28

control somebody like a ragdoll? You kinda had no choice but to be the bad guy."

"You make me sound evil."

"I mean…"

"I feel judged right now."

Junior shook his head as he set up his shot. He wasn't the type to spend much time lining up his sights or analyzing angles. Not to mention, he was a tad bit tipsy from the four beers he had consumed since they arrived at the bar.

"This is a judgement-free zone," Daniel said. "But if you wanted to counter my argument, just tell me what you've done positive with your power. Helped any grandmas cross the street? Stopped any bank robberies?"

"I've done plenty of nice things with it."

"Name one."

Junior took a long gulp from the bottle in his hand to give himself time to think. Daniel smiled.

"Okay, I got one. A couple of months ago, I was at the bar with some guys from work. We hadn't hung out in a while, so we got together to shoot the shit, have fun. There's this guy there that I guess was there scouting for local talent. He was one of those guys that doesn't know when to stop working out. Like, spends all his time in the gym, meathead, steroids - You know the type."

"I've met one or two."

"Let's call him Incredible Hulk. Anyways, I see The Hulk trying to talk to this girl at the bar. She was completely out of his league, I could tell. Everything about him just screamed douchebag. He was even wearing his little sister's shirt which was obvious because it was way too tight. He might as well have had a sign on his head that said 'I don't belong here'. And the girl was like one of those video vixen types. The kind you see only married to athletes or movie stars. She was gorgeous. But I'm not even going to discredit The Hulk's attempt to land a hottie. My cousin used to say, 'one hundred percent of shots not taken are missed'."

"You are like a walking billboard with all these marketing slogans."

"And I didn't have to go to school for it." Junior winked.

"Burn."

"So even from a distance, I can tell that dude is trying his best to start a conversation with the girl. I'm like fascinated with the whole situation. I couldn't help but to move closer, try to ear hustle a little bit. I didn't want to look like I was being too nosey though."

"Of course not."

"He is dropping like an atomic bomb. Just no game at all. And at some point, she's finished her drink, and he hasn't offered to buy her another one. She's annoyed and looking for an escape."

"Let me guess. You ran to a phone booth and quickly changed into your purple cape."

"Captain Save-A-Hoe to the rescue. I see you laughing but you said you wanted to see how I've used my power for good."

"I just don't understand how this is for the greater good."

"She was a damsel in distress. If you could've seen the look on her face or heard the conversation she had to *endure*..."

"This is the fairy tale my mother never read me at night."

"Dr. Seuss could never make Horton hear this Who. I was a knight in shining armor that night. I got him out of there."

"How?"

"I controlled him. I hit him in his bladder. Made it so that he was about to piss on himself but didn't make him actually do it. I didn't want to embarrass him any more than he had already embarrased himself. Then I *walked* him away."

"He didn't fight it?"

"He wasn't smart enough to realize what was happening. I've learned that as long as people don't know what I'm doing, it's not that hard to control them. It's the fear and anger that break my control."

"He didn't come back?"

"If he did, I didn't see him. I had completed my life's mission of proving my power isn't all bad."

Daniel stared at Junior.

Junior kept his gaze on the TV across the room pretending to be interested in the baseball game on display. It was a glaring avoidance to the obvious next question.

"You left with her, didn't you?"

"Did you not hear me say earlier how gorgeous she was? Why the fuck would I pass up that chance? Hell yeah, I left with her."

"Complete trash." Daniel laughed.

"Like, on a scale of one to ten, she was a twenty."

"Trash."

"Plus, how would The Hulk have felt if I had let the drinks he bought her go to waste?"

"I will never know another friend as garbage as you."

"Okay, sir. Since you're on your high horse. What positive things have you done with your power?"

"Plenty."

"Oh yeah?"

"Yeah."

"Name four."

"I'm not gonna name four things. I don't have a list ready to go."

"Then how can you call yourself a good person?"

Daniel stared for a moment, trying to gather his thoughts. He took a deep breath and leaned back on the pool table.

"When I was younger, my uncle was sick with cancer." Daniel said. "We were related through marriage. He married my mother's sister. He was suffering during his last days. I just wanted to make it all go away?"

"You killed him?"

"No, I have never *killed* anybody. Why would that be your first question?"

"Then how did you make it better?"

"I gave him a different reality?"

"A different reality?"

"Yes, I showed him a life past the cancer where he got to meet his grandkids and their kids. I covered him in an alternative where he hadn't gotten cancer and him and my aunt had retired and moved to some small town with acres of land and plenty of animals. I tried to give him some happiness."

Junior shifted from one foot to the other but didn't say anything.

"I sat by his side for two weeks giving him whatever I thought he might like."

"Did he know it?"

"No. He died thinking he had lived a full life."

Daniel looked away from Junior wondering why he had told a fake story. It wasn't true. It was fabricated. He didn't have an uncle that had died from cancer, and he doubted he could bend anybody's reality for two weeks. But the words had fallen from his lips without any resistance. It was easier to lie than it was to admit he had never done anything selfless with his abilities. Junior had caught him off guard by asking a question that Daniel had never thought to ask of himself.

He pushed aside the shame and stood up straight.

"I think I'm done playing," Daniel said.

"Yeah, me too. That sad ass story killed my buzz. Let's go."

Junior paid his tab and followed Daniel out the door.

The weather had changed since they had entered the pool hall. The haziness of a misty drizzle blurred the street lights against the night sky. Daniel made his way to Junior's car, taking the keys out of his pocket. He started to think maybe he should tell Junior the story was untrue, and possibly, they could have a laugh about it.

The first few minutes of the silent drive home didn't give Daniel enough time to confess. Junior still had questions about Daniel's powers.

"So what are your weaknesses? I told you mine."

"That's a really hard question."

"If you're saying that you don't know then you aren't very good at what you do."

"It's not that I don't know. It's like exposing myself. I would be fighting my survival instinct by telling you."

"Is it a really bad weakness? If somebody sneezes, they break out of your spells?"

"They're not spells. I'm not a witch."

"If it barks like a duck…"

"My weakness is that I don't know much. I haven't really had very good training. I'm just kinda floundering along and learning as I go."

"I thought you had a teacher."

"I mean, I do. Sorta. In some kinda way. More like a mentor."

"Okay?"

"There are better teachers out there, but I'm letting loyalty keep me from exploring my other options. My weakness is loyalty to my friends." The last sentence sounded more like a question than a statement.

"That's the most bullshit answer I've ever heard."

Daniel laughed. "It's the truth."

"I want to know how somebody can break one of your curses. Or maybe how you go blind if you don't meditate every night. Something that's a real weakness. Not one of your 'job interview' responses."

"Look. A wise man once said, 'the man that knows something knows that he knows nothing at all'. And I know that I will never know everything."

"A wise man didn't say that. That's an Erykah Badu lyric. I need more than what you're giving me."

"I don't have anything more to give you. I can't even tell you where I'm lacking in power because I don't know where I'm lacking. I don't know enough about what I can do."

"Let's start here. What can you do?"

"I can read tarot. I can travel to other astral planes. I can bend someone's perception of reality. I can communicate with spirits."

"Like ghosts? Can they give us any information about the bank?"

"No, my spirits aren't really the smartest... they're low-level spirits. I just have a lot of them."

"Hmm. You said bend perception? Can you make it so nobody can see you?"

"I guess so. I've never tried that. I usually make people see things, not unsee them."

"If you were to walk into a bank, can you make everybody in the building not see you? Be invisible and walk right into the vault?"

Daniel thought for a moment as the methodical drum of windshield wipers scraped across his view.

"It depends on the number of people, I guess. That would be a lot of people to try to cover in *Grey Matter*."

"That's your weakness? You can only hypnotize so many people?"

"I think so. I've never tried more than a handful. I don't know my limit. This all comes back around to me not knowing enough. But one thing I do know is that I can't fool electronic devices. The people in the bank might not see me, but the security cameras damn sure would."

"Fuck. I didn't think about that. What if somebody were to turn the security cameras off?"

"Somebody like your girlfriend, the bank manager?"

"She's not my girlfriend. And I'm not involving Fatima in this. I was thinking maybe I could get one of the security guards to do it. The only thing is that he would remember doing it. I might be able to hold him for a while to keep him from turning them back on."

"Do you know where the cameras are? Do you know where the security office is? Do you know who has authorization to turn the cameras off? Will turning the cameras off sound an alarm?"

"Good point."

"We could definitely get all this information from your girlfriend."

"How would we ask her?"

"I'm glad you asked." Daniel smiled. "I had an idea the other day that I think might work. I know how we can openly question her but without her remembering."

"A spell?"

"Again, I'm not a witch." Daniel sighed. "It's a *ritual*. While she's sleep, I can use my ability to make her think it's a dream. She won't suspect anything if it's just a dream."

"Then she won't be involved. I think I like this plan."

"So what changed?"

"What do you mean?"

"A few days ago, you were more than eager to involve her. But something's changed. I'm getting the impression that you care more now."

"She's a really nice girl. She doesn't deserve to be used. Or put in harm's way. That's all."

Daniel frowned. He was puzzled. When Junior first ran into Fatima, it seemed as if he wasn't interested in anything more than using her for her position at the bank. But now, Daniel got the impression that Junior was protective of her.

"So are we moving with the dream plan?" Daniel asked.

"Yes. When do you want to cast your spell?"

"Tonight."

• • • • •

Daniel received a text from Junior around 1:00am that Fatima was asleep. He got out of Junior's car, where he had been waiting for two hours, and approached the house. He had told Junior to wait until she had been asleep for at least 30 minutes. Junior had tried to convince him that Fatima was a heavy sleeper, but Daniel wanted to play it safe.

Junior opened the door, and Daniel clutched the items in his hand close to his body. He didn't want to drop anything. Taking a long look around, Daniel noticed the pleasant décor of the house. Everything was arranged and organized. Color schemes carried a uniform theme in each room. And everything looked so clean.

"She keeps a tidy home," Daniel said.

"Better than I ever could."

"Which way?"

Junior waved for Daniel to follow and made his way towards the back. The smell of whatever had been cooked earlier wafted from the doorway to the kitchen as he passed.

The bedroom held the same decorative sense as the other rooms but more feminine. Even without any light, Daniel could tell Fatima took pride in the overall décor of her room.

Daniel sat down on the floor and placed the objects in front of him. First, he lit the candle, being sure not to look directly into the flame since his eyes had already adjusted to the darkness. Next, he licked the coin- the *voleur* had provided a quarter- and placed it on the floor. The metallic taste caused him to frown. He tried not to imagine all the places this coin had been. Lastly, he tied one end of the strand of hair around the Barbie doll's neck, then tied the other end around his finger.

"What now?" Junior asked.

"I wake her up and try to get information from her. I'm going to take her to the bank she works at."

"Will I be able to see too?"

"I didn't plan on having two passengers on this plane."

"I need to see what you see. I don't want to be left out of this."

"It'll be easier if I only have to cover her. I promise she won't be harmed."

"I don't care if it's easier. I'm not going to sit here and wait."

"I could just put you to sleep," Daniel said.

"And I could make you run into oncoming traffic."

Taking a deep breath, Daniel rubbed his thumb across the doll's face. Including Junior in the scenario wouldn't be any harder, but Daniel knew that Junior would be a distraction. He would be forced to not only change his own identity in her 'dream', but now he would have to do the same for Junior.

Daniel shrugged away his irritation and closed his eyes. He wasn't sure what was making Junior so paranoid about Fatima's well-being but he didn't care.

A dog barked somewhere in the neighborhood sending a wave of annoyance as Daniel pulled *Grey Matter* into the room and changed their location. For Junior, it would look as if they suddenly moved from Fatima's dark bedroom to a sunlit street in front of the bank. Cop cars lined the entrance. Yellow police tape framed the door. A few uniformed officers stood to the side interviewing civilians and lights flickered across the windows, echoing the blue and red reflections from the police cars. A crowd of onlookers stood on the sidewalk behind a barricade, Each of them holding their cell phones up to take a picture of the robbery scene.

"Why isn't there any sound?" Junior asked. "Shouldn't there be some noise or background conversation?"

"It's not real. It's supposed to be a dream. Do you remember hearing background noise in dreams?"

Junior took a moment to think. "No. I guess not."

"If you're going to question everything I do then this is gonna be inefficient. Let me do what I'm good at."

Junior held up his hands in resignation. "You're the boss."

"And let me do all the talking. You came to observe. Why? I don't know. I'm not gonna harm your girlfriend."

"She's not my girl. I told you that."

Daniel took the doll, still in his hand, and wiped his thumb across her face.

Fatima opened her eyes and stood up from the bed. Her eyes scanned the scene, and she clasped her hands to her mouth in shock.

"Ma'am," Daniel said, "are you the bank manager?"

"Yes, I am."

"Good. My name is Detective Smith. I've been assigned to the case. This is Officer Bloom. He was the first to arrive on the scene."

Fatima nodded at Junior. Daniel had changed both their appearances to remain anonymous. This ensured there wasn't any confusion from her recognizing either of them. Junior was wearing the standard police uniform while Daniel was dressed in a plain grey suit.

"I'm Fatima Davis. Was anybody hurt?"

"We do not believe so. First, we want to account for everybody that would have been at work today. Can you tell me what employees you have on the work schedule today?"

"Oh. Um… I don't know. What day is it?"

The candle was doing its job of clouding her ability to think clearly.

"Wednesday."

"Today, we would have had Crystal and Jackie on the counter. John and Tyrone on drive-thru. Shelly is in new accounts and loans. Greg in mortgages. Chris, the assistant manager-"

"How many people total?"

"Twelve, if you count me. Why wasn't I here?"

"I don't know."

"I should have been here. I work on Wednesdays. I'm so glad nobody got hurt."

"Our officers are taking statements from your employees now. Would you be able to provide us with the security footage?"

"Yes, definitely. The control room is this way."

Daniel shifted the setting. The bank entrance faded away and was replaced by a carpeted office. The wall was littered with TV monitors, each displaying a different angle of the bank lobby and various areas throughout. Even if the generic looking location didn't match Fatima's memory of the security office, the candle would make everything hazy.

"There's nothing on this footage," Daniel said. "It looks like everything has been erased."

"What? That doesn't sound right."

Fatima leaned forward and banged on the keyboard. The screens in front of her remained blank.

"Is it possible somebody could have deleted the tapes?"

"No, the security cams don't record to a tape. They're digital and save to remote servers. We should have six months of video saved." The tone of Fatima's voice was starting to sound frantic.

"Is it possible somebody deleted the files? Who would have access?"

"I'm the only one with access. You have to be a branch manager or above. You don't think one of my employees did this, do you?"

"So the security guard couldn't have done it?"

"We don't have a security guard. Never had a need for one... Am I a suspect?"

"No," Junior said. "You are safe. We would never suspect you."

Junior glared at Daniel and patted Fatima's shoulder. Daniel had felt the tension rise in Junior as the stress level in Fatima increased.

"*Thank* you, Officer Bloom." Daniel sprinkled his voice with a warning. "Fatima, walk us through robbery procedures."

Now, they were in the lobby of the bank. In the distance, a dog barked and Daniel knew it was the same dog from earlier.

"What do you need to know?"

"Are there security alarms the employees can set off if they are being robbed?"

"Yes, we have multiple alarms. We have pedals on the floor so the employees can be discreet. There's also a button in each of the cash drawers. Once the button is pressed, it sends an alert to our security center."

"What happens then?"

"They give us a call. If nobody answers with the security code, then a call is placed to the cops for emergency services."

"And that call would go to you, the bank manager?"

"No, the call will go to the teller room."

"And what's the security code?"

"It's a combination of things. First, the person that answers has to provide their employee number and a series of digits from their assigned token."

"Token?"

Fatima nodded and reached into her pocket. "Oops. I guess I don't have mine. It's a little digital key that is programmed to display a combination that changes every 30 seconds. I don't understand the algorithm behind it. I'm not a technology expert."

"No, no. That's fine. So how would the robbers have gotten into the vault?"

"They would have had to arrive during one of the scheduled times that the vault is opened."

"You can't open the vault between the scheduled times?"

"We can, but it takes 30 minutes. I can enter the combination from my token and coordinate with our Regional manager to unlock from his side."

Daniel rubbed his thumb over the Barbie, and Fatima's head slumped forward. The scenery of the bank faded and they were once again in Fatima's bedroom. Daniel shook his head.

"The more questions I ask, the more difficult this becomes," Daniel said.

"She was really upset about this whole thing. Are you sure she won't remember anything?"

"People have nightmares all the time." Daniel waved his hand in annoyance. "I think I'm going to have to find another way to rob this bank. There are too many safeguards and policies in place. And I feel like I don't know the right questions to ask."

"Do I need to ask how you got a strand of her hair?"

"I can't use the *voleur* because then I would need to feed them." Daniel continued to ignore Junior. "I don't want to ask Javier for any more advice. I've already involved him enough."

Junior muttered something about helping Fatima lie down. Daniel glanced at his cell phone to see what time it was.

"Do you have anything you think we should ask?" Daniel asked.

"No."

"I guess we can come back if we have more questions."

"Yeah."

"What's wrong, Junior?"

"Nothing."

Something was bothering Junior, but Daniel didn't want to push the issue. He hoped maybe Junior was having second thoughts about the bank robbery idea. If so, they could discuss it later.

Daniel gathered the doll and candle, left the coin, and satisfied his curiosity with giving one last look to Junior.

●　●　●　●　●

Daniel took a left into an alleyway two blocks from his destination. He carried a small box with a rodent inside that he had purchased from a pet store. The rat's movements caused its carriage to rock back and forth. When Daniel had first learned of the form of payment that *voleur* expected, he had been disgusted. He wasn't an animal activist, but he didn't believe in inhuman treatment of any animal, no matter how small. As time had passed, his disgust waned; he grew immune to the feedings.

At first, he worried that the pet store would wonder why he was purchasing rodents so frequently. To avoid being recognized, he tried to stagger the stores from which he obtained the rats. He eventually came to realize that purchasing rodents wasn't considered an anomaly due to the popularity of pet snakes. The pet store employee would assume Daniel owned a snake and ask questions about the type of serpent. One employee, overeager to share, had told him about a customer that bought mice from the store to feed his pet octopus.

Nothing was unusual anymore.

Daniel placed the box on the ground and checked to make sure he was alone. Closing his eyes, he reached inward and turned his thoughts to the fact that he was in need. It didn't take long to receive a reply.

"We can provide."

"We want to please you."

"We can serve."

What once had taken some practice now came with ease. Daniel squirmed at the feeling of goosebumps running down his arms. Before he could second-guess himself, he stated his request.

No need for clarification; he felt the *voleur* vanish. The chill in his limbs dissipated and he stepped out of the alley.

The area of town he walked through wasn't really the best of neighborhoods. It wasn't due to the nature of the people that resided here but the long line of bars, nightclubs and tattoo shops. So many alcohol-based businesses in one location were prone to have a bad reputation. Daniel knew the turn in atmosphere would occur after dark, so he had chose to come during the day.

Daniel walked the two remaining blocks and entered the establishment. A neon sign that read 'Psychic Readings' hung from the window. The large crack in the glass of the door, framed by iron metal bars, hardly gave Daniel a pause.

"Welcome." A middle-aged lady with a plump face and short hair waved him in from the doorway. She was dressed in an oversized purple smock that hung loosely from her shoulders. Her smile, anchored between her lips with a prominent and wide gap, invited him closer with a warmth that one experiences from family. "What service can we provide today?"

An elderly man that Daniel assumed was her father glanced up from his magazine and stared. Daniel acknowledged him with a nod and returned his focus to the glowing charm of the woman.

"I was looking for a tarot reading," Daniel said.

"Sure. We can help you with that. Come on in, baby. Don't be shy."

Daniel approached the counter and let his eyes wander around the shop. It was a simple store with crystal balls, incense and religious candles. He knew most of the items would probably be for show and didn't spend too much time inspecting them.

"How much is a reading?" Daniel asked.

"Normally, we would charge $40. But I can tell this is your first time, so how about we give you a first time customer discount? I'll knock it down to $35."

"Thank you. I appreciate that."

It wasn't much of a discount, but he would take it. Being unemployed had forced Daniel to count every penny. The reserve he had saved while employed had dwindled to almost nothing. It had taken hours of internal debate to commit himself to part with the money for a second reading.

"My name is Regina."

"Daniel."

"Nice to meet you, Daniel." She reached out to shake his hand. "Follow me into the back. That way we can have some privacy."

The back room was definitely for show. A red-and-purple velvet sheet covered a round table, flanked by two plush, matching chairs. The walls were draped with silk curtains that overlapped light fixtures, causing a dimmed ambiance that was intended to create a feeling of authenticity to any customers.

Taking a seat across from Regina, Daniel looked down at the cards spread face up across the table. He watched as she swiped the cards up from the table and set them in front of him before he had a chance to spot the Death Card. He could hear harmonic dissonance of the cards and knew that they were authentic.

"Daniel, what brings you to the shop today? No, let me guess. Love life issues? I can usually smell those from a mile away. Special lady in your life giving you the blues?" She took a sweeping glance at his clothing and raised an eyebrow. "Or a special man?"

"No, nothing like that." Daniel's eyes kept returning to the cards.

Regina laughed. "This is a modern time. I don't judge, baby. But if not for love then my next guess would be money. Those are the two most common reasons people come for a reading. They try to say it's only out of curiosity, but the questions they ask always tell the truth."

"It's a financial question, I guess."

Daniel watched a smirk dance across her lips as she fondled the cards with her long finger nails. He recognized that her conversation was a part of the performance intended for the reading. She had a motherly attitude that was inviting. It helped ease his nerves although he suspected he knew how this was going to end. Her skin glowed with a youthful appearance that contradicted her attire that was similar to a style worn by his aunts. He wondered how much of her character was performance and how much was genuine. He couldn't find any faults or cracks in her demeanor that belied what she was portraying, but any psychic had to be Oscar-winning actors.

So Daniel endured. He knew what his need was. Regina didn't have anything to entice him to play along.

"Daniel, I need you to shuffle those for me, baby doll. And while you do that, tell me what questions you're looking to have answered." She folded her hands on the table and leaned forward.

"I have been asked to participate in a… *business opportunity* that includes some illegal activities. I need to know the best course of action."

"Well, oh my." Her eyes lit up. "I haven't had a question that good in a while. My last few readings were questions for dead relatives."

Daniel shuffled the cards and placed them face down in front of Regina. Her gaze steadied on Daniel, and she tilted her head to the side.

"I'm not most guys," he said.

Regina turned the first three cards turned over in the pyramid formation. She frowned.

Three Death Cards.

"I'm so sorry. I think I must have mixed up the decks."

She swept them up to keep Daniel from seeing them. She continued to apologize as she rushed out of the room, returning with a new deck. This sound of the tarot cards, a high pitched wail that only voodoo practitioners could here, rang from this deck louder than the first.

Daniel repeated the procedure of making his request as he shuffled the cards.

Regina smiled at him when he placed them back in front of her. He assumed she was still embarrassed by the earlier mishap.

The smile faded when she overturned the first three cards. This time they were blank.

She blinked but didn't speak.

"Regina?"

"I don't understand. I've never had this happen before. You must forgive me."

"No, it's not you."

"You came in for a reading, and this is twice that the deck has..."

"No, no. It's not the cards. It's me. I had a feeling this would happen, but I hoped..."

"Who are you?" She whispered.

Daniel looked at her but didn't speak.

"You are a student of the arts? You are here to test me?" Her tone shifted and was no longer warm and inviting.

"I know some voodoo. But I am not here to test you. I came to..."

"You are here to ridicule me? Make me look like a fool?"

"No, not at all."

"Then tell me why you're playing these games? Why do you come into my place of business and make these cards do this?"

"It's not intentional. I really wanted a reading."

"Daniel, what are you not telling me, baby?"

"Everything okay back here? You okay, baby girl?" The elderly man poked his head through the curtain.

"Yes, I'm fine." She rose from her chair, and the smile returned to her lips. Her voice resumed its normal charm. "We are having a little issue with the cards. I think this reading might be a little out of my league. Would you mind helping me?"

The man stepped into the room but left the door cracked.

Regina took the cards into her hand and tossed them down on the table face up. They scattered across the velvet tablecloth, their vibrating pitch unending.

"You see what he has done. These cards ain't good no more. Ruined."

"I see."

46

Regina shrugged and guided the man to the table by his elbow.

"I didn't do this," Daniel said. "I came to get a reading. I'm trying to find a way out of a situation that my own cards put me in."

"You've tried to read yourself?" The man asked.

"Yes. And I got the same results as the first deck she used. I got five *Death Cards*."

They stared at Daniel. Regina sighed and nodded with a frown of sympathy pulling at her eyes.

"Go watch the front." The older gentleman brushed his hand against Regina's back, guiding her to the door.

"Are you sure? I think this might be a good learning experience for me to watch."

"It's okay. I've got this. Plus, I don't think he meant any harm."

"Intended or not, it is disrespect." Regina turned to Daniel. "In the future, it's considered common courtesy to announce your credentials when you meet with another practitioner. Otherwise, it looks as if you're hiding something or trying to spy."

She left, and an awkward silence covered the room. The elderly gentlemen walked to the chair, slumped forward. Daniel debated on whether or not to offer to assist him.

"I'm sorry for my niece," the man said. "She was a happy child even after her mother, my sister, died. She usually isn't so quick to get upset or jump to conclusions. But when you make her question her confidence in her tarot readings, it makes her a tad bit snappy."

Daniel nodded even though he wasn't sure when Regina had been 'snappy'.

The man groaned as he lowered himself into the seat. His wrinkled hands gathered the cards from the table, arranging them back to a solid deck.

"From what I heard earlier, your name is Daniel. I am Mr. Toussaint. My friends call me Clyde."

"Nice to meet you, Mr. Toussaint."

"Very respectful. I like that. Now, tell me who you are. Introduce yourself, so I don't think you're here with any ill will."

"My name is Daniel Leonard. I am a student of Javier Manzón."

"Oh, Javier, huh? Well, that explains some things. I have lived a long life and seen many things. The faces change, the voices echo, but the essence is forever. You say you are a student of Javier because you don't know who you are yet."

"I don't know what you mean."

Mr. Toussaint handed the cards to Daniel.

Daniel, unsure of what to do, shuffled the cards even with the knowledge that they were blank. The confusion was obvious on his face, but Mr. Toussaint didn't acknowledge his question.

"What do you want to know, Daniel?"

"I want to know… "

Daniel couldn't finish. He wanted to know how to avoid being involved in this bank robbery. He wanted to know why Mr. Toussaint seemed to know more about Daniel than he was saying. He wanted to know when he would find a job. He wanted to know if his loyalty to Javier was holding him back from reaching a goal he didn't know he wanted.

All the questions raced to his mind in a stampede of disarray and left him speechless. Some were just feelings of insecurity that he didn't even know how to verbalize.

Mr. Toussaint reached across the table and plucked the deck from Daniel's hands.

"We can answer a few of those for you."

The elder man flipped the first three cards and didn't react to the obvious result. Daniel tried not to show his surprise that the cards were no longer blank.

"The only alternative to continuing down this predetermined path is death. Do you believe in reincarnation?"

"I don't know what I believe."

"Death isn't necessarily the end. Maybe you come back. Maybe you wait for Judgment Day. Maybe you just cease to exist." Mr. Toussaint began turning more cards on the table. "But these are the choices that you have in this situation. Death doesn't have to be the end. Death can be a teacher... or five."

"Oh."

"There are lessons in everything. Do you know who you are yet?" Mr. Toussaint flipped a few more cards in the reading pattern.

"With all due respect, continuing to ask me who I am isn't gonna make the answer mystically appear in my head."

"No, but it will at least make you think." He tapped his temple with the hand not holding the deck. "Daniel, there's nothing I can tell you here that will help you. You will leave with the same information that you came in with. What did you hope to learn by coming here today? Or was this just a way to waste time while your gremlins retrieved something for you?"

"I wasn't trying to waste your time." Daniel sighed and reached into his pocket, pulling out his wallet.

"You didn't waste *my* time. And we won't charge you for a reading we couldn't provide."

"I can't leave here without paying you for your service. I won't have the thought of owing you a favor hanging over me."

"Fair enough. Let's make the charge out to be one dollar."

Daniel paused before nodding and handing the man a single bill. A feeling of gratefulness and relief shifted through Daniel at the thought of not having to part with $35.

"I'm sure you've been told before how powerful you are." Mr. Toussaint said. "From the moment you walked in the door, I could feel your power. The only way for you to accept who you are is to transition to the role you were meant to play."

"What role is that?"

"You aren't meant to follow Javier forever. And if you wait too long, you'll be too big to follow Comtois."

Daniel stood up from the table and shook the man's hand.

"Thank you for your help. I'll keep all this in mind."

"The kids today listen to you, but they never hear. I suppose some people prefer to learn by trial and error. So hard-headed."

Not knowing how to respond, Daniel exited the shop, avoiding eye contact with Regina although he could feel her eyes on his back. Making a turn into the alley he had visited earlier, Daniel reached down and knocked the dehydrated husk of a rat off the cover of the red book, the remnants of the box torn to shreds.

This wasn't how he originally planned on obtaining the tome, but he had accepted that in order to come up with a full plan, he needed it. The *voleur*, whom Mr. Toussaint had referred to as his gremlins, had provided. Tucking the stolen book under his arm, he made his way back to Junior's apartment to begin translating.

●　●　●　●　●

Daniel spent the weekend translating the scarlet book he had nicknamed, *Le Mini Livre*. It wasn't as big as Madame Katrine Comtois' *Livre Des Esprits*, but Daniel was almost certain the book contained some information that might also be in the bigger tome.

The Spanish classes he had taken in high school didn't help with the translation process. The internet became a major resource in translating the text word by word, phrase by phrase. At times, he would sit and process certain pages he had converted in order to determine if they were or weren't what he needed. The closest he came to a solution was the mention of a 'revealing spirit'. There hadn't been much detail, only half a page or so, and so he had continued on but kept this reference in the back of his mind.

Three days after stealing *Le Mini Livre*, he hadn't completed translating even a quarter of the book and decided to visit *The Grey* for a breather. He figured that contemplating in the dull environment would clear his mind and help him see a solution.

It wasn't long until Daniel ran into Javier at a quaint café situated at a four-way intersection of a road with very little foot traffic. With his piercing gaze fixed forward, Javier sat at an outside table in deep silence. Daniel stopped for a second, wondering if he was interrupting something important.

Before Daniel could decide to leave or stay, Javier's glazed trance evaporated, and he focused on Daniel as if suddenly realizing he was no longer alone. He beckoned Daniel to have a seat.

"I hope I'm not intruding," Daniel said.

"No, not at all. Just waiting for Veronica."

Daniel sat down and sighed. As much as he had resolved not to involve Javier in his situation, it seemed as though he was destined to continue to come to him for advice.

"So?" Javier said.

"I went to see a psychic."

Javier raised his eyebrows but didn't speak.

"They got the same result that I got. I left more confused than when I entered."

"I don't know why you thought it would be different. If the cards you used were *true*…"

"I didn't think it would be different. I just needed somebody with more experience. I hoped that maybe somebody who specialized in reading tarot would be able to find a loophole or… an alternative."

"Got more than you bargained for, huh?"

"Who *am* I?"

"Who are you?"

"One of the psychics seemed to know more about me than I know about myself. And it got me thinking about when you and I first met. You said you had met me before. And then that led me to start thinking about the fact *everybody* seems to know more about me than they're letting on. What are you guys keeping from me?"

"Well… your reputation does precede you. Did you expect to remain anonymous after the uproar you've caused?"

"I expected to not feel like I'm being herded like a calf to slaughter. I can't shake this feeling that I'm being forced into a fate that I didn't agree to. And I'm going to get to the end of this hallway of decisions and realize I could have turned around and exited at any time."

"I feel like I know where this is going."

"Everybody keeps telling me about how much power I have and how I'm different. Is this what power is? A one-lane highway into oncoming traffic while wearing a blindfold?"

"So you think your best bet is to leave? You've outgrown us?"

Daniel shook his head but kept his attention on Javier who refused to look at him. This conversation was not planned. He had wanted to come to *The Grey* to think and clear his mind. Again, destiny was pulling the puppet strings on his life.

"I have a book in my possession now. It gives a lot of information about spirit communication and summoning. I think it can be helpful if the group wanted to expand their knowledge."

"We leave all that to La Marieé des Espirits and her followers. If you want to join their cult, then go ahead. But you won't bring *that* into our house."

"Madame Comtois didn't create this form of voodoo. It was here long before her. It's not something that her followers have a monopoly on. I don't understand why you don't embrace change."

"That's not change. That's a complete transformation. This is *my* faction. I run it how I want to. If you aren't happy, you are free to leave. Start your own community. Go join another one."

Daniel stood up from his chair with the intent to leave but didn't step away. Taking a moment to breathe deep, he sat back down. Javier still refused to look at him.

"Veronica said that I need to do whatever I need to survive. So I used the power I had available to bring a book to me that I think might help me. Only problem is that it's in French. Translating it hasn't been difficult, but it's time-consuming."

No response.

"I think I found a possible solution, but the book doesn't give me much information about outcomes or repercussions. I don't want to end up taking a road that leads to death while trying to avoid another road that leads to death when I could've taken an alternate road that lead to... I need more information. The only way I can get that information is from Madame Comtois."

"She does not *give out* information. You got your first lesson from her for free. Do you hope to get another one? You have taken a bite from her tree of knowledge, and now you want more."

"I don't *want* more. I want to survive."

"Then go survive. Go become the Prince of Veils that everybody wants you to be. Because you obviously can't achieve that while sitting under me."

The Prince of Veils. Daniel had heard that title before but couldn't remember where.

Javier ran his hands through his hair and rose from his seat. Daniel noticed Veronica standing a few tables over and wondered how long she had been there.

"If you want to leave," Javier said. "Then leave. I'm not holding you back."

And he was gone. With the suddenness of his disappearance, Daniel was sure Javier left *The Grey* to return to the real world.

Veronica patted Daniel on the shoulder and took Javier's seat.

"I think I'm starting to notice a trend," Veronica said. "It's beginning to look like my job to give history lessons to help explain shit as if I'm the group historian."

"I'm sorry I ran him off. I know y'all were meeting up."

"It wasn't anything important. We can arrange another meeting."

"How much did you hear?"

"I heard enough. You have this desire to feel complete and staying with us isn't filling that void."

"I feel like we could be so much more if we just expanded. Keith has explored and learned about other aspects of this life before he joined Javier. Dwayne taught me a little bit about tarot reading. Hell, even you know more than you let on with what you mentioned about *The Vale*. Why don't I get an opportunity to explore and learn like everybody else did?"

"It could all be so simple. Do you know why Javier is so upset with the thought of you leaving?"

Daniel shook his head.

"When he first found you in *The Grey*, what did he say to you?"

"He said it was nice to meet me again or something."

"Javier knew you in a previous life. You both actually started this group together. He had the idea, and you had the charisma. You guys wanted to create something to rival anything seen before."

"Is this the big secret everybody knows except me?"

"I wouldn't say everybody knows. Just a few."

"So why the secrecy? Why not just tell me?"

"Even with your soul in a new shell, you're not the same. Every incarnation of you will be different. You grow with each life. You change. You evolve."

"So he's mad because I'm not... the *old* me? What was my name?"

"I think you know."

"Sebastian."

"You both built this group member by member. I was around early on even though I left for a bit to… that's not important. I think that's healthy. Sebastian – or you – seemed to think so too. You preferred that people be here by choice, not obligation or coercion. Although they had differing opinions on how the community should be run, they found ways to make it work. Then Sebastian met a woman, a follower of La Marieé des Espirits, and things changed."

"A woman?"

Veronica smirked, leaned back in her chair and folded her hands in her lap.

"You changed. You evolved. She was your type. Believe me. As you grew closer to her, you grew more distant from Javier. It's inevitable. To gain something, you have to give something up. Javier could see the change and fought as hard as he could. But you relinquished your status with us and became a follower of Marie Leveaux. It crushed him."

"Why didn't he tell me this?"

"I'm not sure. But I do know it caused resentment in him."

"Explains why he doesn't think too highly of Madame Comtois."

"You have a responsibility to be true to yourself. If you think the best course of action to survive is to go to join Marie Leveaux's group, then you should."

"I have this feeling that I will never be able to make a logical decision because I don't know all of the facts. Everybody is withholding information. Javier didn't tell me who I was. A psychic yesterday wouldn't tell me who I am. And Madam Comtois will only help me if I join her."

"It could all be so simple."

"Who is the Prince of Veils?"

"Why do you ask?"

"Javier mentioned it earlier. And the name sounded familiar."

Veronica paused. Taking a moment to smooth her dress down, she looked Daniel in the eye.

"It's an old title," she said. "There have been conversations about what it means or who should be called what. But to be honest, with all the egos running around here... There's not a definitive definition."

"What do *you* think it means?"

"I believe it's a title for whoever holds the most power at the time in *The Grey*. Which right now, in my opinion, would be you."

"Me?"

"Yes. Everywhere you go, your power amazes us. The speed at which you learn how to do things. Your desire to know all the tricks of the trade. You truly are *The Grey* incarnate."

"But I can't learn anything if I'm sitting under Javier. He only knows so much."

"And you'll have to be careful because there are a lot of people out there that will use you. They see the power you have to offer and will want to control that. Be mindful of who you trust."

"What if I don't want to be the Prince of Veils?"

"Then stay here with Javier and wallow in ignorance."

"Or leave and betray him a second time. So that's what the psychic meant by learning who I was. He knew. But was it something he saw in the cards? Is that why the tarot was pushing me to rob this bank? So that I would learn more voodoo and move into this Prince of Veils' role?"

Veronica was silent. Daniel realized he had let it slip about his robbery plans.

"I'm at another crossroads," he said. "Another avenue that's keeping me from living a normal life. How much of everything that's happened recent are just events conveniently placed to see me move in this direction? My job loss? Junior's random idea to rob a bank? The tarot cards?"

"One of the many joys of life is the ability to make your own decisions. You don't have to accept the obvious choices provided."

"You're right. If I want to shake this feeling of being manipulated, then I need to stop being so predictable and allowing myself to be pushed. I'm going to take a careless leap and see where I land."

"Unless that's what the tarot cards intended you to do." Veronica smirked.

"Please don't make this more complicated. This could easily spiral into a rabbit hole of paradox."

Veronica waited, not speaking.

Daniel felt she had more information but was feeding it to him as she saw necessary. This was a form of control, and he wanted it to stop.

"I know what I need to do."

CHAPTER TWO

Daniel was a geek in high school. He didn't participate in any extracurricular activities because he didn't know how to explore where his strengths may lie. As a result, he hadn't ever felt like he was a part of anything. Having watched as young athletes achieved sports accolades or awkward nerds strive for higher learning, Daniel didn't have a sense of belonging to any particular group. At times this bothered him. He could remember staring at a member of the popular crowd and daydreaming what it would be like to befriend that individual. Or thinking about life as the school rebel who rarely attended classes and always had an intriguing story to share about something that happened when they were skipping school.

For the majority of high school, Daniel had flown under the radar. If you were to ask any of his former classmates to describe his personality, they most likely wouldn't even remember who he was. This was effectively a positive attribute when he was first coming into his powers. It gave him a chance to remain unnoticed as he came to terms with his abilities.

There was one occasion when Daniel received attention. In his junior year, Daniel was confronted by a classmate for the type of attire Daniel chose to wear. Fashion was a major factor in determining your social standing in the hierarchy of High School popularity. Name brand clothes and fashion trends changed often but Daniel never paid much attention to what sneaker was relevant for a semester or which designer was in season.

His Biology classmate, Christopher, noticed Daniel's disregard for trends and decided to berate him about it for the amusement of the class. Daniel had laughed off the jest. His mom had told him that inciting a bully would only fuel the fire and so he had waited for the classmate's attention to pass. The students laughed, thinking the japes were hilarious, and Christopher was like a pride of lions on an injured antelope. His jokes continued for the full class session with relentless conviction.

Daniel endured, knowing the scheduled class only lasted an hour and a half. The incident fell from his mind and he had left the class thinking he would return to his mundane attendance in adolescent life.

When the next class period convened, the verbal joust commenced again as if it had never been interrupted, and Daniel felt the weight of distress layer itself beneath his sternum. Before Daniel could consider the consequences, he lashed out with a verbal reply that was not only humorous and intelligent but damaging to Christopher's reputation.

On the waves of his remark, the students' laughter cascaded throughout the classroom. No longer were they enamored by Daniel's embarrassment, but now they were infatuated with Daniel's witty comebacks. Daniel vomited a barrage of slanderous retorts and turned the tables on the bully. He couldn't say if it was the adrenaline from his temporary popularity or the confusion from the rollercoaster of teenage hormones one experiences at that age, but he stepped outside of himself and became somebody he didn't recognize. On a whim, he heightened the experience of banishing the evil dragon of the school with *Grey Matter* to give Christopher the impression that the students were laughing louder than they actually were. Daniel's temporary popularity fueled his own fire. He pushed the degrading feeling of being a public focal point down on to Christopher and relished in the oppression. Daniel had taken on the persona of Karma.

Christopher, unaccustomed to being ridiculed at such gross level, snapped and turned the battle from verbal to physical. The pain of the punch or the confusion of suddenly being on the floor took a moment to register within Daniel's brain. This was the first time in his life he had been in a physical altercation and his mind didn't know how to process it. Christopher barraged Daniel with fists of fire for what seemed like an eternity before the other classmates and the presiding Biology teacher broke up the fight.

A full week of suspension was handed down as a punishment to Christopher. Whispers of the incident followed Daniel for a day or two but was soon forgotten as more interesting news and rumors washed away the memory of old events the same way waves erased sand markings on the beach.

After a week of suspension, Christopher returned with a vendetta. This confused Daniel since everybody knew Christopher had won the fist fight. But Christopher's vengeance was fully engorged as he relentlessly made insidious remarks to Daniel.

Daniel could see that time would not heal the wound he had inflicted on Christopher. His sarcastic mouth and hidden powers had heightened a tense situation. In retrospect, Daniel knew that it was his abilities that caused the situation to get this far so using them again would be a stupid idea. But he was young and didn't always make the best decisions. At the time, he figured that if embarrassment didn't deter a bully, then maybe fear would.

He pulled from *The Grey* more than he had ever attempted to pull before. The amount of *Grey Matter* that ran through his body made him feel as if his skin were burning from the inside out. He would later describe the sensation as somebody peeling the muscles and tendons from his bones by each individual fiber. But even with the essence of pain flowing through his veins, he felt invincible. This was power that begged to be molded, sculpted and used. And Daniel knew that this wasn't his limit. He could pull more if he wanted. With the strength of a deity lightening through all the nerves in his body, Daniel created a scene that he had seen in an old black and white movie. Daniel covered Christopher in an imagined reality where spiders crawled from the air ducts, scurried from under the tables and dropped from the ceiling. Arachnids of all variety and sizes raced toward a victim, not necessarily with the intent to harm, but to reach a destination. To Christopher, it was real. But nobody else in the room saw it.

Christopher's reaction was everything Daniel had ever wanted to savor in a moment of revenge. It was the most delicious form of retaliation he had ever tasted.

Christopher went insane.

He slapped. He stomped. He yelled. He spit. He ran.

He didn't return to school for three days. When he did return, he was different. His personality was not the same. Where Christopher once joked with other students, even at the expense of his peers, he was now jumpy and anxious. The smallest movement out of the corner of his eye sent spasms of flailing as he swiped at his clothes in fear. Dark circles began to form around his eyes from what Daniel assumed was a lack of sleep. Ironically, his desire to be impeccably attired and admiringly fashionable waned. The most relieving side effect, the daily ritualistic ridicule for Daniel was replaced with the need to watch for anything that crawled. Daniel had instilled arachnophobia in Christopher.

Intrigued by the fact that he had used a scene from a movie as a weapon with his power, Daniel became obsessed with watching horror movies. He devoured them with an insatiable intensity. Where once he enjoyed reading science fiction books and watching reality tv shows, he now became infatuated with Stephen King novels and Nightmare Before Elm Street movies. He feasted on stories of urban legends from his classmates and ghost stories from relatives.

With his new love of movies, Daniel applied for a job at a local movie trading store. It was there that he got to see all the movies he could consume in his spare time for free. With access to an unlimited supply of fantastical material from the most grotesque of horror movies to the simplest of thrillers, Daniel learned.

In his search for arsenal to add to his cache of mystical weaponry, Daniel didn't stop to acknowledge the news that Christopher's phobia migrated into psychotic symptoms which included hallucinations and delusions. Christopher, the former high school bully, was later committed to a mental institution in Terrell, Texas.

● ● ● ● ●

Daniel stood in the bathroom staring at his reflection in the mirror. For the first time in his adult memory, he regretted being such an avid fan of the horror movie genre. Daniel couldn't stop thinking about all the possible scenarios in which this could end in tragedy. The spirit he was going to call on could break the mirror and jam it into his neck, severing an artery. Or maybe just gazing on the face of the spirit would cause his body to deteriorate where he stood, leaving a gaunt skeleton of what he once was.

One scenario continued to move to the forefront of his mind. An old urban legend that he had heard as a kid, not to mention the many variations, that told the tale of a group of teenagers who gathered in a dark room. With a mirror in front of them and the lights off, they would chant 'Bloody Mary' three times. And when you turned the lights back on, the apparition of a gory figure could be seen for an instant before fading away. The teenagers would leave in fear, each with a bruise somewhere on their body from where Bloody Mary had touched them. If you didn't turn the lights on quick enough, it might be more than a bruise.

As with all horror stories, Daniel had enjoyed that one and written it off as entertainment. But a lot of people would have disregarded tales of voodoo. He questioned that if he believed it was fake then why hadn't he tried it himself? Somewhere in the back of his mind there must have been a shadow of doubt that lingered behind his sense of realism.

Now he was going to have to face his skepticism with something that could possibly be more dangerous. At least with Bloody Mary he had a broad range of stories that held information. With this mid-level spirit he was about to summon, he had half a page from a stolen text.

"Why are you staring at yourself in the mirror?" Junior asked from the doorway.

"Something major is about to happen. I'm building up some courage to take a leap."

"There should be a second person here if you're trying to lose your virginity."

"I am about to jump into the ocean, and I hope I figure out how to swim before I drown. Or before something that lives in the deep blue eats me."

"All these analogies. Just say what you mean."

"I'm about to summon a spirit, and it might be an evil spirit. I'm not sure. But I think it can help us with getting information we need for that… *thing*… we plan on doing."

Junior walked around and stood behind Daniel, grabbing his shoulders and massaging them. Daniel tried not to show how much he enjoyed the physical touch.

"You got this, champ," Junior said. "Before every fight, my dad used to have a routine to help him get mentally prepared. He would listen to this cheesy salsa music while throwing air jabs at his coach. Then he would kneel for a minute to pray, kiss a picture of his mom, and put his hands up in the air as if he had already won the fight."

"I don't think music or kissing pictures will help right now."

"I'm giving you a story to help you with your dilemma."

"I'm having a hard time deciphering the moral."

"He surrounded himself with symbolic items that meant something to him and soothing habits in order to get past his nervousness. A lot of boxers play this role like they ain't afraid of nothing. But they're basically fighting for respect and to put bread on the table. Who wouldn't be a little bit afraid of that? But he didn't let it stop him. My dad made sure he kept his reasons for doing it in sight so he would have the motivation to make that plunge into the ocean."

Daniel made eye contact with Junior's reflection and nodded. That actually made sense.

Junior smiled, reached into his pocket and pulled out a dollar, placing it next to the sink.

"Let this be your motivation. Text me and let me know how it goes."

"Where are you going?" Daniel asked.

"Going over to Fatima's. I don't want to be around when the spirit of Christmas past jumps up from the depths of Hell and devours you."

The Gate, 1987. A group of kids finds a hole in the ground that leads to the doorway of Hell. A horde of demonic trolls exit from the ground and attempt to sacrifice the children to fully open the gateway and release bigger demons upon the Earth.

"That's not funny," Daniel said.

"I won't be back tonight, so you can have the bed… but only if you're not bleeding from this encounter. I just washed those sheets. And I rarely ever wash."

"You'll regret these jokes if I die."

"I want that dollar back when you're finished too."

Daniel listened as Junior gathered his things and left. The sound of the door closing and the lock being turnt sent a shiver up his spine.

"Let my motivation drive me to overcome this fear…"

Daniel scooped the dollar off the counter and stared at it.

"This isn't my motivation. I'm not in this for the money. I'm trying to *survive*." He tossed the bill over his shoulder and watched it flutter to the floor from the reflection in the mirror. "If I'm being honest, *I'm* my motivation. Not to mention my pride. My ego is too big to go ask for help. I'm one hundred percent sure if I just asked for help..."

Daniel thought about how this scenario would be different with Veronica or Javier beside him. Or any of the other members of the group that had experience with voodoo.

"More manipulation by Destiny? Everywhere I look now, I'm going to see doubt and traps. I'll never truly know if I'm being manipulated into situations or if this is my own decision. Unless I do everything that goes against my intuition and common sense.

"That's why you have to do it this way. What voodoo master would attempt some stupid shit like this without guidance? A fool, that's who. So if they want a fool for a leader, let's give them one."

Daniel straightened his back and stared into his own eyes. As he tried to clear his mind, the memories of horror movie scenes elbowed its way back into his thoughts.

Crystal Lake, 2001. A college-age girl wakes up one morning to find the words 'Aren't you glad you didn't turn on the lights?' written with her roommate's blood on the wall. The phrase was referencing the fact she had come home and heard her roommate having sex so she didn't turn on the lights as she made her way to bed. But it hadn't been the throws of passion the girl heard but instead the sound of her roommate being killed.

Daniel breathed deeply then exhaled slowly. Taking dry erase marker he had purchased earlier, he composed the necessary summoning symbols on the smooth mirror surface. He closed his eyes and gathered his thoughts. He projected a desire to commune with the spirit known as Ghiy-āthu'd-Dīn, sending out thoughts while his mouth formed the chant he had transcribed from the *Mini Livre*.

With the *voleur*, he didn't have to call. Any random desire that resembled covetousness awakened them. Throughout a normal day, he would see single individuals from the collective scattered in random nooks and corners waiting to serve. A token of lust in his eye sent them into a chorus of begging. Daniel learned early that if too many of them caught wind of his desire, the volume of the cluster chanting in unison would give him a severe headache.

The lesson he had taken away was not to yearn for anything too hard. He also acquired the ability to overlook the creatures scattered throughout a crowd or clinging to a passing car or hanging from a restaurant ceiling. His eyes slid past them as if he was staring at a page looking for Waldo camouflaged in normal reality.

But Ghiy-āthu'd-Dīn was not the *voleur*. It was stronger. It was singular. It was not waiting to attend him. He had to call for it and hope that it answered. And if it did, then he could try to bargain with it.

And he felt it when it answered his call. There wasn't a sound to announce its arrival. Nothing unusual like a flicker of lights or a chill of up his spine. Daniel just *knew* it was there. It was the feeling that he was no longer alone, a pair of eyes on his back, static from a television before the screen showed a channel.

Daniel looked at his reflection in the mirror and to his left was a dark figure. He turned from the mirror, somewhat afraid to have the spirit so close, but there wasn't anything beside him. Only the single dollar lying on the tile floor.

A simple moment of confusion swept over Daniel as he realized the figure could only be seen in the mirror. The gender of the shadowy shape was indeterminable, but it was human in appearance. The head could have been cloaked or shrouded in hair. No recognizable arms but definitely a torso. Taller than Daniel but slender. He would have to lean closer to the mirror if he wanted to see its feet over the reflection of the counter. The scene from the horror movie, *Redemption Creek*, where a hand reached out of a mirror to strangle a blonde victim played in Daniel's mind. He decided getting closer wouldn't be a good idea.

Daniel waited, wanting the spirit to speak first. The silence became awkward.

The Silent Tale, 2010. Patrons of a bed and breakfast awaken to find themselves shackled in a basement with their mouths sewn shut.

"I have come with... a request," Daniel said, breaking the silence.

"You have fear draped over you like a cloak."

Its voice couldn't have been any more different than the *voleur*. Where their voices were carried on shuffling footsteps on carpet or passing of air by a window, Ghiy-āthu'd-Dīn's voice was a low rumble that felt like a synthesized organ on a techno song. It was deep and melodious but left an impression of artificiality.

"There's nothing here for you to be afraid of," it said.

"I need some information."

"I know what you seek. I can provide everything you could ask for."

"What is your price? How much will this cost me?"

The *voleur* required a small sacrifice. Daniel usually offered a mouse or small rat. He had determined before calling upon this higher level spirit that the most he would offer was a cat. Because who really liked cats anyway? But if the being asked for a larger animal, such as a dog or a goat, that would be his limit. Daniel didn't want to see all his humanity swallowed in an attempt to appease this apparition.

"I am not one of your minions that feeds off the blood of vermin. To offer such a ragged fair would be offensive."

"If not blood, then what?"

Little Shop of Horrors, 1986. Mistreated, orphaned nerd finds a talking plant that provides fame, fortune, and love but in exchange for blood.

The figure in the mirror shifted, distorted, and moved closer to Daniel. He could see an aura of darkness expand that gave Daniel the impression the figure was growing as the conversation continued.

"For most, I would require more than what they could offer. Most cannot afford even the smallest of my services. But you... I would gladly reduce my fee for the opportunity to attend one with a future as plentiful as yours."

"I expected you to talk in riddles to try to confuse me. Adding in some flattery is surprising."

"Flattery? I am not here to pretend to adulate you with pretty words in to boost your ego. I'm choosing to align myself with you for personal gain. I'm not one who feeds from the essence of blood nor the arousal of fear - which I must say, you *are* projecting immensely. No, I want the reparations and residuals from standing beside the Prince of Veils."

"What *exactly* do you want?"

"I would propose being in my debt but I expect you to be cautious for those terms."

"I'm not accepting a deal when I don't know the details."

"I wouldn't expect anything less."

"How do I know you have the information that I want?"

"This information?"

Daniel's attention shifted to the countertop in the reflection. A stack of papers visible only in the mirror.

"What is that?"

"The architectural blueprints for the bank, the work schedules for the employees for the next two weeks, the vault deposit schedule, the algorithm for the bank tokens. Location of the security camera database. Wiring schematics for the alarm system. And the personnel files for the bank staff including previous work history for your roommate's girlfriend."

"And what do I give you?"

"My request is that you hold an item for me. Take a burden upon yourself."

Curse of the Djinn, 1988. The genie grants a man three wishes and in return, the man exchanges places with the genie, trapped in the oil lamp, until another unfortunate soul makes three wishes for him to grant.

"I'm listening."

"I have a mirror, ostentatious and burdensome, passed down from the times when Victorian ladies adorned the cheapest of merchandise with the most expensive of décor. I've never had a taste for extravagance. Maybe you'll find a use for it?"

"A mirror?"

"A gaudy hand mirror."

"What's the catch?"

"None. You take it off my hands, and you'll fulfill your part of the payment. You are allowed keep it, trash it, *destroy* it. It makes no difference to me. It'll grant an equal exchange in this trade which is all that matters. It's the least expensive form of payment I can offer you for this information."

"What does it do?"

"What do all mirrors do? Reflect light back, I suppose."

Daniel couldn't help feeling this was a trap. Once again, he wasn't asking the right questions.

"What do you get out of this? I need to know."

"I get the opportunity to be in your good graces. There was a time when I was called upon regularly by a priestess in France and temples in Kemit. Today, I am parched to find any such remembrance. You can bring me back to relevance. With you is power and a way back to prominence."

"I'm not a member of a spiritualist community. You might be sorely disappointed if you think I can re-introduce you to them."

"It's not who you are today but who you will be tomorrow that piques my desire for alignment. Let me be a weapon in your arsenal."

Daniel took a mental step back and reviewed the conversational phrasing, looking for loopholes.

"You seem hesitant," Ghiy-āthu'd-Dīn said. "So let me make my offer more enticing. Allow me to take this off your hands."

The spirit raised what Daniel assumed was a hand and displayed one of the tarot cards that started this situation. It was one of the five Death Cards. The picture of the hooded figure holding a scythe seemed to grow a dark aura of its own to match Ghiy-āthu'd-Dīn's.

Daniel wanted to ask what taking the card do for his situation but didn't want to show the spirit how ignorant he was in his own voodoo arts. If it was offering to take the card, then that must be something significant. Daniel would just have to find out later what was important about the gesture.

He had taken a risk to summon this spirit, not knowing how dangerous it could have been, and now he was going to have to take another. Before he could second guess himself, Daniel nodded his head.

"Deal. I agree to your terms."

"As do I."

Daniel waited, expecting the documents he had been promised to appear on the counter. But they remained a reflection in the mirror.

"Well?" Daniel said. "Are you going to give it to me?"

"It has already been given, Simple Prince. You asked for information and I have provided. Here, you can see all the information of which you asked."

Daniel smiled. "So that was the small print in this contract? I can only see the information in the mirror. I should've known."

"You are mistaken if you think it was my intention to deceive. I only give that of which you asked. Do you want to send your minions to retrieve the hand mirror or should I bring it myself?"

"My *voleur* are capable."

"It is apparent you are an amateur in this aspect of the arts. Growing in the practice is something that will be necessary if you want to avoid those Death Cards. Perhaps, I can offer you some advice on this bank robbery…"

"What kind of advice do you have to give?"

"Advice that would make this information you have asked for irrelevant."

"What's the price?"

"My Prince, this one will be free of charge…"

• • • • •

Brad sat in his car and refreshed the webpage one more time on his phone. He had been checking the same web address every fifteen minutes to see if his grades had posted yet. His Calculus II and Physics II class had both posted his well-earned 'B' earlier in the day. The Psychology class hadn't posted, but he wasn't concerned about that grade. He was confident he had passed with an 'A'. It was the Chemistry I class that was fraying at his nerves. Something about the logic of chemistry didn't compute in his mind, so this class had been a struggle.

Throughout middle school and high school, Brad had been a straight 'A' student. His brain had absorbed knowledge as quick as his teachers had been able to supply it. He coasted by without learning the proper ways to study or learn. Doing homework and assignments had been sufficient enough for him to pass any exams.

But college was a different beast. Information was provided at a faster pace. Assignments didn't have to be completed on a regular basis, and attendance was optional. Brad had struggled to pass classes his first semester. He remembered instances when he would leave a class and brag to his peers that the exam he had just finished seemed a little too easy. Only to later find out he had failed the test. Collegiate level courses required Brad to do more than regurgitate text from the expensive textbooks.

So Brad had started to teach himself how to study. He gave himself homework. He reached out to classmates for study materials and practice exams. He figured this was his first obstacle into adulthood, and he was determined to succeed. Although sometimes he wasn't sure if he was ready to enter the adult world.

There always seemed to be something that needed to be done. Always some stressful event that required his attention. Between school and work and social events, Brad was tired.

Seeing that his Chemistry grade still hadn't posted, Brad stepped out of his car, an old four-door Nissan Altima that had been passed down from his older brother, and walked into the building to start his work shift.

"Brad. Where have you been?" Sharon asked. "You're late. We've got orders piling up and Mario is a no-show."

"Great," Brad mumbled.

"I need you to cover his area today since it's next to yours. Here's six orders that have already come in."

Brad snatched the order slips from the counter and flipped through them. Four of them he was familiar with because they were in his delivery area. The other two he assumed were in Mario's radius.

"This shouldn't be too bad."

"Oh," Sharon snapped her fingers. "The new guy started today. I want you to let him tail you. Show him the ropes or whatever. He's over there. Eric, sweetie, this is Brad. He's the driver you're going to be shadowing today."

Brad glanced up from the order slips to allow the new guy a brief nod before returning his attention to a map on the wall to trace out the most efficient route for deliveries. One order caught his attention and he frowned in confusion.

"Hey, Sharon, where is this restaurant, The Chip Hut? I've never heard of that?"

"I think it's downtown." Sharon said.

Brad felt the new guy walk up next to him. Taking his gaze away from the map, he got a better look at Eric. He was a tall and skinny nerd type with tight pants and an oversized shirt. He looked young enough to still be in high school. Brad had been working at FoodHub, the fast food delivery service, for six months and the number of employees he had seen come and go was phenomenal. He didn't expect this kid to last long.

"You been there before? Chip Hut?" Brad asked, waving the ticket slip for the unfamiliar restaurant.

"No, never heard of it. That address is downtown though."

"I guess we'll find out when we get there."

The kid shrugged and Brad turned to leave, beckoning Eric to follow.

"Don't forget your hat," Eric said.

Brad took the blue hat with the FoodHub logo from Eric not bothering to put it on. He avoided wearing the hat when he could not only because it gave him hat hair, but because he was embarrassed about where he worked and didn't want to advertise his place of employment.

Eric placed the empty warming bags for the food into the backseat and climbed in. Brad checked his phone to see if there was any update on his Chemistry class.

"I'm going to go ahead and warn you now," Brad said "I'm going to be a little bit distracted while training you because I'm waiting on some grades from a couple of my classes."

"That's fine. I learn by observing anyway."

Brad put his phone away with a frustrated sigh and started the car. Grades should be posted by the end of the day, so if he could just make it through these four hours of work, then by the time he got off he would know whether he passed or failed. So he decided to use some of his will power and stop checking his phone. That should make the day pass faster and keep him from being stressed about something he couldn't control anymore.

"No offense, but you look too young to be working," Brad said. "How old are you?"

"I get that a lot. I'm 19."

"I would never have been able to tell. Is FoodHub your first job?"

"No, I worked at a gas station prior to this."

"It's a pretty good job for college students because the schedule is flexible. The tips aren't really reliable though. Some days I can rack up a good stack. But other days…"

"How long have you worked for FoodHub?"

"Six or seven months." Brad handed his order cards to Eric. "So each driver has a specified area to deliver to. These are the orders we've received so far. We go pick up the food from the restaurant and deliver it to the customer. Everything has been paid for online so we provide the order card and get the food. I try to be efficient and plan my orders and deliveries for the best possible routes."

"Okay."

"Saves on mileage on my car. I need this lemon to last me until I graduate."

"I can understand that."

"First stop is that place downtown, The Chip Hut."

A ten-minute drive later, with the music blasting so Brad wouldn't have to make small talk with Eric, they pulled up to the restaurant. Brad exited his car and looked up at the building. The restaurant looked out of place stuck between all these office buildings.

As he walked in the door, Brad received a text message from Gina, a girl from his Psychology class.

-Party tonight at Kappa House. U going?-

-Not sure… depends on mood-

Brad got in the line behind some customers. He figured with the restaurant being so small, they probably didn't have a system in place for delivery men to skip the line and pick up orders.

-Rough day?-

-not really… just waiting on some final grades-

-What's your major again?-

-today… Biomedical engineering…. Tomorrow… who knows-

-Why would you choose such a hard major?-

-money-

-LOL-

-I'll let you know if I decide to go or not-

The customer that ahead of Brad moved away from the cashier. He walked to the counter and handed the employee the order card along with the warming bag.

"It's not a very big order. We should be able to get everything in the bag," Brad told her.

She read the order card then looked up at him. Brad frowned at the look of confusion on her face. Then a flash of something else before she began loading the bag with the food order.

He started to ask if anything was wrong when his phone chimed with a new text message. Gina again.

-Anna was asking if you were going to be there. Just FYI-

-what's her deal? Does she seriously think we're going to hook up after she already hooked up with Steven and Trey?-

-I don't think they would care. They're still friends.-

-I'll pass… she's not my type… somebody should let her know-

-LOL-

-by somebody I mean you… you're her friend- Brad was annoyed that she didn't get the hint.

-She's not really my friend. Her brother used to sell really good weed and he was hot-

The cashier returned with the bag and handed it to Brad. He smiled and glanced at her name tag. She was cute, and he hoped to run into her again if he ever had another delivery from here. Might even chance asking her out.

"Thanks, Sharon," He said as he turned away.

-I'll come out if my grades don't have me down… but gotta go… at work-

-OK. Text me later. Bring tequila.-

The bag was heavier than he expected and he ended up dropping it. Embarrassed, he didn't turn to see if the cashier noticed and rushed through the lobby out the door. Eric, following behind, offered to carry the bag but Brad shook his head.

With a nervous feeling of remorse for breaking his promise not to check, Brad opened the app to see if his Chemistry grade had been updated. Still nothing.

"After we get the food," Brad said. "We take it to the customer. I keep two warming bags in the car because sometimes two restaurants are kinda close. Two birds with one stone. It sucks for the customer if I've picked up their food first but my scheduled route doesn't take me into their area until the last stop. But oh well."

Brad looked over at Eric. The poor kid was hanging on to Brad's every word as if there would be a test afterward. He had seen kids like this in high school that were over-achievers and always eager to complete tasks. Brad wondered if kids like this ever lost their virginity before graduation. Just from the mannerisms alone, Brad couldn't help but think this kid had probably only seen a naked girl on the internet or when he walked in on his mom changing.

And an idea tugged at the back of Brad's mind.

"Hey," Brad said. "Do you drink?"

"I'm not old enough yet."

"You got any plans tonight?"

"No."

"How would you like to go to a party tonight? I got a girl that I think you would be perfect for."

Ten minutes later, Brad pulled up in front of a bookstore. A shorter guy wearing a bookstore uniform greeted him.

Brad watched as the man removed the sandwiches from the FoodHub warming bag and transferred them to his own red duffle.

"That's a lot of food for this small store," Brad commented.

"We're having a book signing later today and wanted refreshments."

Brad tried to contain his reaction to the fact the guy's voice didn't match what Brad had expected.

The guy handed Brad a nice tip which surprised him. Turning, he found Eric standing a little too close for comfort; especially since Brad had forgotten Eric was even behind him. Brad hoped Eric didn't expect to get a portion of the tip.

"What kind of business is this?" Eric asked. "We deliver more than food?"

"No, just food. Why do you ask?"

Eric didn't answer but seemed to hesitate before getting back in the car. Brad pulled out his phone, ignoring the two missed text messages and logged in to the school's website for an update.

The Psychology and Chemistry grades had been posted.

•　•　•　•　•

Daniel didn't wait around to watch the delivery guys leave. He took the duffle bag and walked to Junior's car, trying his best not to rush. Placing the bag of money in the passenger seat, he buckled his seatbelt and drove off.

•　•　•　•　•

Daniel walked into the apartment and dropped the duffle bag on the table. His face felt warm with adrenaline. The smile he had tried to contain on the drive home escaped into a full grin as he ran his palms across the front of his pants.

"We did it."

The reality of their actions kept him from being able to sit down. On the drive home he had even screamed a couple of times.

He unzipped the duffle bag and looked at the unorganized clumps of money. It had been an almost flawless plan.

Earlier that morning, Daniel told Junior that he had a plan for robbing the bank and the most opportune time to follow through would be that afternoon.

"Today?" Junior asked. "I guess your experiment last night in the mirror was successful?"

"This entire time we were over-thinking the plan. We were trying to come up with a plan that involved the two of us being on the front line."

"If not us, then who?"

"Whoever we want. Random stranger on the street. Corporate asshole from Park Row. Broke college student. Doesn't matter."

"I wouldn't mind seeing the Corporate asshole go down for this. What if we use the manager that laid you off?"

"As tempting as that sounds, it's best we use somebody we don't know. Plus, we're not doing this for revenge."

Junior shrugged.

Daniel pulled out the sheets of typing paper with his familiar handwriting on them and spread them across the table. The employee schedules, bank blueprints, and bank policy and procedures. He had a difficult time at first trying to duplicate the documents from a mirrored reflection but after some time his mind had becoming accustomed to reading the ever-altering documents in reverse and transposing to printer paper.

"Where did you get this?"

"Results from yesterday. And a few *other* things."

Daniel glanced at the hand mirror laid face down on the end table.

Junior shuffled through the papers with a look of satisfaction on his face. Daniel slipped a page from the stack and pointed at a paragraph that was most interesting.

"Look here," Daniel said. "There's a bank policy that states if a potential robber comes in with a note and hands it to the bank teller, there won't be an alarm sounded. To protect the staff and the customers, the teller will completely empty the cash drawer and allow the robber to leave before sounding an alarm."

"A note?"

"Yep. A note that basically just conveys that this is a bank robbery or give me all your money. Something to that effect."

Junior scanned the paragraph with a sense of disbelief. When Ghiy-āthu'd-Dīn had explained the policy to Daniel, he hadn't believed it either. But examining the policy and procedures document helped to push aside any skepticism.

"Bro," Junior said.

"I know. But that's not all. We don't have to do this ourselves. I can give anybody a note and have them go into the bank for the money. I can change their perception so that they don't even know that they're robbing a bank."

"Somebody else can go down for the crime."

"Yes… Wait… No!" Daniel shook his head. "Nobody has to go down for the crime. We need to do everything we can to make sure they don't get caught. Treat them as if we were the ones actually doing the crime."

"Why?"

"Junior, I don't want anybody to get hurt. This will be an innocent person." A discomfort pinched the back of his mind at the thought of the hand mirror.

"I don't care either way. So how do we keep them from getting caught?"

"Well, first we need to take out the security cameras. Fatima said the data is stored off-site, so we don't have a way to erase it. But what if we disable the cameras?"

"Who has access to do that?"

Daniel smiled and reached down to pick up the sacrifice he hadn't had to use with Ghiy-āthu'd-Dīn . He placed a small, clear cage on the table and looked at Junior.

"A rat?" Junior asked.

"A rat!" Daniel was excited to explain this part of the plan to Junior. "You said you can control animals. We just need a few of them to chew through the security cameras. Three in particular." Daniel picked up a pen and began circling sections on the bank blueprints. "One at the right entrance door, one in front of the teller and this one to the right of the lobby. That will create a blind section for our guy to get in and out."

"I don't want Fatima involved in this. How do we keep her from getting involved?"

"She's going to be involved no matter what we do. We're robbing the bank that she works at."

"But I don't want her to be anywhere near this. You saw how she reacted when you were messing with her mind about the hypothetical robbery. She's a cool girl and doesn't deserve-"

"Look." Daniel held up his hand to stop Junior. "I agree. I'm assuming you'll need to be in the bank anyway to move the rats and distract the guard. Maybe your excuse at the time can be that you were there to take her to lunch. Isn't that what couples do? Go on lunch dates or whatever?"

"I can be there in case anything goes down."

"Right, but I need you aware of everything so don't let her distract you because I have one more task you'll need to handle."

"Damn, why am I getting so many fucking tasks? What will *you* be doing?"

"I'll be bending reality so that nobody in the bank will know what's going on? I'll be guiding our robber to and from the bank and then collecting the money. I'll be making sure he doesn't know that he's robbing a bank."

"Okay. Fair enough. What is my other responsibility?"

"I need you to knock the teller out after she gives him the money."

Ghiy-āthu'd-Dīn had suggested killing the teller. Perhaps by making her heart stop working. But Daniel wanted this to end without any fatalities. His primary goal was to not have any casualties. He needed to delay the teller from pressing any alarms. The alternative option was to incapacitate her.

"Knock her out? I ain't trying to go to jail for battery."

"You said you can stop hearts. You can't stop anything else? Her lungs from breathing? Maybe raise her blood pressure until she faints? We don't want to kill her, but we need some time to let the robber get away."

"I never thought about that."

"You're only limited by your own imagination."

"We're about to rob a bank." Junior smiled.

"We're about to rob a bank." Daniel echoed.

Daniel watched the excitement dance across Junior's face and saw the spark in his hazel eyes that all the women he came across fell in love with. They were going to rob a bank.

"Now," Daniel said. "Let's go over the plan again. We need to comb through everything and make sure there aren't any holes or possible weaknesses."

"Let's do this shit."

But no plan was flawless. No matter how much you planned ahead or tried to accommodate for possible contingencies, there would always be something that would be unexpected. Daniel had learned this lesson from the day to day work at the call center and incorporated it in the plan. He had decided that if the robbery was looking to go south at any point, he would abandon it. It was better to not get caught and be able to rob another day.

Daniel's first task was to find the puppet. His ideal candidate was a delivery person. Spending an hour camped outside a FoodHub branch provided a suitable participant. A young delivery driver that seemed distracted by his cell phone. Daniel's eyes drank in the man's athletic body and charismatic confidence and assumed he was a lady's man. These assumptions evolved to include the constant attention to his phone as a frat boy's need to be included in a popular social life. Every characteristic the guy displayed screamed that he would be an easy and distracted target.

Daniel found out afterward that there would be a tag-a-long. He didn't see much foot traffic going in and out of the food delivery service center, so Daniel accepted the pair and followed his initial instinct, enveloping the young man and his companion in *Grey Matter*. They saw what he wanted them to see, and the first switch was the order card. Daniel displayed an address on the note card guiding them to the bank. The message for the teller was simple and direct.

This is a robbery. Empty the cash drawer.

The pair drove to the bank as Daniel followed. Junior texted Daniel that the rats had successfully chewed through the security camera wires, and the security guard had been hit with the pains of a stomach flu that would have him occupying the restroom for ten to fifteen minutes.

Daniel distracted the delivery guy by supplying him with a faux text conversation, not only to keep him occupied but to keep his head down in order to prevent the other customers from seeing his face. Daniel didn't need to enter the bank and sat in his car, watching through the glass doors. When the pair exited, Daniel led the way to the drop-off point, not waiting to see if Junior completed his final task of incapacitating the bank teller.

During the robbery, Daniel had trouble with the delivery companion, the unnecessary tag-a-long. His powers didn't work on the kid as it did with most. This had happened once when Daniel was in high school with one of his cousins, and he had never been able to figure out why. *The Grey* kept slipping off the kid as if he were covered in oil. At the drop-off, Daniel was almost certain the guy saw everything. The money in the unzipped duffle and Daniel's face. There had been a reaction that was unmistakable. But did he know where the money had come from? What they had just done?

Junior texted Daniel that Fatima was dealing with the police and he wanted to stay with her for moral support.

Daniel stared at the money in the duffle bag remembering how many times they had reviewed the plan before Junior left for work. Junior had wanted to call in sick since it was a special day but Daniel said their days should continue as normal. Daniel even filled out a few job applications.

They had done it. They had robbed a bank.

Daniel sat down on the couch and removed the money from the duffle bag, amazed at seeing so much money at once. Some were in loose, single bills. Some was wrapped with a paper band, denoting the quantity.

So much money.

Daniel began organizing the bills by note and daydreaming about how he would spend his portion.

Of course, they wouldn't be able to deposit all of it at once, but this would give him some cushion while looking for a job. Maybe he could even get a hotel room for a few weeks so he wouldn't be crowding Junior's space. Although Junior hadn't said anything to make Daniel feel unwanted, nobody wanted a houseguest when they were used to living alone.

But Junior wouldn't say anything. At least, not yet. Daniel knew he couldn't stay here forever. He wasn't sure how long Junior would keep his home open.

"A vacation would be nice too," he said to himself. "I've never been to a beach. I hear Mexico is warm year round."

Daniel pulled out his phone and opened the calculator app to start calculating totals.

"I need a new interview suit too. One that fits a little bit better to impress interviewers. They'll definitely want to hire a professional that *reeks* of money. Junior will probably spend all his funds on alcohol and women."

Daniel imagined Junior taking Fatima to a nice restaurant to 'cheer her up'. Every time Junior became infatuated with a new woman, Daniel felt a slight pang of envy. Fatima would take up a lot Junior's free time. It was a feeling that had taken a while for Daniel to identify because he had never experienced it before. Jealousy.

He paused and looked at the figure on the calculator.

"That can't be right."

With the bills organized into stacks, it looked like a lot less than loose, bunches of cash. And there were a lot more one dollar bills than he had originally anticipated.

He counted the money again, a gleam of sweat coating his forehead. His hands were shaking, and he dropped a few dollars, having to start over a couple of times. But the end result was the same.

They had robbed a bank for $8,218.00.

• • • • •

Daniel was nervous about the upcoming conversation and couldn't sit still. Junior was going to be home soon, and Daniel needed to explain why their bank heist had such a low reward. He had played the hypothetical conversation in his mind.

First, he had considered putting Junior into a good mood with a meal and a six pack of beer. Maybe even hire a masseur to help ease him into the bad news. But a masseur would require money, and that would have to come out of the $8,000. Next, he thought about writing a note and leaving the apartment for a few days. That would give Junior time to digest the bad news and have a cooling-off period. Daniel had even considered taking his portion of the money and moving back home with his dad.

All the scenarios had consequences. Daniel knew he had to face the wrath and confess that his plan had been flawed despite his confidence.

Junior arrived later in the evening, having stayed with Fatima for emotional support. Daniel could only watch as the rollercoaster of satisfaction paraded through Junior's emotions since he had been forced to contain his excitement all day.

"We did it!" Junior said.

Daniel smiled, the script from his practice conversations evaporating.

"I couldn't stop thinking about this shit all afternoon," Junior said. "I think the first thing I'm going to do is take my little girls to Disney World. I think they would like that. I've always wanted to take Izzy and Amanda on a trip the way my parents used to take me and my brother places when we were little. Hell, with all this money, I might take their moms too."

Daniel let out a nervous giggle.

"Aw, man. And of course, I'm going to have to give my own mom something too. She doesn't get half the shit she deserves for being such a good parent."

"Let me get you a beer."

"Get us both one. We need to celebrate."

Daniel took the time in the kitchen to take a breath and try to calm the awful feeling in his stomach. He returned with the beer and handed it to Junior, not bothering to bring one for himself. Junior looked at him and frowned.

"You're not celebrating?" Junior asked.

"We need to talk first before we celebrate."

"I already know what you're going to say. We don't need to go crazy with spending money because that's attention on ourselves that we don't need. So that's why I'm only going to go on the trip with my little girls then I'm going to lay low. Maybe only spend a few thousand a month. Maybe invest a little bit because that's what the rich people say to do. Make your money work for you."

"Junior..."

"Oh, and I will have a fun night at the strip club. But that's a part of celebrating. That doesn't count. Why aren't you drinking? We worked hard for this. This is an accomplishment. I know you're used to finishing shit. Hell, you graduated college and that's major. But I ain't ever finished nothing. This is... this is something real."

85

Daniel didn't know what to say as Junior spread his arms and pulled him in for a hug. In all of their years of friendship, Daniel had never seen Junior this affectionate. It felt good, but Daniel couldn't enjoy it.

"We need to talk," Daniel said.

"We need to celebrate."

Junior took a long swig to finish his beer and went into the kitchen to fetch another one.

"Junior," Daniel's voice cracked. "We weren't as successful as you think."

"What was that?" Junior called from the kitchen.

"We didn't... We didn't get a lot of money?"

"What do you mean?" Junior held the opened can of beer and watched Daniel from the entryway to the kitchen. "

"I have been thinking about where we - no - where I went wrong. I think I should have maybe specified with Ghiy-āthu'd-Dīn the amount we were trying to walk away with."

"The amount? What does *Guy of the Dean* have to do with the amount?"

"I trusted his plan to be solid. We had an in and an out. We had a sure-fire way not to get caught. We used our powers to our advantage and... Basically, I failed."

"How much was the haul?"

Daniel paused and glanced away.

"You've avoided telling me how much money we walked away with," Junior said. "So I'm not sure how disappointed I should be?"

"About eight grand."

Junior dropped his beer and balled up his fists.

Daniel's first reaction, thinking he was about to be punched, was to flinch. But instead, he pulled from *The Grey* and created an image of himself where he was standing and stepped away. His power provided a reactive response assuming Junior was frustrated enough to lash out, physically or magically. Daniel didn't want to be the recipient. From Junior's perspective, he saw Daniel standing in the same spot with a look of regret on his face. Daniel saw a dimmed reflection of himself watching as Junior screamed in frustration.

"What the fuck are we supposed to do with eight grand? Who the fuck robs a bank for eight thousand fucking dollars? Wait… please tell me it's eight grand each?"

The shadow of Daniel shook his head.

Junior screamed again and kicked the beer can into the kitchen. The aluminum cylinder banging a few cabinet doors and vomiting the remaining liquid as it spun in violence.

Daniel started to say he was willing to sacrifice his portion to try to pacify Junior but something held his tongue. Was he willing to give up something he had pushed his morals aside for? He had earned this money, no matter how small, as much as Junior had. He deserved every penny.

"What went wrong?" Junior said, breath heavy and fists still clenched. "How did we only get eight thousand dollars?"

"We slipped a note to the bank teller. She emptied out her cash drawer with everything that was in there. That is the protocol."

"And when the FoodHub guy left, I knocked the bitch out. She fainted like we planned. Did the delivery guy take a few dollars for himself?"

"No, it was the bank teller. Or not so much the teller but the bank. Their policy and procedures say to empty the drawer, but I guess they don't keep much in the cash drawer. That's a minimal loss for a major bank with billions in assets."

"I knew for sure we were going to get at least a hundred thousand dollars. How many cash drawers would we have to hit to get that much?"

"Twelve or thirteen."

"Do you feel like doing this twelve or thirteen more times?"

"I didn't even want to do it the one time."

Daniel saw Junior's posture slump. He searched for something to say to make this better. He wanted to say they could rob a different bank, make a new plan. But the words wouldn't leave his lips. He didn't want to do this again. He wasn't a villain. Last week, he hadn't even been able to provide any anecdotes that showed he had used his powers for the betterment of somebody else. But now, he had a story of how he had used his voodoo for self-gain.

Daniel looked inward, searching for some sign of guilt or remorse. And he couldn't find anything. He might have felt something if somebody had gotten hurt or one of the delivery drivers got caught or if a story was released that the funds stolen belonged to an elderly lady. But there was nothing.

"So what now?" Junior asked.

"We go on with our lives."

CHAPTER THREE

Daniel plucked at the gems surrounding the frame of the hand mirror. Ghiy-āthu'd-Dīn's description of it being gaudy was inaccurate. The mirror was hideous. It was overlaid with so much gold and gems that it was an eyesore. And Daniel was sure that at any moment the handle was going to break from the added weight.

Junior, beer in his hand, sat dozing off in the chair next to the couch. He hadn't said anything else to Daniel, choosing instead to turn the television to a basketball game and get drunk enough to forget the fantasies he had created when he thought he was one hundred thousand dollars richer.

Daniel had looked for an escape from the awkward situation. His first inclination was to get a hotel room for a few nights. But the frugal adult in him told him to save his part of the robbery bounty to help carry him while he continued his job search.

And so they sat in silence.

Daniel wasn't interested in the game and decided to learn more about the mirror. He figured it was a trap, but it intrigued him - like a puzzle that he needed to solve. Daniel assumed that if he could figure out how the trap worked maybe he could learn something from it.

The rubies, emeralds, opals and other stones were impossible to remove from the mirror with just his fingernails. He had tried to pry them loose with his keys and later a pair of scissors. He would have tried more appropriate tools, like a hammer or a screwdriver, but that would have required talking to Junior because he didn't know where Junior kept his toolbox.

It was when he covered it in *Grey Matter* that the mirror began to do something. The reflection changed. Daniel no longer saw his depressed face. The image of a brick house replaced his image. Green lawn, tall trees and a curved driveway covered the mirrored view.

Without being able to explain how he knew, Daniel became aware that this mirror was a gateway. The house he was looking at was a plane of reality similar to *The Grey*. The colors weren't muted, and he didn't see any flashing apparitions of persons past, but it was another astral plane, nonetheless.

The internal debate whether to explore further was short-lived. The best way to get more information about this mirror would be to ask questions, so he ran through a list of individuals who could provide answers. Javier was still upset with him. Madame Katrine Comtois would probably focus more on the fact he had spoken with Ghiy-āthu'd-Dīn and question how he had learned about the spirit. Then he would have to admit he had stolen the red book. Veronica might be able to provide some insight, but he had bothered her enough with his problems. Keith might know more about the mirror, except it could be months before they crossed paths in *The Grey*. He didn't want to wait.

So Daniel decided to venture forward with the same bravado he had when he summoned Ghiy-āthu'd-Dīn. He plunged headfirst into deep waters and hoped for the best. It was becoming his theme song.

A deep breath, a clear mind and a focus of desire was enough to submerse himself in the ostentatious trinket.

Upon entering the mirror, the first thing he noticed was the brick house was not isolated. To the left and the right, houses of various shapes, sizes and colors lined the streets. All of their lawns were perfectly manicured and shaded with giant oak trees. Daniel could feel the sun on his skin from the partly cloudy skies. The sudden plunge into the high humidity environment constricted Daniel's airways, and he struggled to pull air into his lungs. Whatever plane he had moved himself to was different from *The Grey.* Although dreamlike in context due to being so overly perfect, he could feel every sensation with a striking sharpness.

The birds chirping seemed higher pitched. The swift movement of the clouds across the sky appeared over exaggerated. The humidity so constricting that Daniel was positive he was close to a large body of water, maybe an ocean.

Daniel didn't move, looking around for the signs of a trap. In nature, the most beautiful colors on insects and plants always turned out to be a way to ensnare prey. Daniel was the prey here. A skimming thought moved to the front of his mind about how he probably should have warned Junior what he was doing before proceeding. Then that thought moved to the memory of a few weeks ago when Veronica had mentioned every trained voodoo practioner had access to their own astral prison, *The Vale.* This remembrance led to the realization that he didn't know what *The Vale* looked like and this place could be Ghiy-āthu'd-Dīn's *Vale.*

Faster than the mind's ability to process a thought, Daniel pulled himself out of the mirror, focusing on the spiritual umbilical cord that tied his essence to his body and following the lifeline back onto the couch in Junior's living room. It was more of a reflex than a reaction. The hand mirror still reflected the house, the basketball game still played on the television and Junior slumped in his chair asleep. The empty beer can had slipped out of his hand and fallen to the floor.

"All these unnecessary risks are going to eventually pay off," Daniel said. "Or they're going to get me killed."

But he knew now the mirror wasn't a path into *The Vale* since he was able to leave at will. This was something else. Daniel's curiosity had been piqued.

He drifted back to the hand mirror's flawlessly structured neighborhood and walked towards the front door of the brick house. In the distance he could hear a lawnmower and dogs barking. A bead of sweat slithered down his temple as the humid heat dampened the shirt to his torso. Behind him, a car horn honked, and he turned to see a man waving his hand out of the car window as he drove by.

Daniel didn't wave back. Friendly neighbors annoyed him.

He braced himself for what could lie on the other side of the door. His body was on alert and ready to jump back out of the mirror at the slightest threat.

The interior of the red brick home surprised him although it shouldn't have. It was just as pristine and perfect as the rest of the neighborhood. A plush white couch stood on cream carpet. A glass coffee table wiped clean, green house plants, matching lamps. It reminded Daniel of the model homes that real estate agents showed you to plant the idea of the houses available in a new-build neighborhood might look.

The artwork on the walls was basic and unattractive. He didn't spot any pictures of the family that lived in the home.

"Daniel's home," a voice said.

He turned to see two girls run toward him and wrap their arms around him in an embrace. Daniel restrained his urge to pull out of the hand mirror and instead looked down at the children in confusion.

They looked up at him. The taller one looked familiar. He had seen her before but couldn't recall her name. The second, shorter girl was faceless. She had no eyes, no nose, no mouth. He assumed that beneath the twist of dark hair she would also have no ears. And even without lips to smile with, the girl was obviously glad to see him. The rise of her cheeks denoted a grin.

"Come see our drawings. Daddy told us to draw our family."

They pulled at his arms and led him into the dining area where the table was littered with colored paper and crayons. The faceless girl held up her art, and Daniel struggled to identify any significant objects. The older girl's artwork was more legible, and he could make out two taller stick figures, most likely the parents, the two girls and a pet. He wasn't sure if it was a dog or a cat.

"We were going to hang these on the fridge, but we want them in our room now. We'll draw something else for the fridge."

A muffled noise came from the younger girl that Daniel assumed was her voice, but he couldn't make out what she was saying.

"Are these your parents?" Daniel asked.

They giggled, and the smaller girl made more sounds that Daniel assumed was a response. He stared at the older girl, and her familiarity dawned into recognition. She was Junior's daughter, Isabel. It had been a couple of years since he had seen her, but she looked exactly the same. That would mean the faceless girl was Junior's youngest daughter, Amanda. He had never met Amanda so he couldn't assign a face to her. Which explained her lack of facial features. The hand mirror was using his memory to create this environment. That explained why Isabel hadn't aged.

As if on cue, Junior walked into the room carrying a pizza box and a six-pack of beer.

"So Michaelangelo and Picasso couldn't wait to show you their latest masterpieces?" Junior asked.

"We're going to hang them up in our room, Daddy."

"But then we won't be able to see them," Junior said. "We wanted to hang them up in the kitchen so we all could see them. And anytime we have visitors, they could enjoy them too."

"We'll make more for that. We're keeping these."

The faceless one made more noises.

Junior smiled, patting Amanda on her head. And before Daniel had a chance to react, Junior leaned in and kissed Daniel. The movement was so swift that Daniel didn't have a chance to process the quick peck, but the casual affection seemed familiar to Junior.

"You're just in time for dinner," Junior said. "I got sausage with mushrooms and jalapenos."

"Mushrooms? Eew," Isabel said, her sister echoing the disgust.

"Don't worry. I got pepperoni for you two ladies. Now, go wash your hands."

A duet of cheer escaped them as they ran out of the room.

Daniel stared at Junior with bewilderment with the shock of the kiss still on his mind. Junior grabbed some paper plates and placed them around the dining room table, a setting for four. The children returned and sat at the table, pizza waiting on their plates.

Junior sat at the head of the table and bit into a slice before looking up at Daniel.

"You gonna just stand there or what?" Junior asked with a mouth full of food.

The girls stopped chewing and looked up, watching for Daniel's answer. The stare of all three individuals, two sets of eyes, unnerved him. He realized what this was. Ghiy-āthu'd-Dīn was dangling a carrot. The feelings Daniel had for Junior were no longer a secret. Ghiy-āthu'd-Dīn knew.

Daniel didn't understand if this was a warning or an offering. Was this the bait for the trap or was this the trap? Daniel was uneasy with Ghiy-āthu'd-Dīn being privy to this information. He had been content with knowing he would never get the opportunity to explore his attraction to Junior.

But what if he could? Was this Ghiy-āthu'd-Dīn giving a chance for Daniel to experience a life with this man in a romantic way?

He shook his head. He couldn't stay here and play this out. It would be too weird. And he definitely didn't want to play this game with Ghiy-āthu'd-Dīn. There wasn't anything that he could learn here. So he decided to return to the couch and destroy the mirror.

But the look in Junior's hazel eyes, the tone of his voice as he asked Daniel to sit as a family tugged at Daniel. It glued his feet to the floor and prevented him from leaving. With a sigh of resignation, he found himself walking to the table and taking a seat. The girls smiled and continued eating, the faceless one chewing although he hadn't seen how she was able to take bites from the partially eaten pizza.

Junior took a long swallow from his beer can, and Daniel thought to himself that even in a false reality, Junior was still an alcoholic. Junior reached across the table and grabbed Daniel's hand. The feeling of Junior's rough calluses from working construction sent a shiver up Daniel's spine. He was flooded with a wave of joy from being able to experience affection he had only dreamed of.

Junior squeezed his hand and looked at him. "Are we good?"

The hazel eyes that Daniel had watched devour women with lust and torture them with a piercing gaze were directed at him. He now understood why some of the smartest women were willing to make stupid decisions for this man.

A brief memory tickled the back of his mind. Daniel saw a younger version of himself sitting at a table with his mom and using *The Grey* to provide the same faux reality of a family dinner with her loving husband.

"Yeah," Daniel nodded.

"You sure? You seem a little distant."

"Just thinking about the fact that karma is a cold-hearted bitch."

• • • • •

"I think the problem is," Junior said. "You were never one hundred percent invested in this heist."

Daniel swallowed the eggs he had in his mouth and frowned. They were seated at a late-night diner because Junior hadn't wanted to go straight home after leaving the bar. The only places opened at this late hour were drive-thru food establishments and 24-hour diners. This breakfast diner was empty save the two employees.

Daniel preferred not to frequent these types of places during certain times because they seemed a little shady to him. The restaurant felt like an ideal target for a late night robbery, so he was on constant alert, scanning the near-empty parking lot for any suspicious activity.

Junior had remained somewhat distant since the low haul from the bank robbery. He hadn't been his jovial, talkative self which was a stark contrast from the hand mirror doppelganger. Daniel had been worried that things would never be the same between them. But a few days had passed, and Junior had asked Daniel if he wanted to go out and get drunk. Daniel accepted without hesitation.

"I took a lot of risks to accomplish what we did." Daniel's words slurred from the alcohol in his system. "I explored parts of my abilities that could have endangered me."

"That's a part of the problem. You don't know enough about your power. You experiment here and try this over there. But what could you do if you mastered this?"

"It takes a long time to master voodoo."

"How long does it take a normal person?" Junior leaned forward across the table. "How long does it take someone who doesn't want to learn? You don't even experiment with what you have. You could be learning by trial and error. I didn't have a teacher, but I know more about my powers than you do."

"I want to learn but…"

"But you're staying loyal to a friend. Yeah, yeah, yeah. That's cool and all. Loyalty is a great thing to have… if you're a character in a romance novel."

"It's more complicated than that. In a previous life, I betrayed this person. I'm not the type of person to hurt somebody twice."

"So when the heartache happens again it shouldn't hurt him as bad as it did the first time. Do you think that learning at the pace you are that you're going to become the Master of Shadows ever?"

"Prince of Veils," Daniel corrected. "Master of Shadows sounds so evil."

"And Prince of Veils doesn't? You're not going to get that throne by learning one new trick and telling yourself that it was a big leap for you. How long would it have taken you to get that degree if you spent your 16 years in school being taught by one teacher who only specialized in Astronomy?"

"I'm beginning to think your superpower is horrible analogies."

"How's this for an analogy? What we're doing is a business. We're generating revenue, and we had a small *setback* with our first production of inventory. But we can't let that stop us. We move on and keep pushing to make the business profitable."

"Anti-Analogous Man?" Daniel smiled. "Sergeant Symbolism? Okay, I'm sorry. I'm sorry. Let's be serious. So you wanna keep going forward on these heists?"

"Hell yeah. If at first you don't succeed, dust yourself off and try, try, try again. We evaluate what we did wrong, and we learn from it."

"Okay. Sounds like you've been thinking about this a lot. Tell me what did we do wrong? Give it to me straight, Captain Correlation." Daniel pushed his plate away and leaned back in the booth, folding his arms.

"Well, for starters, we're not at our maximum potential. And by 'we' I mean 'you'."

"I'm not comfortable with all the blame being pushed on me. I ran this plan by you before we set out and you were in total agreement."

"I hear your complaint and empathize with how you feel-"

"You don't have to patronize me with call center script, Junior."

"Then take *accountability* for your shortcomings. Stop acting like a fucking child and man up."

"Everything okay over there, boys?" The waitress asked with a hint of warning.

Junior waved his hand and smiled in apology for raising his voice. The waitress stared for a moment, refusing to be pacified by Junior's good looks, before returning to her conversation with the short order cook.

"You want to make everybody happy," Junior said in a hushed tone. "And make sure everybody likes you but that ain't realistic. Go out and get what you deserve."

Daniel looked out the window at passing cars. Years ago, his father had reprimanded him for having an insatiable need to be liked by everybody. At the time, he hadn't been self-aware enough to evaluate the characteristics that led his dad to this assumption. But now, he could see how Junior could mistake loyalty for a need to be liked. That seemed like baggage or personal issues that Junior would need to resolve, not Daniel.

"Another shortfall of the *business*," Junior said. "We need to expand beyond banks. Maybe start in other areas that ain't so well guarded until we get a better handle on how to best exploit our gifts."

"What kind of areas are you talking about?"

"Armored trucks, wealthy businessmen, older widows with their husband's pensions."

"I'm not robbing old women."

"I'm just throwing out suggestions. But that brings up my next bullet point. You gotta let go of this ethics clause. It's not good for our brand."

"We have to have some kind of morals."

"No, we don't. We're stealing shit for our own personal gain. There ain't nothing good about that. You can't cancel out the bad with a good deed. We're not Robin Hood."

"I think there are levels to being a crook. Yeah, we might have robbed a bank, but that's a big corporation, and they won't miss that. But taking from elderly or innocent, that's just…"

"A thief is a thief is a thief is a fucking *thief*. You can't be okay with the reward but hesitant about the pursuit. It's like you want to do the crime, but you don't want to carry the guilt."

"I wasn't raised to be a criminal. My parents taught me the difference between right and wrong."

"You don't think mine did?"

"I can't tell. You're so hellbent on becoming a supervillain."

"You don't know shit about where I come from or how I was raised, so it's probably best you shut the fuck up."

"I know enough," Daniel said.

"If you want to talk about families, then why don't we talk about why you decided to crash on my couch instead of moving back in with your dad?"

"Or a better topic: how long before *your* dad is up for parole?"

Daniel felt his mouth clamp close; his hands stiffen on the table. Junior had lashed out and taken control of Daniel's body, stopping him from saying anything further. Daniel had overstepped and pushed Junior too far. The reaction to losing his ability to move was to pull from *The Grey* and cover Junior with darkness. The amount of *Grey* smoldering Junior was on the edge of crossing the limit Daniel had set to avoid causing permanent damage.

But it was enough to prevent Junior from having sight. Daniel knew that at this point Junior was blind.

"Did you boys want a refill on coffee?" The waitress appeared at their table.

Daniel couldn't move. He remembered Junior couldn't hold him in extreme emotion such as anger or fear. But he couldn't conjure enough of any emotion to break Junior's hold. Daniel blamed the alcohol.

Following the sound of the watress' voice, Junior turned to where he believed she was standing and smiled. It was a good attempt.

"No, thank you," Junior said. "We're fine."

She nodded and walked away, her soft heeled tennis shoes squeaking on the floor with each step.

Daniel felt his jaw relax. Junior had released his hold. He peeled back the field of *Grey* he had used to covered Junior's eyes and sighed. Arguing and fighting weren't going to help them move forward.

Junior arrived at the same conclusion. He looked at Daniel, his eyes squinting due to the sudden return to the lights.

"I won't bring up your parents if you don't bring up mine," He looked at Daniel, his eyes squinting due to the sudden return to the lights.

Daniel nodded.

"I'm not scared of prison," Junior gave a half-hearted smile. "I have a few relatives in there. I don't think you should be scared of prison either. Do you think there is a prison that can hold us? Is it possible to contain us with the things we know how to do?"

"If you get caught, you can *compel* a guard to release you. I don't doubt you would be able to find your way out within a few days."

"If not, I'll just kill all the guards. Cardiac arrest, brain aneurysm, deflated lungs... I have options. But you have even more options. Would they see you if you left? Can you make them see you sitting in a cell even if you weren't there? Could you make them all go blind – good trick, by the way. I didn't even know you could do that."

"Thanks. I got it from a movie. First thing I could think of."

"But the point is we shouldn't be afraid of getting caught. Because if we do, what can they do to us?"

"They could kill us," Daniel whispered.

"Can they?"

Daniel picked through the food left on his plate with his fork.

"So what's the next move?" Junior said. "How are you going to get more training on your witchery?"

"I need to let my loyalties go and see if Madam Comtois can help me with the spirit world."

"Just her? Why not multiple people? Remember, this is college. Full load is 4-6 classes."

"I don't know. I guess… there was this psychic reading place I went to a few weeks ago. I can see what they have to offer in the way of training. Veronica is pretty knowledgeable about astral planes. If I want to learn doll manipulation, I'll need to talk to Keith, but I think he already taught me everything he knows."

"This is a start. I think we might be moving in the right direction."

"Damn," Daniel snapped his fingers. "I should've said Señor Metaphor."

• • • • •

Daniel approached the cathedral and watched the magnificent towers, stacked on the steeply slanted roof, grow bigger and bigger. His memory of this place had diminished over time, and the familiarity of awe from the building enveloped him. Even through the hazy mist of *The Grey*, Daniel couldn't help but admire the intricate architecture of the building. He wondered if it existed in the real world or only in *The Grey*.

Madame Katrine Comtois' instructions to him had been not to return until he was ready to devote his life to the teachings of La Marieé des Espirits. And yet here he was returning to the place where he had been bestowed with the *voleur*.

He needed a teacher. Madame Comtois was the best possible mentor for learning spirit communication. If he were to join her community, Daniel was certain she would take his teaching into her own hands.

He stood at the bottom of the steps and peered at the doors in anticipation.

"Here goes another dive into the unknown," Daniel said.

Daniel wasn't sure how long after he had received the gift of the *voleur* before he saw the trap. When he was younger, his Uncle Jimmy told him about the crack epidemic of the 1980s. Usually, Daniel didn't pay much attention his uncle's stories. His uncle was the type to tell his over-the-top stories to anyone that would listen. If you gave the tiniest hint that you would give him an audience, he would talk your ear off. And Uncle Jimmy had a million stories.

His dad never had anything good to say about his brother. They had gone in separate directions in life. Daniel's dad had served in the military and later worked a government job where he excelled. In contrast, Uncle Jimmy had been a hustler, finding ways to earn a living through street work, some of which was legitimate.

A master of all trades, Uncle Jimmy could fix cars, lay tile, patch roofs, file taxes. He could also find the best hooch for parties, knew all the locations for underground gambling and would sell you any drug you desired, no matter how obscure or new the drug was, prescription or otherwise.

His tales were associated with his many jobs. In one story, Uncle Jimmy described the climb of crack in the 80s because he had seen it first hand while working as a manager at a car wash. He was positioned on the front lines because this particular car wash was the high traffic marketplace for drug deals.

The best way to introduce the product into the neighborhood was to market it with a free sample. Anybody willing to try the new street drug would receive a courtesy taste at no cost. It was confusing to anybody who sold any other drug because how could you make money if you were giving away the merchandise for free? But the answer became apparent soon enough. It was like that Lay's Potato Chip ad, "Can't Eat Just One." And nobody could try crack once and not want to try it again. That was the hook.

This story helped Daniel realize that the *voleur* was Madame Comtois' free sample of crack. You got a taste of what the *voleur* offered, and eventually, you would want more. But Daniel had found immunity to their appeal. He didn't have the heart for the sacrifice. Daniel hadn't needed the *voleur* to show him his distaste for animal cruelty. In college his dorm roommate had had a scorpion that glowed under black light, and Daniel had never been able to watch it eat the live crickets it was fed.

But sooner or later everybody becomes immune to something that disgusted them. And Daniel could see himself slowly becoming desensitized to the offerings. It explained why he was willing to offer a cat to Ghiy-āthu'd-Dīn to appease him for his help.

It made Daniel consider what offerings would he have to make if he did get Madame Comtois' to agree to teach him. What did more powerful spirits consume? He doubted all of them would be generous enough to offer him hand mirrors into fantasy worlds.

Daniel pushed aside the sudden intruding thought of Junior holding his hand at the dinner table and climbed the steps.

He entered the foyer to find a young man cloaked in a dark green robe.

"I'm looking for Madame Comtois," Daniel said.

"And you are?" The volume of his voice, projected across the entryway, seemed blasphemous to Daniel's ears given the setting.

"Daniel Lebeu"

The man's eyebrows rose. He signaled for Daniel to stay before rushing off down the aisle and around the altar into a door.

Looking around at the familiar but forgotten décor, Daniel admired the stained glass story of Marie Leveaux portrayed across the walls. Her followers had used *The Grey* to create this extravagance that didn't exist in the real world. Javier preferred to appreciate dilapidated locations without enhancement whereas it looked like Katrine preferred decorations to rival Daniel's new hand mirror.

Daniel verified he was alone in the foyer before he approached one of the massive stone statues placed near the entrance. During his previous trek into the cathedral, Madame Katrine Comtois had informed him the statue was a powerful, yet dormant spirit. This particular statue was composed of black marble that did little to highlight the detailed muscle in the arms and legs. The body was crouched in a squatting position. Daniel knew if it had been structured in a standing position it would have been twice his height. The face was contorted in what initially could be taken as a grimace, but a longer look at the face convinced him the immobile creature was just as much animal as it was human.

A deep hum, communal in nature, vibrated from the crouching gargoyle and reminded Daniel of a gong. He paused, trying to ascertain if the hum had been present when he entered. Maybe he hadn't noticed, and it had just gotten louder. Or had it started as he approached?

Setting caution aside, he stepped closer, trying to focus on identifying the face, unable to discern what kind of animal the head was structured to show. The stone was dark and seemed to swallow the shadows and highlights that would have helped define its characteristics. The features didn't change, but it took all of his concentration to see them. It felt as if his eyes wanted to shift away, or that *The Grey* was too dense to penetrate by sight. The warning from Katrine

Comtois about the power of this being kept him from giving in to his urge to explore with the *Grey Matter*.

The vibration shifted to a lower tone, and Daniel was surprised the windows in the temple weren't rattling from its power. He closed his eyes and inhaled the sound through his mouth, the power was thick enough to taste. It was but a fraction of the power he could obtain as The Prince of Veils. A shiver rippled down his back as Daniel wondered if this was an offer. Was the spirit communicating with him?

An offer for what though? Daniel opened his eyes, exhaling the charged vibration of energy from his lungs, his body complaining at the loss of so much power.

The stone gobline had shifted slightly and turned its head to peer at Daniel causing him to jump back in surprise, almost stumbling over a pew. The statue's face was clearer than before.

The green-robed man returned as Daniel was composing himself from the surprise.

"Please follow me," he said.

Daniel strolled towards the altar, embarrassed but trying to hide the shock he had just experienced. Taking multiple glances behind him at the gargoyle, he walked around the altar and through the door where   he found Madame Comtois standing with pride, her hands on her hips, watching him enter.

Seated in chairs to her left and right were four other individuals, two on each side, dressed in the same green robes as the young man but laced with decorative yellow lining. They peered at Daniel, each with a different expression that made him uneasy.

"*Mon fils prodigue,*" she said. "You have returned as I knew you would. Please come have a seat."

Daniel let the reluctance drag his feet across the carpet as he approached the seat planted in view of the staring eyes. This felt like a judging panel.

"You surprised me." Her French accent was thick. "I expected you back a lot sooner. *Mieux vaut tard que jamais.*

Maybe that just proves how much strength you hold, no? Not only the sheer force of your power but the willpower to contain it. I love it."

Daniel smiled and offered her a timid nod. It wasn't possible to sweat in *The Grey*, but he was sure he was sweating at home.

"Garrison was skeptical of the fact that you had so many *voleur* in your possession."

Daniel assumed she was referring to the man on her left who had only afforded Daniel an intense glare. The man had a thick mane of silver hair that contradicted his smooth face. His lips remained taunt in a frown that should've been uncomfortable, and his posture seemed poised as if to strike at any moment.

"Why would he doubt that?" Daniel asked.

"Because it's such a rare thing. Plus, he had not seen it with his own eyes. He wanted to know an exact number, so he has tried to count your *voleur*. *Plus facile á dire qu'á faire.* Easier said than done. It looks like your *voleur* don't behave as others. They move and shift and… I do not know the word"

"Transition," Garrison said, his eyes remaining locked on Daniel.

"Yes. They *transition*. They are here. They are there. Sometimes they are yours. Sometimes they are not yours. It's a fascinating event. But enough of that." She waved her hands to dismiss the topic. "Where are my manners? Let me introduce you."

Madame Comtois strutted to stand behind Daniel and placed her hands on his shoulders.

"Of course, everybody knows you. And you've already learned the man with the charming personality is Grand Seigneur Garrison."

Daniel preferred not to make eye contact with the man and his intense gaze.

"Beside him is Seigneur Alexandre."

A tall, slim Italian that could have passed for a distant relative to Junior nodded. Daniel felt an instant attraction and knew it was due to the resemblance. The only thing missing were the hazel eyes. A distant urge to return to the mirror world fluttered through Daniel.

"Be careful with that one. He's the type to feed you great food and great sex, then steal all your possessions while you watch. But then again, look who I am warning. You are no stranger to robbery."

The group laughed, and Daniel felt his ears grow warm with embarrassment. They knew about the failed bank robbery?

"The round Spaniard over there is Seigneur Oscar Elizondo. You might find this hard to believe, but when I first found Signeur Oscar, he was a matador."

"Don't let my size convince you it is not possible, *hermano*." Oscar's smile brought a warmth to his face that almost made Daniel want to reciprocate. "I may be bigger than the bull, but I was never slower. I did not start off as the prettiest bullfighter, but by the end, with all the scars everybody collected, I ended up the best looking."

A nervous smirk crested Daniel's face as more laughter filled the room.

"And lastly," Madame Comtois continued, "Seigneur Maxence."

"Max," the petite man said. He wore glasses and seemed to twitch involuntarily. Daniel wondered how this was possible in *The Grey* since everybody here was just an astral projection. Daniel assumed something was wrong with the thin man's ability to move into this plane?

"And there you have it," Madame Comtois moved to stand in front of Daniel, her bosom eye level. "I cannot tell you how excited we are to have you join us."

"May I ask," Alexandre said. "How did Javier take the news? I was not around the first time you betrayed him, but I've heard stories about it. I'm sure the second time was maybe less painful since it was to be expected."

"*Mi diablo Italiano.*" She shook a finger at him. "Betrayed is such a poor word choice. Daniel did not betray anybody. The only thing keeping him shackled to Javier was his desire to remain loyal to a friend. I think it is beautiful that a love such as theirs has crossed through death and returned anew."

Garrison grunted.

"Was he angry?" Alexandre asked.

Daniel paused, not knowing how to proceed with answering.

"Oh," Alexandre's eyebrows shot up. "You did not tell him. That is delicious. I would pay to be a condom in the whorehouse when that john cums to pay."

"If it is a matter of safety, you do not have to worry, Daniel," Comtois said. "We will be here to protect you. He could not harm you the first time and he damn sure cannot do it now."

"It's not like that small group of misfits has enough power to do anything substantial anyway, sitting in opera houses and waxing poetic about the ghosts of Dr. Frankenstein."

Oscar and Madame Comtois couldn't contain their fits of laughter, and Daniel looked away. He swallowed any retort in defense of his friend and soaked up the information they had provided. They didn't think too highly of Javier and his followers. And since Daniel followed Javier, what did they think of him?

"I say we send him a note." Alexandre wasn't finished. "A message in true voodoo fashion. I have three or four spirits in mind to help deliver it."

"Alexandre, *s'il vous plait.*" Madame Comtois composed herself. "What Daniel must think of us."

"My apologies, Mr. Daniel. I did not mean to offend."

"No offense taken. Actually…" Daniel paused. "I think there has been a misunderstanding."

"We misunderstand how?" Comtois asked.

"I did not come here to join you. I came to ask for your help."

Silence filled the room. A look of confusion decorated Alexandre's face while Oscar's face expanded with delight. Madame Comtois was unreadable.

"You did not come to join?" she asked. "I instructed you to return *only* when you were ready to commit, and yet here you are."

"Yes. I'm here on a long shot, I know. But I didn't see the harm in asking."

"Leave us."

For a moment Daniel thought she was speaking to him until Oscar, Alexandre and Maxence faded out of the room, leaving him alone with Comtois and Garrison.

"Tell me why I should not find you where you lay and kill you as you sleep? You come into my house and embarrass me in front of my leadership. The disrespect that you have-"

"Madame Comtois, I did not intend to disrespect—"

"Silence when I am talking," she yelled. "You may not know the proper etiquette when addressing me but you will learn today. I am not Javier. I do not have the same reservations about harming children."

Daniel stood up and didn't flinch as Garrison stood in response, ready to strike. If it came to a show of power in *The Grey*, Daniel knew he was the strongest, although he didn't know how he knew.

"I didn't come here to be threatened or talked down to. So you can keep your threats."

"These are not threats. What was really your intention for coming here? You cannot have been stupid enough to think we issue favors here. Did the atmosphere fool you? Even headquartered in a cathedral, we are not in the market of providing charity."

"To be honest, I don't know what I expected from you."

"You have power, I will admit. But you are doomed to die. You will never reach your potential without us. So why fight it? This teenage rebellion will have to end eventually. It would be best to grow out of it before it is too late."

"Stop calling me a child. I am an adult."

"Okay. Fine, *mon fils prodigue.*" She took a breath and let a moment of silence pass to let the tension in the air dissipate. "Let us speak as adults then."

"Good." Daniel sat back down and tried to ignore the fact Garrison remained standing.

"What do you want from us? What is it that you are asking of me?"

"I need training. I need the knowledge that you have regarding spirits."

"Why do you think you need this knowledge?"

Daniel paused. The memory of Veronica warning him about people that would use him for his power surged in his mind. He wasn't sure how much Madame Comtois knew about the Prince of Veils, and he didn't want to bring it up.

"I need this knowledge to grow. To move to my full potential."

"And you think that by joining us, we would feed your growth? If you cannot offer us your membership, then what do you have to offer? What do I get in exchange for us training you?"

Another memory of Madame Katrine Comtois telling him that communing with spirits was nothing more than a session in bargaining. And that's what she was doing here. Daniel had to be able to offer her something that would be equal in value to her training him.

"I can also train you. I am expert at *The Grey* and *Grey Matter* manipulation. It would be an exchanging of knowledge."

"Parlour tricks." She waved her hand in dismissal. "I have no desire to learn how to create fantasies or make people go insane."

"I have a book. A tome like yours. Train me, and you can add it to your library."

"We have thousands of books. What is so special about this one that makes it worth my time? For all I know, it is another journal from an amateur spiritualist who probably died while experimenting with the unknown. A fate that I see you will probably share."

Daniel didn't know what to say.

"Anything else?"

"Money?" Four thousand dollars to be exact.

"I see." She sighed. "I like you, Daniel. I liked you in your previous life also. Your power is interesting, but it is not what is saving you right now. I will tolerate this disrespect once, but this will be the only time. You have nothing of value to me except your commitment to follow La Marieé des Espirits. Next time you enter this building, be ready to bleed, either in matrimony or death."

She faded away. Grand Seigneur Garrison remained a moment longer to stare with dramatic effect before vanishing.

Daniel left the sanctuary and exited the building, trying not to let his despair show in his stride. He had taken a gamble, and it hadn't paid any rewards. At least he knew more now than he did before. He knew Madame Comtois underestimated him. And he knew she didn't know how powerful *The Grey* was. The tome he had procured was one of many and wasn't as valuable as he thought, probably written by somebody like himself who was just figuring it out as he went.

Daniel decided he needed to find Javier and apologize for upsetting him with his quest to be trained by Madame Katrine Comtois when a short, plump man stepped from the shadows, blocking his path.

"So the black widow released you without eating you alive?" Oscar said.

"I guess this means she did not fight you?" Alexandre stood between Oscar and Maxence.

"Oh, she would never fight him in *The Grey*. He has too much power here. This is his element. She would want to take advantage of him in an arena she's more familiar with."

"Are y'all following me?" Daniel asked. "What's going on?"

"We just wanted to make sure you were still alive," Oscar said.

"And we also wanted to pledge our support to you," Alexandre said. "Because we would be fools not to recognize the Prince of Veils."

●　●　●　●　●

The house in the mirror was quiet this afternoon. Mirror Junior had sent the kids to their respective moms which had given him and Daniel some time alone. Daniel's mind had been pre-occupied with worry after being approached by Alexandre and Oscar. He watched Junior, who was sitting on the floor, legs crossed, as he scratched out a drawing in a sketchbook.

"What?" Junior asked, not looking up, feeling Daniel's eyes on his back.

"Nothing. Just watching."

"You think you can do better?"

"At drawing? Definitely not. You know how people that can't cook say they can't cook toast or they can't boil water? Like they name the simplest task that an average person can do and say they can't. That's how I am with drawing. I don't know what the equivalent is though. A straight line, maybe?"

"A straight line is harder than you think. I'd go with stick figure."

"Okay. I can't draw a stick figure to save my life."

"What hobbies did you have in school?"

"I don't know," Daniel said. "Watching movies, playing video games and torturing bullies, I guess."

"Oh, you were the big bad wolf in school? I don't believe it."

"I wasn't a wolf, but I had voodoo on my side. I might not have been able to physically beat somebody up, but I could definitely break them down."

"I can't see you being a torturer. You come off as the shy kid in the corner."

"I think I'm more of a hawk, hiding in the sky waiting to strike."

"Sure. If you say so."

"I made a boy go crazy… in high school."

"No shit?" Junior paused from his doodle, and looked up to see if Daniel was serious.

"It wasn't on purpose. I just didn't know the amount of power I had at the time."

"He must have really done some fucked-up shit to you."

"Now that I look back on it, he didn't do anything that I couldn't have gotten over. I regret what happened. When you're a teenager, everything just seems more serious than it really is. All those problems that were 'world ending' back then I would *pay* to have now."

"You couldn't reverse what you did?"

"Nobody knew how. Nothing like this had happened to anybody else. Javier didn't have any experience with this much ability. He said whatever I did to the guy would eventually just fade away."

"That's crazy." Junior returned to his drawing.

"You do anything with your power that you regret?" Daniel asked.

"I don't regret anything that I've done. I'd do it all over again, the same."

"There has to be something. You never told me why you came to Texas, but I know something went down back home."

"Something…"

Daniel didn't speak and allowed the dreamy silence to fill the room. The scratch of Junior's pencil across the page was soothing in this false reality. His leg began to tingle from the position he was sitting in, so he leaned forward to peer over Junior's shoulder.

"One thing I remember about New York is the graffiti," Junior said. "I don't think I knew until I was older that it was considered defacing property. You could pass a building, and see all different styles of art and signatures and gang paraphernalia. It really made me want to become an artist. The streets were my own personal art museum. I think that's what I miss most about New York."

"Not the winters? Or the snow? The crowds?" Daniel paused. "The smells?"

"I think if I had stayed in New York I would have eventually done something that I would've regretted."

"Like what?"

"I would've killed my dad."

"Oh, damn." Daniel waited.

"My dad was abusive. He used to beat on my mom. And if I ever got into trouble at school or did anything to piss him off, he would hit me too. I remember my mom making a comment once, after one of his rampages, that he only got hot-headed after he had lost a match."

"He was a boxer, right?"

"An amateur boxer. He wasn't very good. Lost just about as many fights as he won. No chance of ever becoming a pro. I had hung around the gym enough to have picked up some things. I was learning about my powers, and figured I could help him never lose another fight. That way he would never hurt my mom again.

"I told him what I could do, and he didn't even look at me crazy. I've told other people about this before, girlfriends or whatever, and they always go through this script where they ask me am I joking or just write it off as me making shit up. But right away he told me to prove it. I showed him. I made his body move and start boxing like I had seen him do during training. I thought I could help him during a match to fight better."

"By making him swing harder or faster?"

114

"I didn't really think about how. Just wanted to help. But he had other ideas. He wanted me to stop his opponent from hitting back. Maybe get the other guy to lower his defense just enough for my dad to get a good shot in. I really had to step up and learn the limits to my powers. I couldn't let my dad down. So I trained just like he did. I moved people on the way to school, in class, in the grocery store, on the train. I got better and stronger.

"During matches, we had signals. He didn't want the match to look rigged. I had watched him train so much that I could tell when his feet moved out of the rhythm of his normal cadence, or when a combo looked slower than usual. I didn't have to help him *every* time, but he stopped losing matches."

"And the domestic violence stopped?"

"For a while. But he caught the attention of some important guys, and they involved him in some shady shit. I don't know the details, but we suddenly had a lot more money. My mom got more special gifts, and I got more spending money. My brother got a regular supply of comic books and video games. The money was coming, but his attitude started to swing again. I think it must have been whatever he was involved in. Looking back, I think it was either drugs or gambling."

"What makes you think that?"

"Some nights, he would be out later than gym hours. I remember him telling my mom he was providing security. But at the same time, when he won a fight, he would claim the title prize money *and* more. I saw guys delivering cash to our house sometimes after a match. I think they were betting on him to win as a sure thing and giving him a portion of the proceeds. Maybe it was just snippets of conversation I heard around the house. I don't know. Kids always pick up on more than what their parents think they do."

"Yea, tell me about it."

"I don't know if it was the stress or what, but the beatings started again. One night it just became too much. I jumped in between him and my mom, and I told him to stop. I used my power on him. I stopped him. I grabbed the closest object I could find, a metal clock that my mom had bought from a garage sale, and I swung it at his head as hard as I could."

"Damn, did you knock him out?"

Junior laughed. "Not even close. My dad was a prized fighter. He had a strong chin so it would take more than that to knock him out. My powers didn't let me hold him long, and he slipped out of my hold, even angrier than before. All I knew was that I had to protect my mom. I couldn't let him keep hurting her."

"So what happened?"

"I woke up in the hospital a couple of hours later. I didn't even remember the punch."

"Fuck."

"I know, right? It had scared my mom so bad she called the police. They arrested him for domestic disturbance or battery or something. I told her this was too much. I knew that we had to leave. But even with me in the hospital bed, she didn't want to leave. I tried to convince her that he would eventually kill us. It wasn't getting any better. Reasoning didn't help, so I had to threaten to run away. And if I left, I was taking my brother with me. He was too young to be exposed to all this. Plus, if I left, my brother would have to take the beatings my dad gave me. My brother was still innocent and young and naïve. Hell, he still believed in superheroes. Those comic books, he believed that some of them really happened. Like the stories of Brotha Man and Sista Girl. He didn't deserve that.

"She came around when I told her she would never see us again. And we left that weekend while my dad sat in jail. Came to Texas to live with her cousin because I thought her sister in Miami would be too obvious. I wanted to get away and make suere there wasn't any chance he would find us."

"So how did he end up in prison? Domestic violence doesn't get you put in prison unless somebody gets hurt really bad."

"He ain't have me to help him with his fights anymore. I heard the first fight he had after we left, he lost. Whatever mob or gang he was dealing with wasn't happy about that. He didn't have a way to pay them for the money they lost, so he ended up having to work for them, running drugs. Got busted and sentenced to 10 to 15 years."

"That's so sad."

"That's not the worst part. My mom *writes* him. She still loves him. He knows we're in Texas, and I'm sure we'll be his first visit when he gets out. My brother is 18 now. He'll be 21 or older by the time my dad gets out. Not forced to suffer because our mom is blinded by love… or whatever you wanna call that."

"Love will make you do stupid things." Daniel sighed.

"Tell me about it. I've watched people be blind to obvious character flaws. It's amazing how they can be so infatuated with a person that they can't see their own life spiraling towards destruction right in front of their eyes."

"I robbed a *bank* for you."

"And from what I can tell, you're going to do it again." Junior set his pencil down and took a gulp of his beer. He stared at Daniel, daring him to argue.

Daniel wondered how much of this Junior was real. He had learned that Real World Junior didn't know what happened in the mirror. But Daniel suspected that Mirror Junior knew everything that happened in the real world. Sometimes Junior would address or mention some things and sometimes he wouldn't. Daniel wanted to know if Mirror Junior knew he was a fantasy, but he also didn't want to ruin the illusion of what they had here. This was Daniel's escape.

"I'm not robbing banks because I love you," Daniel said. "What we have here, this is lust. You should know what lust is more than anybody. We fuck because you look good and have a nice body and can charm the thong off a nun."

"You're not a nun."

"And I don't wear thongs."

Daniel got up from the bed and started getting dressed. He knew he didn't need to be clothed to leave the mirror. The only way to leave the mirror was through the front door of the house, so he had learned, and when he returned to the real world, he would find himself sitting on the couch, same as when he entered.

"Hit a nerve, huh?" Junior asked.

"No, I have things I need to think about. I need to get out and get some fresh air. You're a distraction."

"Yeah, I get that a lot." He smirked. "You still thinking about those three guys from *The Grey*? I thought I would have been enough to take your mind off of them."

Daniel rolled his eyes, sitting back down on the bed to put on his shoes. Another thing he pondered was why he didn't enter the mirror wearing the same clothes he was wearing in the real world.

"Like I said," Daniel sniffed. "You distracted me from thinking about it, but that doesn't make it go away."

"Do I need to feel threatened by these dudes?"

Daniel didn't answer, choosing instead to bite back a snappy comment. Getting up from the bed, he kissed Junior on the neck and headed towards the front door. He could hear Junior following behind him.

"So you want to try and make me jealous?" Junior asked. "Two can play that game."

"Whatever you say."

Daniel walked out the front door and found himself back in his body, on Junior's couch with the mirror in his hand. A pair of eyes stared at him from the other end of the couch.

"You sleep weird," Isabel said.

Junior's daughter looked at him with her wide, expressive eyes. Her appearance was a small shock to him, and his mind took a brief pause to verify he wasn't still in the mirror.

"Somebody's been calling you," she said, gesturing to his cell phone on the table.

Daniel swapped the mirror in his hand with the phone and saw two missed calls from his dad, a call from an unsaved number, and two voicemails.

Isabel moved closer to get a better look at the phone screen.

"Is it your girlfriend?"

"No, it's my dad," Daniel said.

"Oh, are you in trouble?"

"No. I'm not in trouble. I'll call him back later."

"Izzy, I told you to leave him alone." Junior walked out from the kitchen and chased Isabel into the bedroom. "When we came home, it looked like you were in a trance or something. I figured you were doing something with your witchcraft."

"I need to clear my head." Daniel was slammed with a feeling of déjà vu as he started putting on his shoes.

"Everything okay?"

"Yeah, I'll tell you about it when I get back." Daniel looked over Junior's shoulder to see Isabel peeking around the corner. "It's nothing major. I just prefer to discuss without the chance of being overheard."

Junior nodded and returned to the kitchen. Daniel slipped the mirror into a duffle bag of dirty laundry, making sure he positioned his body at an angle so Isabel couldn't see, then left the apartment.

• • • • •

Klyde Warren Park was a 5.2-acre public park located in downtown Dallas between the city's Arts District and it's Uptown. Constructed on top of a bridge covering a three-block area of Woodall Rogers Freeway, the park produced a splash of green in an area of concrete and windows.

During the week, at lunch time, food trucks lined the road next to the park, and business-casually dressed employees, shackled by the professionalism and structured workload of corporate America, would line the sidewalks to grab a quick meal while enjoying the quasi-natural view.

Klyde Warren Park was no more than five years old, and any visitor or non-native could tell its youth by the still vibrant brick walkways and the slim trunked trees.

Daniel sat at a table on the east end of Klyde Warren Park, allowing the warm breeze to wash over his face. Children, most likely on a field trip, played in the grass, their voices screaming in delight. A nearby restaurant mingled the symphony of children's laughter with the less enjoyable conversation of businessmen. Daniel stared at one of the art sculptures decorating the lawn, a brilliant red tangle of metal that his mind refused to interpret as more than a failed construction site. Overlooking the artwork and active children, he let his gaze focus on the tan-and-gray building situated across the street.

The Federal Reserve Bank of Dallas, with its over-sized logo mounted on the south side of the building, sat on a diagonal from the park. Daniel had learned in school that the Federal Reserve Bank was a central bank for the United States and served as the depository for federal funds. He tried to remember if the banks housed physical bills, though. Now was one of those times when he wished he had paid better attention in his college Finance classes instead of worrying about sex, clubs and drugs.

A stiff vibration from his pocket interrupted his thoughts. He took his phone out, glanced at the text message notification from Junior and chose to ignore it. But a missed call from his dad kept him from returning to his daydream. He had avoided calling his dad since he got fired but knew he would have to return the call eventually.

He watched two kids run past screaming with joy as he placed the call and waited while the phone rang in his ear.

"Hello."

"Hey, Dad."

"Who is this?"

"Daniel." He knew the routine. These conversations always started the same. "Your only child."

"Oh, sorry about that. It's been so long since I heard from you I didn't recognize the sound of your voice. You sound familiar, so I'll take your word for it."

Daniel awarded him an awkward fake laugh. "Yeah, sorry about that. Things have been busy here."

"Oh. Working hard, huh? I think you get that from me."

"Yeah, things at work have been kinda hectic. We have a new vendor, so we're learning script for troubleshooting internet connectivity."

"Oh, so you're not with billing anymore?"

"No, I made a move. I didn't see much of a way to advance from the billing side."

"Sounds like you're outside. Are you off today?"

"Yep." Daniel closed his eyes and clamped his mouth shut. Maybe this would keep him from moving any further with the lies.

"Oh, okay."

There was a silence as Daniel tried to think of what to say next. "Yeah, I took off today to come downtown so I could do some market research for a business me and my friend started." The lie flowed so easily from Daniel that he blinked in surprise.

"That's great. Putting that Marketing degree to good use, huh?" The tone of his dad's voice transitioned to one of interest in the new topic. "What kind of business is it?"

"Search engine marketing. We're going to help small businesses become more visible on search engines like Google and other sites. We want to manipulate the system so that when people search certain words, our clients are higher up on the search page. I know for myself, when I'm searching for something, I don't ever look past the second or third page. It's a very lucrative business venture from what I've seen so far."

"Sounds like a good idea. Definitely something you millennials can get behind. Do you have start-up capital, yet?"

"We didn't really need much. We got our first client a few weeks ago, and we've already made about eight thousand dollars."

"Well, isn't that something."

"Yeah. If we start making enough, then I might leave my job and do this full time."

This gave Daniel a back door out of the lie.

"My son, the entrepreneur. I'm proud of you."

"Thanks."

"So you said you and a *friend*? Is it a boyfriend?"

"Nope... just a friend."

"There was a pause there."

"Don't read too much into that. We're business partners and friends. I wouldn't cross that line."

"Smart. But if you..."

"One issue I do have." Daniel interrupted to avoid going too deep into his and Junior's relationship. "We have a couple of individuals that say they are interested in investing in our work."

Daniel's mind focused on a way to get his dad's advice about Oscar and Alexandre.

"What's the issue?"

"I can't tell if they're serious or not. I want to be sure I can trust them before I bring them into my circle."

"Do you have any reason to *not* trust them?"

"Other than them being strangers?"

A buzz on his phone alerted him to another text from Junior.

"You can't say somebody is untrustworthy just because you don't know them. That's no way to live life."

"What signs should I look for?"

"Well, when I'm interrogating a suspect or a potential informant or anybody really, I look them in their eyes. You might not be able to tell if they're giving you the whole truth or what their motives are, but you can see if they are genuine.

There's always something inside of you, a feeling or an intuition, whatever you wanna call it, that reads what you see in people's eyes."

"I haven't had a chance to look them in the eyes. Our communication has been all verbal."

"You kids and your technology. There are ways to look them in the eye."

Daniel pondered for a second. If Oscar and Alexandre were serious about helping him, then he should suggest they come to him. It would be a lot easier to read them if they were in person.

"I'll have to try that."

"And you'll have to keep me updated on your business. I wouldn't mind an early retirement if this thing takes off."

"I'll keep you updated."

Daniel hadn't expected good advice such as this from his dad. He had planned on asking Veronica her opinion, but he hadn't been able to find her in *The Grey*. And Javier had avoided him since their fallout. Not as if Daniel would have asked him anyway. He pondered the situation on the Uber ride back to the apartment.

CHAPTER FOUR

Daniel walked through the door to find Junior seated on the coffee table with a lady sitting on the loveseat across from him. She turned and looked at Daniel.

"Sorry," Daniel said. "Didn't know you had company. I can come back."

"No, don't leave," Junior said. "This is why I've been texting you. You should really check your texts more often."

Something in Junior's tone was odd and alerted Daniel to the mood. He walked around Junior and got a better look at the woman.

She was dressed in black clothing, jeans and V-neck shirt. Her hair was short and spiked with a single streak of purple and a single streak of pink in the front. His first thought was to wonder what grunge rock band from the 90's was she performing with later. Her face showed her to be older than Daniel and Junior, maybe late 20s.

Daniel shook the woman's hand as she introduced herself as Nicole.

"What's so urgent?" Daniel asked.

"His texts were probably trying to tell you about how impressed I was with your bank robbery," she said.

Daniel's forehead ran cold, and his heart thundered in his ears. "I'm sorry. What bank robbery?"

"I've already gone through this with your friend. Please don't make me do it again."

Daniel looked at Junior who nodded his head. "Take me through the short version of this hypothetical bank robbery, if you don't mind."

"It was a coincidence that I was even outside the bank when your FoodHub associate went inside. I was scoping out for potential marks and saw him withdraw that large sum of money. My initial thought was this idiot will definitely be an easy target."

"You planned on robbing him?"

"Yes. Fortunately for you, I always follow the money. I saw him exchange the haul with you, your *first* mistake."

"I'm still not admitting to anything. And if this conversation is being recorded, I do not consent and would like to speak with a lawyer."

"I'm not a cop." She rolled her eyes. "And that only works on TV. You didn't check to see if you were being followed and you led me here. I backtracked to that FoodHub employee, approached him first. That's when it got really interesting because he doesn't even remember robbing the bank."

"What idiot would admit to committing a crime?"

"One who knows there isn't any evidence of the crime. News reports say the security system and the armed guard were both incapacitated during the robbery. I figured this has to be a big-time job for everything to go so strategically haywire at the most opportune time." She paused. "Although, I guess it would be the most *inopportune* time from the bank's point of view."

"I think," Daniel said, "you have the wrong idea about who we are. We aren't involved in any organized crime. If we had robbed a bank, then we wouldn't be stacked two people deep in a one-bedroom apartment."

"I know it's not organized. If it were, then your other mistakes wouldn't have been as detrimental."

"What mistakes?" Junior asked.

"Like robbing the cash drawer. The cash draw holds anywhere from three thousand to ten thousand dollars at one time."

Junior glared at Daniel, no longer making it a point to pretend they hadn't been involved in the robbery.

"How much did y'all get away with? Five grand?"

"What other mistakes are on your list?" Daniel wanted to avoid having this argument with Junior again.

"Did you know the bills you took are marked?"

"This just gets worse and worse." Junior stood up and started pacing.

"Not marked exactly, but the serial number on some of those high dollar bills were recorded in the system when they were deposited. It's not a normal occurrence for that bank. Nobody would have expected you to know that. But if a large volume of those marked bills gets deposited into a single bank account, you'll have the Feds at your door within an hour."

"Fuck!" Junior said. "I've already started spending this money."

"Calm down," Daniel said. "We don't have to worry about marked bills. We have a method to locate them."

"Is that your superpower? Finding traceable money? I already know one of you has the power to erase memory. Although it must not work on everybody because..." Nicole let the thought trail off.

"We haven't made any deposits into our bank accounts. We're just going to spend the cash."

Nicole got up from her chair, holding her bottle of beer, and strolled around the living room. She made a show of picking over the artwork on the walls and the dust layered on the electronics.

Junior sat down next to Daniel.

"You know," she said, "there are better ways to do this. Me and my associates have been doing this for a long time, so we've gotten past the mistakes that you haven't touched on yet."

"Are you willing to share those tips?" Junior asked.

"Depends…"

"On what?"

"First tip, start a business. Something small like a Laundromat – or what do the locals call it in Texas? A washeteria? Any form of business that you can use to launder your money?"

"Launder our money?" Junior asked.

"You know, convert it from stolen to spendable. You don't want to keep large amounts of cash laying around."

"If we start a business," Daniel said. "We can take cash and make large deposits without it looking suspicious. It'll look like we're making money from the business."

"Any business will do. A tax service or car wash." She looked at Junior with a hungry gaze. "Personal trainer."

"Nicole," Daniel said. "What do you want? You're here accusing us of robbing banks and giving us tips on money laundering. I'm trying to figure out why you're here."

"I want to propose a partnership. No, I want to… how do I say this?" She placed her finger on her lip and gazed upward in thought. "I want to audition you for a role in my company. The business is expanding, and I need to hire some new talent."

"Audition?" Daniel and Junior said together, one confused and the other intrigued.

"But you still didn't tell me what it is that you do."

Nicole's slow stroll around the room brought her to the suitcase that Daniel had been using to store his clothes and personal items. She bent down and plucked something from the top of the disheveled stack and held it up for Junior and Daniel to see.

"Tarot cards?" she asked.

Daniel couldn't remember leaving those out in the open. He tried not to leave any voodoo related items unattended while Isabel was around and thought he had put everything away before he left for the park.

"I read tarot," Daniel admitted.

"Hmm." Nicole seemed to consider for a moment before tossing the cards back down into the suitcase of jumbled clothes. "I don't think fortune telling and magic tricks are going to be the assets we need to add to the team. Sorry to have wasted your time."

She began to move towards the door and stopped mid-step. Her body stiffened, rigid and trembling, and the air hissed between her teeth. Daniel realized that Junior had stopped her. He turned to Junior and shook his head. She dropped down on the couch with a clumsy twist.

"That's what I can do," Junior said. "Could've knocked you out if I wanted to."

Daniel couldn't tell if the look of amazement that swept over Nicole's face was from her awe of being restrained by Junior or from the thought of what she could do with his power.

She rose from the couch and patted Junior on the chest, her hand lingering longer than Daniel would have liked.

"I could definitely use that."

"Just name the place, and we'll be there."

"We?" She glanced at Daniel. "For what I had in mind we really didn't need Ms. Cleo."

Daniel sighed.

"It's both of us or neither," Junior said.

"Cool." Her face was unreadable for a second, but a smile crested as she reached a decision. "Let's go."

"Now?" Junior asked.

"Yes, my friend is waiting downstairs. I have a two-seater, so you'll have to take your own car. Follow us and try to keep up."

Nicole introduced Daniel and Junior to her friend downstairs as Tiffany. Short, petite Tiffany gave Daniel the impression that she was young, maybe high school age, although he had a feeling she maintained a youthful look on purpose. He used the advice that his Dad had given him earlier to see through her timid voice and reclusive mannerisms. He didn't see any genuineness in her eyes.

"You'll follow us," Nicole said. "It's party time."

Junior drove a safe distance behind Nicole to keep her in sight. After a few minutes, Daniel couldn't hold it in anymore.

"What the fuck?" Daniel said.

"I know, right?" The excitement in Junior's voice irritated Daniel.

"This is the most fucked up coincidence. How did she just *happen* to be at the bank at the exact moment we were robbing it?"

"Of course it ain't a coincidence. This is fate. This is your power doing its job."

"You can't blame every coincidence on my power."

"You've given us a taste of bank robbing and in the process introduced us to something bigger."

"What if she's part of some mob or gang?"

"Trust the process. You can't spend your life distrusting everybody you meet."

"Stranger danger. Isn't that what they taught us in school?"

Junior shrugged. "You know, I think you're only being hard on her because she's female. You have a real catty personality sometimes."

Daniel stiffened in his seat. "I don't have anything against her. The only reason you're following behind her is because you want to get laid. If it had been a man who came to the apartment and started talking about our heist, you would have popped a blood vessel in his brain or pushed him into a coma."

"Not if he was telling me shit that made sense. She offered us some good tips as a token of good faith. What more do you want? It ain't like your plan was successful."

"My plan was successful *enough*."

Junior scoffed.

Daniel watched the gray concrete whiz past the window. He wished he could have this conversation with Mirror Junior. At least that version of Junior would have been more empathetic about how he phrased certain observations.

"Look," Junior said. "What's the worst that can happen?"

"They could kill us."

"Could they? We have power that we can defend ourselves with. We're just going to check things out and get some information."

"But we don't know what they can do. Think about it. She knows that you can control people, and she thinks that I can erase memories. You gave her too much information and didn't get anything in return."

"You think she has power?"

"For her to believe that we can do supernatural things without having to be shown means either she has powers of her own, or she knows somebody that does. It doesn't shock her."

"Her friend…"

"If you thought somebody could erase your memory, would you go into their home and confront them about a hypothetical crime?"

"No."

"She must have some ability to negate anything she thought we could do. And as a safeguard, she left her friend outside."

"That's smart."

Daniel had a neighbor growing up who was expert level at chess. He had taught Daniel how to play. One of the lessons the neighbor had given Daniel was to assess the skill level of the opponent early in the match. The best way to foresee an opponent's plans on the chess board was to know the difference between a beginner and an expert. If you mistake an expert for an amateur, you wouldn't last very long on the board. If you mistake a beginner for an expert, you would go crazy trying to figure out their strategy. Random moves, without rhyme or reason, would have a chess player second-guessing their own strategy.

Daniel took a step back to look at the heist situation. Nicole knew they were amateurs. She had been able to discern that early in the conversation, maybe even from just observation. But she didn't know everything about them. They could use that to their advantage. He was certain that Nicole and her friend were more advanced in this heist business. They knew more than Junior and himself, but not enough where they could retire. Unless they were unable to satisfy their greed, they needed help moving into the high-level game.

"We need to let her continue to think I can erase memory. I don't want her to know everything about us."

"That distrust is going to keep you from meeting a lot of great people."

"Until we know more, or we know what power they have, we need to keep it to ourselves. Let's not show everything in our hand."

"Okay, whatever you say, bro."

"You should be more wary of her since she knows where you live. What if she had popped up while Izzy was there?"

Junior didn't say anything.

"Let's set a game plan," Daniel said. "We need to find out as much information about them as possible."

"I'm not playing this game. I'd rather learn what they have to teach us and make a profit. You do what you want to do."

The whispers of the *voleur* pelted against the doors of the car matching the sound of the wind passing. Daniel ignored them.

"Junior, you know this could be a trap, right? We're following Gene Simmons and her friend to an unknown location. And we haven't let anybody know where we're going. We don't know what to expect when we get there."

"This is one of those moments when it's obvious you have seen way too many movies. This is real life. Not some mafia movie."

"I know this is real life. You know what else this is? A city where they find a dead body floating in the Trinity River every other week. There's reality shows dedicated to following detectives around as they solve murders in this city. I've never turned on the TV and heard the news station say 'well, there weren't any murders today'."

"Stop being dramatic. If you're so worried about something bad happening… if you don't want to do this then say so. I'll pull over and let you out."

Daniel wanted to tell Junior to pull over. But then he thought about the fact Junior would have to face this alone. And what would Daniel do if something bad happened to Junior that Daniel could have prevented? He needed to be there to help Junior defend himself against anything that might happen.

He crossed his arms and sulked under the growing pressure of the *voleur* begging for his attention. Was he being dramatic?

"So you staying or you want out?"

"Just drive."

"I should've grabbed a beer on the way out." Junior sighed. "Your anxiety about this has stressed me out, and I need to bring myself down."

They exited the freeway and followed Nicole through a residential neighborhood in an area of town where the cheapest car you would see cost more than Junior and Daniel made in a year combined.

"You think this is where they live?" Junior asked.

"No way."

"If they're living like this from bank heists then I think we definitely need to join them. This is exactly how I want to live with my kids."

The volume of cars parked on the street increased. Nicole pulled her car to the curb. Junior slid his car behind hers and looked out the windshield at the mansion-sized home where a stream of people filed inside.

"A house party?" Junior said.

"Looks like you're gonna get that beer you wanted."

• • • • •

Daniel and Junior found themselves in Highland Park, a city located in the northern sector of Dallas County. Surrounded on all four borders by the City of Dallas, it is one of the wealthiest cities in Texas and boasts the most affluential suburb in the state. With a population of under 10,000 residents, Highland Park prides itself on the level of exclusivity it demands from the Dallas natives. Homes in the area start at $1.2 million with the most expensive home costing $31.5 million (the second most expensive home in Dallas County).

It wasn't an area of the city that they were used to exploring. 10,000 square foot homes and $200,000 cars were the norm.

Junior sat on the hood of his car, knowing its faded paint job stood out in comparison to the other cars lining the street and watched Nicole and her friend approach.

Daniel hadn't spoken since they arrived and attempted to fade into the background. The approaching women exchanged a glance, and Daniel could see the hunger in Nicole's eyes. She was attracted to Junior and didn't make any attempts to hide her lust. Daniel's upper lip curled up into a snarl before he realized it, and he forced himself to slip back into a neutral, unreadable face.

"Is this your party?" Junior asked.

"No. It isn't."

"Were we invited to this party?"

"In a way. You could say that."

"I'm not really into crashing parties. Not to mention, I don't think we belong here." Junior waved his hand at the expensive homes.

"You'd be surprised," Nicole said as she took a spot next to him on the hood. "Take a look at those girls entering the house. You can't see the name brand labels on their asses or the designer logo on their shoes, but you can tell they're dressed nice, right?"

"I don't need to see their clothes to know we're in the wrong area."

"Notice how they don't even look twice at the guys dressed in equally priced clothing? Watch who they gravitate towards."

The pair spent a moment watching the women move up the sidewalk. It was dark and Junior's eyesight wasn't the best, so he wasn't sure what Nicole expected him to see.

"Who are they looking at?" Junior asked. "The hired help? Is that why you brought us? Because I look like the gardener?"

Nicole laughed and leaned her head onto Junior's shoulder. Tiffany exchanged glances with Daniel before rolling her eyes.

Then Daniel saw it. There was an exchange between one of the girls and a guy that didn't fit in with the aesthetic of the party. The guy's clothes were more average than luxurious, the fit not as tailored. A hand-off between the casual male and a random blonde made Daniel frown. If that was what he thought it was, they weren't trying to be inconspicuous about it.

"Was that a drug transaction?" Daniel asked.

"Sshh." Nicole shushed him. "Not so loud. You want them to think you're the police?"

Daniel tightened his lips and placed his hands in his pockets. Tiffany shook her head.

"I thought we were here to hit a mark?" Junior asked.

"We're here to test out you guys' skills. I need to see what you have up your sleeves and how we can best utilize your... *abilities.*"

"So what's the plan? What do we need to do?"

"Just follow me for now. We'll get to the fun part later."

Nicole grabbed Junior's hand and started the march towards the party. Tiffany and Daniel followed behind, not speaking or looking at each other. It felt like they were the third wheel to this duo.

The atmosphere became hazy the closer they got to the house. The flashing lights and buzz of the party inside drummed against Daniel's senses. Once inside, the clouds of smoke muted his vision to the point that if he didn't know better, Daniel would have assumed he was in *The Grey*. The fragrance of marijuana and other burning chemicals assaulted his nostrils. The music thudded louder, and he recognized the base line of a popular song that had been over played on the radio since the beginning of the year.

Daniel took a moment to collect himself and look around. The party was comprised of college students holding red cups of alcohol, screaming to be heard over the music. From the hallway, he could see into one room on his left where liquor bottles were lined up for self-service. The room to his right was the source of the weed smell. A dotted array of burning joints and lit blunts flickered in the gray haze of the smoke-filled room.

Nicole was speaking in Junior's ear and pointing to the table to their left. He nodded, and she walked away.

"Do you want anything to drink?" Tiffany asked Daniel.

"No thanks." He wanted a clear head.

"It'll be harder for you to blend in if you don't have something in your hand. Who comes to a party and doesn't drink?"

"Fine. I'll make myself a drink."

Tiffany didn't take the hint that Daniel didn't want to be babysat and followed him to the liquor table. Daniel's preferred drink was rum and Coke. He knew it would be too tempting to drink if he made himself his favorite drink, so he settled for vodka and Sprite. Thinking he could slip a minimal amount of alcohol in the cup, Nicole tipped the bottle forward causing him to pour more than he intended. She gave him a lazy smile and winked with two cups in her hand.

"Just place the cup to your lips every minute or so," Tiffany said.

"What?" He struggled to hear over the music.

"Nobody will know if you are really drinking or not. Just make it look like you're drinking." She placed the cup to her lips as an example, and Daniel couldn't tell if she were showing him the trick or drinking.

"Thanks."

Junior and Nicole had moved to a less crowded room with less noise and a thicker layer of smoke. Daniel blinked a few times to push moisture to his drying eyes and watched as Junior pulled his head up from the table, rubbing his nose in irritation. Nicole rubbed Junior's face. The traces of white powder and a rolled up dollar bill on the table signaled what this room was for.

"So much for staying sober," Daniel said.

"You're so uptight." Nicole frowned at him. "Maybe you should take a bump. That will loosen you up."

"I thought we were here for a test."

"The test is coming. But until then, relax."

Nicole picked up the rolled bill and offered it to Daniel. He shook his head and took a pretend sip of beer, noticing that Tiffany hadn't taken her eyes off of him.

"So, Junior," Nicole, seated on the arm of the couch, leaned in and wrapped her arm around Junior's shoulder. "Is that your real name?"

"Juan Carlos." He stopped rubbing his nose long enough to talk. "It's my dad's name too, so I go by Junior. Everybody calls me that."

"I'm gonna call you Juan. I don't want to be like everybody else. Or maybe JC."

He shrugged.

"Where are you from?"

"New York. You can't tell?"

"I hear the accent, but I think you've been in Texas too long. You're starting to get that twang."

"Please don't say that. That's an insult. I'm Brooklyn all day, every day. Nobody will never be able to take that away from me. When I first got here, hearing this Texas accent, it used to kill me. It was like I died and got sentenced to life in the Beverly Hillbilly section of Hell. My brother lost his accent quick. He would walk around saying 'y'all'. Shit irritated the fuck outta me."

"What's wrong with 'y'all'?"

"Ain't nothing wrong with it. It's just not something people from New York say. It sounds stupid."

"Oh, and people from the south are dumb?"

"Your words, not mine."

Nicole laughed and took a gulp from her red cup.

"Why did you move to Texas then? Most people wouldn't want to move out of the castle to live with the peasants."

"It's complicated." Junior patted Nicole's leg.

"Where are y'all from?" Daniel asked.

"I'm from Louisiana," Nicole said. "Tiffany is from Florida. We're all southerners here."

"What made you move to Texas?"

"Profit." She turned to Junior. "So tell me about the bank job. How did y'all make that work? The bank teller couldn't even give an accurate description."

"Well," Junior said. "We had that college kid come in with a bag and hand the teller a note. We found out that it's bank policy that in order to protect the customers and employees, they just empty the cash drawer."

"I already knew that. I guess your girlfriend didn't tell you that the cash drawer only had so much money in it. Did she tell you how much was in the vault?"

"We didn't want to involve her in this. She didn't tell us anything."

"So how were you getting your information?"

Junior opened his mouth to speak, and Daniel interrupted.

"We have our informants. How much information do you expect us to volunteer without any reciprocation?"

"Well, shit. Those are some big words. We southerners aren't all dumb, huh, Junior?"

"What powers do you guys have?"

Nicole and Tiffany exchanged a look while taking a sip from their cups. Daniel could tell that Tiffany didn't drink but Nicole's lengthy swallow said otherwise. They were stalling.

"Look," Junior said. "Daniel is a distrustful person. We had a conversation in the car, and he doesn't know whether you two are genuine or not."

"Junior…"

"No, let's put it all out there. We need to know as much about you two as you know about us. It's only fair."

"You're right," Nicole said. "We should be more open about who we are and what we can do. I can see into the future, and Tiffany *talks* to machines. We have a guy who is a vault specialist."

"A seer and a computer geek?" Daniel said.

"A hell of a lot better than tarot cards, I promise you. Let me show you an example. In about 45 seconds, a guy in a white shirt and blue jeans is going to enter the room with his entourage. His party will be comprised of two bodyguards, obviously well-armed, and two women dressed in clothing that has more in common with lingerie than fabric."

"There's plenty of people here in white shirts and blue jeans."

"He's going to nod his head at the guy in the corner over there in the red shirt," she continued. "It's a signal of some sort. The guy in the red shirt is going to grab a box and take it to the table, and they're going to have a conversation."

"A conversation about what?"

"I'm not close enough to overhear, but that's not important. Once we confirm that the guy is here, we have 47 minutes to complete your test. That's when the audition begins. We have a friend, the vault specialist I mentioned earlier, waiting outside for us. He arrived about ten minutes before we got here."

"Why are we waiting for the guy in the white shirt?"

Daniel had not completely finished his sentence, when a slim white guy, average height wearing a white shirt and blue jeans walked into the room, taking a look around at the partygoers. He pointed to a couch across the room as two muscled men in suits followed behind him. Daniel couldn't see the guns, but he was aware of how the bodyguards carefully scanned each person in the room.

"Y'all might want to look away before they notice you staring." Nicole said.

"Who is he?" Junior asked.

"That is Jeremy Staffle. One of the most profitable cocaine dealers in North Texas. He's the one that supplied the coke for this party. This is his cousin's party. But I guess it must not be one of his favorite cousins because this supply is trash. I know he has better shit than this."

"Do you know him?"

"No. We prefer not to hit targets that we know."

"We're here to steal drugs?" Daniel asked.

"Hell no. I'm not a drug dealer. I wouldn't know how to get rid of that shit. We are here to make sure that he's here. And now that we know he's here, we can leave."

Nicole stood up from the seat and pulled Junior beside her. She leaned in and kissed him. He grabbed her by her hair, pulling her head back and planted his lips on her neck.

Daniel looked away. Tiffany smiled.

They walked out of the room towards the front door, having to stop twice as Junior made pit stops to fondle Nicole.

Nicole led them to a black SUV where a large man wearing all black sat behind the steering wheel. Junior introduced himself and jumped into the back, not wary of the warning most children of the 90s received about getting into cars with strangers. Tiffany climbed into the back with Nicole, leaving Daniel to sit passenger.

"And now," Nicole said, undisturbed by Junior's kisses and roaming hands. "Let's go rob us a vault."

• • • • •

Daniel was annoyed with having to deal with not only Nicole but also a new stranger. The growing party of participants in this scenario was approaching critical overload. Hearing Junior behind them in the SUV making out with Nicole, augmented by her giggles and moans, only increased his annoyance. He turned to the driver, a muscular white man dressed in black with a buzz cut hairstyle and brown eyes, and wondered if the sounds irritated him too.

The guy glanced at him, an expression of annoyance on his face also. But it seemed maybe it was more by Daniel and Junior's presence than by what was going on in the backseat. Daniel shook his head and glared out of the window with the realization that he didn't know where they were. He had lived in the city since college, and the first two years he hadn't had a car. Those two years were restricted to keeping his extracurricular activities to campus and surrounding areas. His junior year, he had moved off campus to an apartment, and his dad bought him a cash car. It wasn't the sports car that Daniel dreamed of owning, but it was his first car and free, so he didn't complain. He didn't have to rely on friends for transportation. It gave him a new sense of independence. His knowledge of the areas in Dallas increased, and he learned about what areas to stay away from at night.

But even with those six years of living in Dallas, four of which he had transportation, he was still amazed when he traveled somewhere that he didn't recognize. It was a stark contrast to his hometown of Abilene, a small town in West Texas. With a population of a little over 100,000, there wasn't a corner of the city Daniel hadn't seen or explored. One of the reasons he left as soon as he could.

"Where are we?" Daniel asked.

"Addison." The man's voice surprised Daniel. He had expected a deeper voice to match the large frame. He tried to keep the reaction from showing on his face, but Daniel was sure the man still noticed. Most likely a usual reaction from people that heard his voice.

Junior whispered something to Nicole, and she giggled. Daniel felt a compulsion to ask them to shut up.

"We live to serve."

"We live to please."

"We can provide."

Daniel suppressed his desire, not realizing it was strong enough to summon the *voleur,* but not before wondering how they could help him silence the noise in the back. Were they offering to steal Junior's ability to speak?

Freddy Kreuger, 2001. Freddy, the metaphysical killer haunting kids' dreams, slices the tongue out of a victim's mouth with the sharp knives attached to his left gloved hand and the newly muted patron clasps his hand over his mouth unable to contain the fountain of blood that gushes out.

Daniel smiled before he could catch himself.

"Right here, Greg," Tiffany said.

The man pulled the car to the side of the residential area and turned off the headlights. They sat in darkness and silence, Junior and Nicole now quiet, and waited as Tiffany typed with fury on her tablet.

"So what's the test?" Junior asked.

"We want to see how your power can help us." Nicole tugged her shirt down. "We're going to hit that tan house over there. Tiffany can disable the security system. I can see if anybody is coming, making sure we don't get caught. Greg is going to open the safe."

"And us?"

"There are people in the house. We need you to take them out."

"He's not going to kill anybody," Daniel said.

Nicole shrugged and looked at Junior, waiting for his response.

To Daniel's relief, he shook his head. "I'm not going to kill anybody, but I can make sure they are incapacitated."

"As long as they stay out of our way, I don't care. The first person you'll need to handle is security in the guest house out back."

"Take me to him."

"You can't do it from here?"

"Nah, I need to see him. It's easier if I can see what I'm doing."

Nicole exchanged a look with Greg in the rearview mirror before nodding.

Daniel climbed out the car and waited for everybody, but Nicole and Junior were the only ones to exit.

"I'm not sure we need you there for this." Nicole patted Daniel on the shoulder.

"Me and Junior travel together."

"He's an adult. He doesn't need his mother tagging along. Believe me, if he gets hungry, I'll feed him." Nicole cupped her breasts and lifted them up to emphasize the innuendo.

Daniel peered at her through narrow eyes and folded his arms.

"I'll be okay," Junior said. "Just wait here."

"Why are you being so trusting? I thought we talked about sticking together."

"Daniel, if they wanted to harm us, they would've done it by now and gotten a quick eight grand. Just chill here. Get to know the meat head guy. He might be cool."

Daniel got back in the car and started to close the door but was stopped when Nicole grabbed the handle.

"If we need help with a bad hand of blackjack or Uno, we'll be sure to give you and your tarot cards a call."

Greg the driver stifled a laugh. Daniel tugged the car door close.

"She's a bitch. You get used to it." Tiffany's voice mumbled from the back.

"So she treats y'all like that too?"

"No, we're not somebody that she would want as enemies. She only talks to people like that who she feels is a threat."

"How am I a threat?"

"You both have the same power. You can see the future same as she can."

"I can't see the future. Tarot reading isn't as precise science."

"Probably best not to volunteer that information to her or else you'll sacrifice your usefulness."

Tiffany set her tablet down in the seat, locking the screen, and sat back with an accomplished look on her face.

"How did you all meet?" Daniel asked Greg. "Y'all are a weird bunch, and I don't see you three sitting at the same table in high school."

"I met Nicole at my tattoo shop, back when I was finishing my sleeves." He pushed his arms forward, flexing to show Daniel the overcrowded sketchpad of inked skin. "Business wasn't doing good. I guess because I picked a shitty place to open a tattoo shop. Nicole said it was because the location wasn't shitty enough. Nobody wants to get inked in area without at least three crackheads, five bars and four liquor stores."

Daniel nodded.

"She came in the shop with this guy, Carlos, and I got the craziest feeling of déjà vu. I knew I had seen her before. I couldn't place her face though. We talked about her getting some ink done. She couldn't decide on where she wanted the tattoo though." Greg smiled with a pause. "I don't think she really wanted a tattoo. She was showing me places on her body she said she was considering, but I know now... she was seducing me. I can't believe I missed that back then."

The smile faded from Daniel's face. "So y'all were together?"

Daniel started getting nervous that Junior was just in the backseat fondling Greg's ex-girlfriend.

"Nope, we had sex a few times but nothing serious. Nicole isn't really the settle down type. She's more of a man than any woman I've met."

A tap on the passenger window made Daniel jump. Nicole was standing at the door with a smile on her face.

"See," she said. "I brought him back safe and sound."

The trio climbed out of the SUV to join Junior and Nicole. Daniel, seeing Greg now standing, hid his surprise at how short Greg was. In the car, with the weight of muscle, he had given Greg the benefit of being at least the same height as himself.

"Well?" Greg asked.

"Smooth as butter. The guard is out like a light. Junior thinks he'll be out for at least an hour. And the security cams?"

"Taken care of," Tiffany said.

"Then let's go."

The group, led by Nicole, walked up the neighborhood to the gray and white house. Daniel glanced around, keeping alert for any movement, but nobody else seemed tense. Once at the door, Nicole produced a set of keys, courtesy of the guard and unlocked the door.

The dark interior, backlit by the glow of light from other rooms, greeted them with an eerie calm. Nicole stepped inside first, and Daniel braced for the screech of alarms. His body on edge and ready to run if needed.

Silence layered over the group like a comfortable quilt as the group entered through the doorway, Daniel following last.

Nicole paused and looked around the foyer, a wash of glee lighting her face.

"Upstairs," she said. "Master bedroom."

Greg and Tiffany took the lead as Nicole wrapped her arm through Junior's, taking a step in front of Daniel.

"We're going to go take care of the other two people in the house?"

"I didn't see anybody else in the house. Are you sure somebody else is here?" Tiffany asked.

Nicole tapped her finger to her temple and nodded. "You forget what I can do with this. Two women. Most likely some of Jeremy's groupies."

Daniel resisted the urge to try to follow them, remembering how Nicole had embarrassed him at the car. He trotted up the stairs and entered the room behind Greg.

To his amazement, the master bedroom was the size of Junior's apartment. Light blue walls with chandelier lighting and a massive bed, Daniel stood in the doorway mesmerized. Everything in the room was over-sized and extravagant. The plush pillows on the bed that looked almost as big as the bean bag chairs he had in college. The wooden dresser that could have been a part of set design for a Disney film. The horribly tacky long hair rug rounding the middle of the floor.

Daniel couldn't keep his eyes in his head. He wanted to touch everything from the movie screen size TV to the rack of video games lined on the built-in bookcase. But he also didn't want to leave any evidence he had been in the house they were about to rob, so he refrained.

"This is a lot." Daniel said.

"Tell me about it," Tiffany said. "This asshole won't even miss the money we're taking. How long do you think it will take him to notice it's gone, Greg?"

"If we run this job right, I'd say weeks."

"We need to find the safe," Tiffany said. "Probably would've been easier if she had just shown us."

They scattered around the bedroom. Greg checked obvious locations, behind pictures and art work. Tiffany opened drawers and checked the night stand.

Daniel didn't know where he would be best needed. He could use Ghiy-āthu'd-Dīn to find it, but he would need a mirror. And he didn't want to release this part of his power yet. So he looked around, trying to make a show of being helpful. Within a few minutes, he had moved to the study, a room adjacent to the master and gazed at the shelving of books lining the walls.

The guy he had seen at the party, the drug dealer Nicole pointed out, didn't seem like the reading type. Taking a closer look, there wasn't any dust on the shelves or on the books, but that didn't necessarily mean they were frequently read. With a house this size, Daniel could assume that Jeremy had a cleaning crew.

Daniel walked around the oak desk, marveling at its sturdy appeal, and looked at the closed laptop. He didn't dare touch it and leave any fingerprints. It was an expensive brand that he had considered buying some weeks before he got fired from his job. He questioned if the laptop could be traced if he took it.

No, he could buy his own laptop after they pulled off this job. There wasn't a point in stealing a second-hand used item. Not to mention the others probably wouldn't let him take it.

One section of the library of books caught his attention. The spacing between the shelves wasn't consistent with the surrounding inlaid bookcase.

Using the tip of his finger to maneuver one of the books, he spied the round numbered knob of a metal safe.

"Found it," he called out.

Tiffany and Greg pushed into the room and peered around his shoulder at the metal dial. Tiffany snapped a picture of the shelf with her cell phone. With less regard for fingerprints than Daniel had taken, she began removing books and stacking them on the floor.

Daniel offered to help, but she waved him away. Greg returned with a small handbag and pulled out various items, placing them on the desk next to the laptop.

"What are those?" Daniel asked.

"My paintbrushes. The tools behind my artistry."

Daniel picked up one tool that looked like a hybrid of a medical scalpel and the mathematical compass he had used in geometry class in high school.

"That is one of the first tools I learned how to pick locks with," Greg said. "Old buddy of mine told me that it used to belong to Frederick Cooper, the guy that kept escaping from prison."

"He used this to escape from prison?"

"No, it's only used to pick key locks like on doors. Every tool has a specialty and purpose."

"Well if Frederick Cooper used this tool then it must be valuable then."

"Not really. Found out later my buddy got it from a pawn shop." Greg plucked the utensil from Daniel's hand and placed it back on the table. "Let's consider this to be an art museum. You can look but don't touch."

Daniel nodded and continued to admire the row of tools Greg meticulously placed in perfect rows on the desk.

After a few minutes, he removed a stethoscope from the bag and placed it around his neck. Daniel's mind flashed to the last time he had seen a stethoscope. It had been around the neck of the doctor as he informed his dad that he was now a widower.

The few minutes of watching Greg listening for the heartbeat of the safe grew boring and Daniel migrated his attention to Tiffany, seated on a chair in the corner with Jeremy's laptop open.

"You're not worried about leaving fingerprints?" Daniel asked.

"Why would I be worried? You think Jeremy is going to report his missing drug money to the police? Trust me, if any drug dealer is that stupid then they deserve to get caught. And I doubt he has access to run the prints himself."

"I feel like I'm not much help to you guys right now."

"I agree." Nicole walked into the room with her hair disheveled and shirt wrinkled.

Junior followed behind with a sheen of perspiration on his forehead. The same look of satisfaction on his face that Daniel knew from the mirror.

"Did y'all take care of the girls?" The sarcasm dripped from Daniel's tone.

"Took care of more than that,"

"Y'all found the safe?" Junior asked.

"It wasn't hard," Daniel said. "I don't think there are too many places to hide a safe."

"It looks pretty big. How much you think is in it?"

"No idea. We'll find out when it's open."

"How long will that take?"

"A lot less longer if I could get some fucking quiet." Greg looked irritated.

Daniel nodded at Junior and ignored the smirk from Nicole as he left the room. Since he wasn't helpful in the study, he could take a tour and fantasize about the luxurious life of a drug dealer.

He found the room with the sleeping women, a guest bedroom a few doors down. He verified they were still breathing, although he trusted that Junior wouldn't have killed them. Further down, he discovered a movie room. Next to that, another bedroom. A gameroom in the interior of the house downstairs to the left of the foyer. But depressingly, no bowling alley.

"This is the life." Daniel said. "How can I get the *voleur* to steal me a house like this?"

No response.

Daniel found himself admiring the guest bathroom downstairs. If this was for guests then he could imagine what the master bathroom was like. He looked at his reflection in the mirror and sighed, wondering how he got here. When he thought of burglars and thieves, the images that popped in his head were vastly different than what was happening in reality at this moment. He imagined people who were addicted to drugs, that were willing to do anything for their next fix. Or ex-convicts that had spent years in prison formulating the one big job that would set them up for life.

Escape or Die, 2012. Recently released prisoner reunites with former cell mates with plans to rob a mansion. Perfect plan goes awry when ex-convicts find out house is set with elaborate traps intended to dismember and decapitate. The game is changed when the burglars are trapped inside the House of Death *they intended to rob as the owner watches and taunts from the outside.*

And yet here Daniel was, a college graduate, unemployed, roaming a drug dealer's mansion with his best friend who may or may not be high off cocaine. And he knew why he had made a pit stop in the bathroom. It was inevitable. He closed his eyes, disgusted that he couldn't admit it to himself that he wanted the contact.

He traced the required emblem on the mirror with the corner of a bar of soap. The symbol of summoning was imprinted in his mind, and he doubted that he would ever be able to forget it. The lights buzzed and dimmed as the shadow coalesced in the mirror, this time more defined than the last.

Curse of the Djinn, 1988. A genie grants a man three wishes. Although not explained in the rules, once the third wish is granted, the man exchanges places with the genie, tortured through every living minute, until another unfortunate soul makes three wishes for him to grant.

And this would be wish number two.

"Why did you give me the mirror?" His intention had been to ask a different question. The urgency behind his voice as the question pour from his lips was surprising.

"An exchange. To do with as you please." Its voice was rolling thunder. "You have forgotten our agreement?"

Did the rest of the crew hear it upstairs?

"I need to know what it does?" Daniel kept his voice low. "You gave me the impression that it was *just* a mirror, but it's more than that. You never mentioned what else it could do."

No response.

Daniel wanted to asked Ghiy-āthu'd-Dīn to take the mirror back, but he couldn't bring himself to say it. It couldn't be as simple as asking the spirit for a refund. One of the stipulations were that Daniel could destroy the gaudy ornament if he wanted. Did he want to?

"You're a fucking con artist."

No response.

"I need the combination to the safe. What gift do I have to accept for that information? Headphones that make me listen to words I'll never hear in real life?"

A condensation of fog appeared on the mirror. Outlined within were the numbers 25-48-07. That was too easy.

"What's the price?" Daniel repeated.

The shadow faded. The lights perked back up.

Daniel clenched at the bar of soap in his hand, his nostrils flaring with anger. He wiped down the mirror with water and toilet paper, flushing the evidence and pocketing the crushed soap.

Junior was waiting outside the bathroom door when he exited.

"You okay?" Junior asked.

"I got the combination."

Junior looked past Daniel at the mirror and nodded. His movements jerky and anxious. "How?"

"Twenty-five. Forty-eight. Seven. There will be less questions if you're the one that opens it. No questions about what I can do."

"You can always say you got it from the Psychic Hotline."

"Her 'Ms. Cleo' comment *was* a good dig. If it had been anybody else..."

"Your Gene Simmons remark was funny too."

"I know, right? I waste all my good material on you."

Junior punched him in the shoulder and shook his head. He always punched a little too hard, but Daniel would never say anything.

"Let's go open this safe so we can get out of here."

•　•　•　•　•

Daniel knew he was cautious. In college and in his adult life, he played by the rules and didn't test the boundaries as most new adults did. It was one of the reasons why he didn't know the extent of his power. Sure he had experimented with various drugs, but not to the extent of his peers.

With all the planning and financial savings and keeping abreast of responsibility, he still ended up homeless and depending on a friend to survive. Playing it safe hadn't paid him much of a return on investment.

Playing it safe was why he didn't speak up while watching Nicole count out fifty thousand dollars and hand it to Junior, praising him for his contribution to the success of the mission, but refusing to give Daniel a share of the profits, claiming he hadn't contributed to the job.

"You can't leave him out," Junior said. "He was there and present just as much as everybody else."

"I'm the boss," she said. "I decide who was vital and who wasn't."

"So why does the meat-head with the stethoscope get a cut? He didn't open the safe. I did."

Greg and Tiffany had parted ways earlier. Daniel assumed they already had their respective portions of the haul. Nicole stood in their living room with a sly smirk on her face.

"You interrupted Greg from doing what he was there to do, but that doesn't make him less valuable. As far as I'm concerned he carried his workload."

Junior dropped the cash on the table and approached Nicole. Daniel could see the look in Junior's eyes and wanted to prevent anything from happening they might regret later.

"Junior, it's okay. I don't need..."

"No, it's not okay. If we do work for somebody, then we expect to get paid. Nobody here works for free." He turned to Nicole, standing dangerously close. "How can you expect us to trust you if you refuse to pay us what we deserve?"

Daniel watched, waiting for her to respond, but she didn't move, not even to blink. Was Junior holding her, keeping her from speaking?

Junior leaned in and whispered in her ear. Daniel wasn't able to make out what was said. But she turned her head to look at him, her mouth still twisted in a smirk. Rolling her eyes, she turned her bag over onto the table, emptying more stacks of money with Junior's pile.

"Just know," she said, "This decreases your paycheck from fifty thousand down to forty, since you want to be generous and split it with your coworker. Forty for each of you."

Junior didn't have time to respond as she kissed him and floated out of the door without so much as a glance at Daniel. When Junior looked up from the stacks of rolled bills on the table and asked Daniel what he was going to do with his share, Daniel didn't know how to respond.

"I guess I can..." *Move out,* Daniel wanted to say.

It had been almost two months since he had started crashing with Junior, and he was constantly aware that he was a guest here. Junior hadn't invited any women to spend the night, choosing instead to sleep over at Fatima's or whoever else he slept with before her. Daniel wasn't sure if Junior was doing it out of respect or embarrassment. Which in turn, made Daniel feel like he was inconveniencing Junior. So the sooner Daniel left, the better for the both of them.

But at the same time, Daniel was still unemployed. He couldn't get an apartment without proof of income. And if he did move out, how long would this money last until he was right back in Junior's apartment?

"Celebrate, of course," Junior said. "That's obvious. But what after that? This is a lot of money."

Indecisiveness reared its head, and multiple options swam before Daniel's eyes. Celebrating was not on the list.

"I need a new interview suit. And I can afford to put gas in my car now, probably get an oil change."

"Fuck the gas and oil change. You can buy a brand new car with the money we have here." Junior picked up a few stacks from the table and waved them at Daniel. "Or even better, I can load up my car with toys and a new paint job. And some new clothes and furniture."

"I think I'm going to take Steven Tyler's advice and launder this. I need to get this in the bank. Can't pay for everything with cash." Daniel looked up from the money and looked at Junior. "Thanks for standing up for me… I appreciate that. I need this money."

"I mean, you could've done that yourself by showing her what you can really do. Who's going to take you serious with a deck of tarot cards as your contribution?"

"My contribution got us in the safe."

"How long do you think they're going to let you in on these heists if you ain't pulling your weight?"

"I don't know if I wanna be let in. I'm really not 100 percent sure I wanna keep doing this."

Junior picked up a couple of stacks of the rolled money and tossed it at Daniel. "Yeah, right. This is the easiest money you've ever made in your life. You didn't have to talk to an angry customer with first world problems or deal with an irate manager who is never satisfied with your work."

"Do you trust them? Nicole and her Company?"

"I don't trust them with my life, but I trust them enough to follow and learn. I figure it's like being an intern under Steve Jobs or Bill Gates or Oprah. You learn as much as you can as fast as you can before the ride is over."

Daniel picked the thrown rolls of cash off the floor and tossed them back on the table.

"I'm starting to figure out," Junior said, "You don't know what you want. You wanted a way to get this done without nobody getting hurt, and you got it. We just cracked a fucking safe, and *nobody* got hurt. What more do you want?"

Staring at the eighty thousand dollars piled on the table, Daniel tried to push aside his indecisiveness and find a way to celebrate. He didn't want to be the responsible friend and longed to be as reckless as Junior in his decision making. He didn't need to ask what Junior would do with the money. Junior would go tip half-naked women and get drunk. Maybe even try to get a stripper to leave with him.

The thought of sex as a reward punched an emotion in Daniel's head, and his eyes darted to the suitcase next to the couch where he had hidden the hand mirror. Sex with Mirror Junior was a prize he deserved.

"I know that look," Junior said.

Daniel's heart lurched from seeing the smirk on Junior's face, and he tried to clear the guilty look from his face.

"What?"

"You just thought of something. What was it? Jewelry? Drugs? A trip somewhere?"

"You know I'm not into material things."

"Sure. Well, I'm going to give myself all the shit I didn't have growing up. And my girls are going to be treated like the princesses they are."

Junior strutted into the kitchen. Daniel assumed he was going for a beer, but he came back with a bottle of water that he guzzled with dramatic expression.

"Why am I so thirsty?" Junior asked.

"Probably the cocaine."

Daniel glanced at the clock. He was scheduled to meet Oscar and Alexandre in *The Grey* tonight and couldn't help but wonder if he had enough time to take a trip into the mirror beforehand. It would be a quickie, but any time with Mirror Junior was worth it.

A knock at the door interrupted Daniel's thoughts, and Junior choked on the water he was swallowing from his second bottle. They exchanged glances, both puzzled, before Junior snapped his fingers.

"Hide the money," Junior said.

Daniel swiped an armload of the cash into a duffle bag and checked around the table to see if he had missed any.

Junior looked out the peephole before turning to make sure Daniel had carefully hidden the money. Receiving a thumbs up from Daniel, Junior opened the door.

"Hey, what's going on?"

"You haven't been answering your phone. Did you forget we were going to the movies with Erica and Ty?" Fatima walked into the apartment with a purse in one hand, and her other hand balled into a fist.

"Oh shit. I forgot all about that."

"I'm here to remind you." She frowned and leaned in for a sniff of his chest. "Go change. You smell like weed."

Junior rushed off to the bedroom, stripping his shirt off on the way.

Fatima sat on the couch, placing her purse on the floor. She opened her hand and stared at an object in her palm and frowned.

Daniel stood next to the couch feeling the pulsing heat from the bag of money, knowing that what he was feeling was imaginary and only in his head.

"Hi," Daniel said. "I don't know if you remember me. We met at the park."

"I remember."

"I know I probably look different because my hair has grown out a little bit. It's time for a haircut."

Fatima nodded and looked around the living room at the overcrowding of clutter that was mostly Daniel's. Daniel picked up a pillow off the floor and placed it on the couch, using the gesture to kick a wad of money he had missed out of her angle of sight.

But Fatima didn't notice. She stared down at her hands and waited for Junior.

"Um…" Daniel said. "I heard about what happened at your job. I was sorry to hear about that, but I'm glad everybody is okay."

"Yes, it was a blessing that nobody got hurt."

"Have they caught the guy?"

She shook her head.

Daniel sat on the arm of the couch and pulled out his cell phone, using it to keep himself from interrupting the awkward silence that had descended upon the room again.

"You want to hear something weird?" She asked.

Daniel peeled his eyes away from the social media app he was browsing and looked at Fatima.

"I had a dream about the robbery before it happened."

"What?" Daniel asked.

"Not the actual robbery but the aftermath. The yellow police tape and the swarm of police and the media attention. I know it's a coincidence though. I don't believe in psychics or any of that nonsense."

"Oh."

She continued to play with the item in her hand, a single quarter, and the room hummed with a low discomfort of silence.

"Are you sure you're okay?" Daniel asked. "You seem really focused on that quarter."

"Sorry." She smiled. "It's a nervous habit I've picked up." She dropped the coin into her purse.

"I understand traumatic experiences. When I was in college, my mom was killed in a car accident. It ended up changing the way I looked at things, and for a long time it kept me from driving myself. It just took some time for me to get past it."

"It's silly because I wasn't even in danger when the robbery took place. I was in my office…" She sighed. "With Junior."

The pause was enough to let Daniel know what they were doing. He swallowed the heat of jealousy that rolled around his mouth. "What do you think the issue is then?"

"I regret not doing anything after having my dream. I could've scheduled extra security. Or reviewed the robbery policy and procedures with my employees. I could've done *something.*"

"Nobody got hurt. Why do you think anything different should have been done?"

"They didn't get hurt physically, but that doesn't mean there aren't emotional scars."

Daniel hadn't thought of that. He also hadn't noticed when she had pulled the coin back out her purse and was rubbing it in a circle motion with her thumb.

Junior rushed back into the room wearing different clothes, the aroma of cologne following him, as he tossed a backpack over his shoulder. "You ready?"

Fatima stood up, grabbing her purse, and smiled at him. "Yes, let me text Erica and tell them we're on our way."

She pulled her phone out of her purse and gave Daniel a brief wave as she preceded Junior out the door.

"I'll see you later," Junior said before closing the door.

Daniel glanced at the clock. He wouldn't have time to visit Mirror Junior before his meeting.

CHAPTER FIVE

"*Le fils prodigue,*" Alexandre said. "We were beginning to think you were not going to show."

"Sorry. I got… tied up."

"I know that look." Alexandre wrapped his arm around Daniel's shoulder and grinned. "The arrogant walk, with your chest puffed out and chin high. The confidence is beaming off you like a furnace. Who was the lucky girl?"

As if on cue, the transparent wisp of a woman passed in front of them and faded.

"I wouldn't say it was the confidence," Oscar said. "I think it's just his power."

"You might be right. I'm not so much used to standing next to somebody so strong. Maybe I used the wrong word. What is the difference between confidence and power?"

"Confidence is an attraction. Power is a repulsion."

"A repulsion. I have never been repulsed by power. I chase it. You, on the other hand, were a matador. It is no question that power is something you would run from. The strength of a bull charging at you with its horns unknowingly dulled but still expecting to damage where it can."

"So, with a bull raging towards you, you would choose to chase it back?"

"I would straddle that bull." Alexandre removed his arm from Daniel and stepped forward with a prideful expression. "Like I do with my lovers. You ride the power and eat it. Devour until they have none left, until all the power is yours. And then you give it back to them slowly. Tease them with the dribbles of what they once had until they beg you to release the floodgates. Nothing shows more power than having somebody beg for it."

"My English is not so good. I'm not sure I still know what we are talking about."

"We are talking about *this man.*" Alexandre thumped Daniel in the chest. "He has been given some power, and the confidence is making me dizzy. It is overwhelming. So, what do you think? What is the difference between confidence and power?"

They stared at Daniel. He didn't know what to say.

"A man of few words. I like that. Keep everybody guessing about what you are going to do next."

"Um…" Daniel paused. "I guess power is based on strength potential. Confidence is based on self-image."

"So articulate and scientific," Alexandre said. "I can tell you have education. Too bad it's an American education which means you're probably three or four hundred thousand dollars in debt now. But don't worry, I hear your kids will be even worse off than that. Better them than you, no?"

"Alexandre, I do not think he came to talk about collegiate debt."

"No, no. Of course not. Forgive me. We came to talk about your throne."

"I don't have a throne."

"Not yet. But we can help you get there."

"I don't think I wanna talk about this here."

Alexandre gave a dramatic performance of looking around the park. "You think we are seen? That there are others to hear what we say? Perhaps you would be more comfortable in the comfort of a theater or auditorium?"

Oscar snorted, the only sign that he was holding in a laugh.

"No," Daniel said. "I think it would be best if we met in person. Have this conversation face to face."

Oscar and Alexandre exchanged glances.

"Ahh," Alexandre said. "You want to look us in the eye and see if we are true to you and not Madame Comtois? That is smart and also not so smart. Here in *The Grey* you have the advantage because you have more power than the both of us combined. But in the real world..."

"Are you sure this is what you want?" The round-bellied Spaniard asked.

"I figure if you both are serious about joining me..." Daniel shook his head. "Yes, I wanna look you in the eye and see what my gut tells me. I need to hear with my own ears the earnest in your voices, not veiled in the hollowness of this place. I can't force myself to trust you when the only interaction I have is in *The Grey*."

"But you know you are safer here, no?" Alexandre said. "If we come to you, no matter how much power you have, you are stepping with trust to have us within reach."

Daniel was confused at Alexandre's reluctance since it would be Daniel in danger and not the two of them.

"Those are my conditions. Take it or leave it."

"We will accept it," Alexandre said. "But you understand what we have put in danger by joining you?"

"Not exactly, no."

"Under Katrine we are signeurs." His tone suddenly somber and serious. "We have status above everyone save for the Madame and her Grand Garrison. Through lifetimes, we have ascended the ranks to get to this point. It was no easy task to accomplish. Stature is not given for free."

"I can imagine."

"Some of the things we do have not been innocent. There is not a sin the Madame or her predecessors have not asked us to commit. You are young in this life, and I can see the purity in you."

"Why are you telling me this?"

"Because you need to know the men you are dealing with. I tell jokes and smile, but I do not want to mislead you into thinking I am an angel. This is me giving you my genuine portrait."

"How did she react when you told her you were joining me?"

The duo exchanged guilty glances.

"She doesn't know?"

"She knows," Oscar said.

"Maxence was not completely committed to following you as we were." Alexandre said. "His demeanor is… misleading. We can never read him or ever really know what his intentions are. He betrayed us and told her of our meeting you outside of the cathedral."

"And?" Daniel asked.

"So we are here as her spies. No, hear us out…" Alexandre could see the look on Daniel's face. "We do not plan on telling her anything you don't want her to know. If you want her to think you are doing nothing, that is what we will tell her. It can keep her off your trail."

"I don't wanna play politics with her," Daniel said. "I can see you want this to be Game of Thrones, but that's not what I need right now. I have enough going on."

"You have to know that she already has eyes on you," Oscar said.

"How did you think she knows about your bank robbery? Or about your employment status?" Alexandre crossed his arms in frustration. "She has a group devoted to studying you and learning why you have the power you have. It is not something you want her to learn so easily. We can make that difficult for her."

"No," Daniel said.

"So stubborn," Oscar said.

"An obvious Taurus," Alexandre sighed. "What do you suggest? What do you want us to do?"

"You're on my side or her side. I'm not gonna spend my time doubting."

"All of my fortune, assets, hell even my family legacy, my name, is entangled in her community. To walk away from that and give it up to follow you would be..."

"A sacrifice. But not one you will be doing alone. I'm going to be breaking something, too. I can't ask you both to leave your groups if I don't do the same."

"You are asking a lot."

"I'm not asking. It's the price of admission. If you choose to join me, you know where I am. Pledge your allegiance in person."

●　●　●　●　●

The House in the Mirror, as Daniel had begun to refer to it, was an escape from responsibility. He realized around his third visit that he enjoyed his time here, not only because he could pretend that any affection for Junior was reciprocated, but because he didn't have to focus on the responsibilities of being an adult.

There weren't any bills to pay or pressure to be the Prince of Veils. No reminders he was failing at life. Here he was able to forget any troubles and do whatever he wanted to do. And Mirror Junior played along, an actor on Ghiy-āthu'd-Dīn's stage.

Daniel and Mirror Junior sat on the couch watching a television show. Still saturating in the adrenaline from successfully robbing a drug dealer, Daniel was viewing everything with a sense of excitement. Any ambiguity he felt from partaking in the imaginary relationship with a mirror entity had faded with his conscious decision to not focus on the many reasons his mirror visits were wrong.

He stared at Junior, admiring how engrossed he became in soccer matches.

"You're annoying when you're being mushy," Junior said without looking away from the screen.

"Sorry. I wasn't trying to be lame. I'm not used to this."

"What's on your mind? You've been distracted since you got home. Been a while since I've seen you in such a good mood."

"Nothing is on my mind. I can be free here. It feels good not to have to be focused on whether I'm about to be stabbed in the back or not."

"You wanna talk about it?" Junior picked up the remote and muted the TV, signaling that Daniel had his undivided attention.

"I took some advice from my dad. You know I really should call him more often. Or better yet, I should go home and visit more often. He doesn't deserve to be avoided the way that I do. I'm a bad son."

"I would believe you, but you're smiling when you say it."

"I'm a *bad* son. How was that?"

"And the Oscar goes to…"

"Did you know I never told him about my power? Like, to this day, he doesn't really know who his son is. I only give him the outer shell, never the layers around the core of me."

"You could always be more open with him."

"I should."

Silence followed, the hum of a passing car being the only sound. Daniel leaned back on the couch and propped his bare feet in Junior's lap, staring up at the ceiling. He closed his eyes and let his ears train on the sounds of the house. Ghiyāthu'd-Dīn had created an amazing environment. One that Daniel began to appreciate once his eyes became desensitized to the vibrant saturation of color and the sharpness of sound.

"So what was the advice?" Junior asked.

"Hmm?"

"You said your dad gave you some advice."

"Oh, yeah," Daniel said. "He told me to meet Oscar and Alexandre in person. That way I could look them in the eye, face to face, and see if they are being real or not. I think in *The Grey* you can't see a person for who they are. You are seeing this dimmed version of what they project."

"I have this theory that some people are so good at lying that they can even fool themselves. I hear that's how spies fool lie detector tests."

"I gave them three days to prove where their loyalties lie. The only drawback is that also put me on a deadline. How can I lead if I'm too scared to do what needs to be done?"

"Part of being an adult is having uncomfortable conversations. Life was easier in high school when you could just go to your room, shut your door, and pretend everything was fine."

"I feel like that's a metaphor for me being here."

"Is it? I thought it was just me trying to be as wise as you right now. You are in a really big 'wax poetic' mood."

"I think I'm just *relaxed*, and this version of you is really easy to talk to."

"Oh, okay." Mirror Junior never responded to comments about there being two versions of himself.

"Alexandre is a lot like you. I noticed that the first time I saw him. He's good-looking, and I get the impression that he sleeps with a lot of women. Katrine made a comment about him being a ladies' man."

"Should I be jealous?"

"A little."

"Me and this Alex guy are fighting on sight. No warning or talking it out. I'm going to show him what I learned from my dad."

"You might want to be careful. He's got about thirty pounds of muscle on you."

"The bigger they are, the harder they fall." Junior whistled the pitch of a tree falling, and Daniel laughed.

"I still have to speak with Javier," Daniel said. "I need to figure out what I'm gonna say. This is just history repeating itself."

"The more things change, the more things stay the same."

"I started daydreaming about how I want my empire to be. I wanna live in the castle on the mountain, or in this case, the mansion on the hill. That way I can look down from the balcony on my subjects. I want my generals to be in the houses surrounding mine. But none of the houses can be bigger than mine. That's my first amendment."

"This sounds familiar. The King and I?"

"That's not important."

Daniel jumped up from the couch and grabbed the blanket draped over the arm of a chair. He tossed it around his shoulders, letting it hang to the floor like a cloak.

"The Prince of Veils decrees for his subjects, and everything he speaks is law," Daniel said. "If he says it is, so then it is so."

"And what is the purpose of the Prince of Veils' rule? What are you and your generals wanting to accomplish?"

He paused. "Shit. I hadn't thought of that."

"I guess you wanted to just sit in a house and give commands to go fetch food?"

"Well… no."

"I'm listening."

"Hmm…" Daniel searched for a quick response. "The purpose of kingdoms is to gain power. And knowledge is power, so my legacy will be the accumulation of knowledge. Ever since I found out what I can do, I've been restricted to learning only one aspect of voodoo. But what if I collected it all? Knowledge from everywhere regarding everything mystical."

"So you want to be a school? A library?"

"No, I want to be an order. A society of members who know selections of information that cover multiple areas. That's what my generals can do, collect. They keep telling me that I'm so powerful, but there has to be a limit. What if I could reach the limit on everything? That would definitely secure my rulership."

"How are you going to do this?"

Daniel paced the room, releasing the blanket he had clutched to his neck and letting it drop to the floor.

"I need teachers," Daniel said. "Instructors from each aspect. Oscar and Alexandre, if they decide to denounce Comtois and join me, can provide me all the instruction I need regarding the spirits and communing with them. And Clyde, the old guy from the tarot reading shop, I think he knew all along that I would ask him to join me. Veronica can teach me about the astral planes."

"It sounds like you want to be Prince of Veils now. Just a week ago you were being indecisive about the whole thing."

"What can I say? Give me a taste of power and I'm ready to claim my birthright."

Junior got up from the couch and hugged Daniel, kissing him on the mouth to punctuate his new-found purpose. They stared at each other for a moment before Junior spoke.

"And what about me? What's my role?"

Daniel opened his mouth to say he would be seated on his left, consort to the Prince, but he stopped. This wasn't the real Junior, and for all Daniel knew, this was Ghiy-āthu'd-Dīn speaking through a false image of his friend. He would need to learn more about the spirit before offering him any position on his counsel.

"Well, as for roles in my First Circle," Daniel said. "I counted on Oscar, Alexandre, Clyde and Veronica. You're asking for the fifth spot... five spots? Five Death Cards?"

A revelation blossomed in Daniel's mind. When reading his tarot, there had been five Death Cards. He was going to learn the five aspects of voodoo and would, therefore, need five teachers. Ghiy-āthu'd-Dīn had taken one of the Death Cards in the bargain for the bank robbery information.

"Damn," Daniel said. "He knew I was in over my head."

Junior didn't speak, his body frozen and staring ahead.

"I can't believe this shit." Daniel sat down on the couch, head back, staring at the ceiling.

No reaction from Junior. His face remained blank, allowing Daniel time to work it all out.

Daniel stared into his eyes, looking for the shadowy figure of Ghiy-āthu'd-Dīn. The hazel eyes stared back at him, emotionless.

"What could you teach me? You're not trained in the arts of voodoo, so I'm not sure there's anything I could offer that would be suitable."

"I didn't necessarily want to be a general. I just wanted to be by your side."

The uncertainty of who Daniel was speaking to broke his illusion of everything he found comforting in the mirror.

"We have time to work it out," Daniel said. "It's not like I'm gonna have to make this decision tomorrow."

"Yep. We have plenty of time."

•   •   •   •   •

Daniel noticed the more time he spent in the Mirror, the less comfort he found in *The Grey*. He wondered if it were a part of his maturity in the arts of voodoo. In high school, he had spent a lot of his time at the movies, consuming anything theatrical. But in college, he began to gravitate towards clubs and parties. His growth as a person moved him to enjoy the party atmosphere as opposed to the isolated movie theater.

The fact that Mirror Junior was available might have also had a hand in his preference. But either way, he hadn't been spending as much time in *The Grey* as he normally did.

It didn't take long to find Javier. He was seated in front of an old orchestra building next to a teenage boy Daniel

assumed was a new recruit. The face of the kid looked
familiar, but Daniel couldn't place where he had seen him
before. Daniel watched from a far enough distance that he
couldn't hear their conversation as to allow not only a bit of
privacy for the pair but also a chance for him to collect his
thoughts.

Javier's demeanor was always sarcastic and humorous.
He treated his followers as if he were an older sibling even to
those older than him. Daniel had appreciated it when he was
younger because it gave him a sense of comfort and didn't
seem as if he were trapped. The feeling he got from Madame
Comtois was ominous. The two times she had tried to entice
him to join her legion, Daniel felt the only way he would ever
be able to exit was death. It wasn't just the blood oath or the
menacing headquarters but a clenching ache he had in his gut
that had warned him to be cautious.

The more Daniel thought about it, the more it seemed
that Javier's community was structured like a gang. They
didn't initiate you with violence as an entry fee, but there was
a family element encapsulated in the bond between members.
It was that bond that filled a void most of the followers
weren't able to find in the real world.

Daniel decided his community would be different. He
would take the best parts from Javier and Comtois and
incorporate them into his own community. Good managers
knew how to learn and grow.

Javier, dressed in the blue jumper reminiscent of an
auto mechanic, looked up and acknowledged Daniel. He
patted the teenage boy on the shoulder and dismissed him.
The boy's figure faded away as he left *The Grey* to return to his
body.

Daniel approached, assessing Javier's mood. This was
not going to be an easy conversation.

"How have you been?" Daniel asked.

"I could be better. When I was younger, I was in a rush
to grow up and be an adult, but the peak of adulthood passes

so fast. I hope in my next life I remember this journey and just take time to savor that peak."

"Who was the kid? The one you were talking to. He looked familiar."

"A new recruit. He has some potential. I could tell from just looking at him. Did you see his aura?"

"Not really. I wasn't looking that closely. I've always had to concentrate to see auras."

"Just work on opening your third eye, and you'll get there. Or you could take Prince's advice and use a 'special code to access your mind'. You might be too young to get that reference."

"My mom used to say that I was an old soul."

"She could sense the past lives in you. I've noticed that if people look too long in my eyes, they become uncomfortable. I think they can see multiple people staring back at them."

Daniel nodded and sighed. Javier was in a good mood, so he hoped that this conversation wouldn't escalate into a fight. He opened his mouth to begin his practiced speech when Javier held up his hand, stopping him from proceeding.

"You know," Javier said, "When we first found this place, me and Sebastian, we didn't know what to call it. He kept comparing it to switching from AM radio to FM. I'm sure you don't know what that means now?"

Daniel shook his head.

"Figures. Sebastian was basically saying that we were moving our minds to a different frequency. Which explains why everything here looks muffled. It's not *tuned* to us."

"I've always thought of it as muted. The volume on everything has been turned down."

"That's another way to describe it, I guess. I never really cared much for the titles or names. I didn't have the desire for knowledge that Sebastian had. I just went along with the flow."

"If you don't pursue knowledge then how do you expect to grow?"

"The number of followers grow. My power grows. It all grows just enough for me to stay under the radar. I don't think we were even noticed by many others until you came along. I'm not blaming you. I'm just stating a fact."

Daniel nodded his head.

"Looking back, I know now that me and Sebastian had different goals. I wanted to build a haven, a safe place. Small enough to not be a threat but big enough to garner interest."

"What did Sebastian want?"

"He wanted to know everything. He was a journalist and had this irritating habit of sticking his nose in everything. It had to be ingrained in his personality because in school, after discovering the things we could do, he set his mind on becoming a spy. He wanted to use these powers to be the best spy in the world. Sebastian was a child at heart even close to adulthood. He would use his power to hide in plain sight. I can only imagine what use the government would have had for him. Can you imagine a U.S. spy with our abilities?"

"That's a lot of secrets to unfold." Daniel smiled.

"It surprised me when he ended up becoming a journalist. Although, it kind of fits since I'm sure he used his resources to get information that normally somebody wouldn't find. It's funny how much those characteristics carried over into his next life."

"Veronica told me about how you parted ways."

"If she isn't the group historian then I don't know who is."

"You've been a mentor to me, and you know that I would never turn my back on you. Taking me in when I was wandering around *The Grey*... Being there when my mom died..."

"Everything changes once you leave us. You know that, right?" The abrupt subject change surprised Daniel.

"Does it have to change?" Daniel asked. "We can still be friends and work together."

"No, this isn't a pact. Anything that you start will be a competition against what I've built here. If you want to be friends and work together, then you'll stay."

"I can't."

"I'm not going to openly villainize you. We have too much history for us to be enemies. But I won't pretend that what you're doing advances anything other than your own agenda. Sebastian always thought about himself and rarely about others."

"So if we're not friends and we're not enemies, what are we?"

"Former coworkers. You've been a valuable asset to the team. I think I might lose a few followers when they find out you're creating something new. I'm going to do everything in my power to lose as few as possible."

"I don't have any intention of taking people from you."

"It doesn't have to be intentional. You're the Prince of Veils. Word has already spread about what you're doing to get money. Other people will want a piece of that."

"Is there anything I can do to convince you to join me? We can have the same thing that you have here but with me as lead. Like the arrangement that you had with Sebastian."

Javier shook his head. "Me and Sebastian were only equal partners until Harry met Sally."

"Javier, please."

"Be careful with whomever it is you're dealing with from Katrine. That's a snake pit of vipers. They don't have scruples and probably just want to use you for the status advantage. If I had the same aspirations, I would follow behind you too."

"I know I need to be careful where I place my trust. I'm not entering into this blindly."

"You enter everything blindly. Your naivety is going to get you killed."

Daniel stared ahead and didn't speak. Javier sighed and reached over to pat Daniel's shoulder.

"If we should meet again in your next life," Javier said, "I hope we do not have the abilities that we have now. It's the voodoo that separates us. You left me for knowledge under the guise of a skirt last time. This time it's money and power. But even with the change in script and cast, this movie has the same theme."

• • • • •

"I don't know if you noticed during your audition, but we take time to plan our jobs," Nicole said. "We don't just *randomly* choose a bank and rob it without intel."

Daniel rolled his eyes. "We didn't go into that heist blind."

"You didn't have 20/20 vision either. Or else you would have known that the cash drawer is a simple man's game. All the information you gathered about that job you pretty much could've gathered from the internet. And we know how reliable the internet is."

"We had a man on the inside with knowledge," Junior said, referring to Fatima.

"Your inside guy sucks. I wouldn't call the janitor your 'inside man'. Let me break down this process for you. You start with a target and gather information. Evaluate your team's abilities and pre-plan. Then you meet to discuss the plan and look for holes or cracks. This is usually when you establish backup plans. *Then* you implement."

"What part of the plan is this?" Junior pointed out of the car to the deserted parking lot.

Daniel peered out into the night and watched a group of guys gathered in front of a convenience store. The streets, still wet from the recent rain, reflected the neon signs.

"This is implementation."

As if on cue, the back car door opened, and a Hispanic male, early thirties, climbed in next to Daniel. Nicole glared at him over her shoulder.

"You're late," she said.

"Anthony is having one of his days," the guy said.

"You shouldn't have spent time on that. He's a junkie. There's no helping that."

"Hey. That's my brother."

"I know. That's why you have my sincerest condolences."

"These the new guys? Hi. I'm Carlos."

"Daniel and Junior."

Daniel shook his hand while Junior allotted him a wave. Nicole started the car and drove out of the parking lot, passing the well-lit convenience store.

"So you made it over the audition process, huh?" Carlos smiled. "What special tricks you got that impressed Nicole enough to bring you on the team?"

A feeling of deja vu washed over Daniel. He had been here before, in this car, having this exact conversation.

"Junior, here," Nicole reached over and rubbed Junior's shoulder. "He can put people to sleep or give them a bad case of the shits. He's our anesthesiologist."

"Oh, for real? I don't think we've met someone with that specialty before."

"I figure it can come in handy when there are guards or security. Or maybe even backup for emergencies where things don't go according to plan."

"Yeah, I can see how that can really be useful," Carlos' tone didn't match his facial expression. "So do you spit gas out your mouth or something? Or hypnotize them with your eyes? What's the secret?"

"No," Junior said. "I just… think it, and it happens."

"That's so cool. What about you, guy?" He turned to Daniel.

Nicole laughed. "He reads tarot cards."

"Tarot cards?" Carlos frowned. "So we need another future teller."

"I haven't really decided how we can utilize that yet. Right now he's just a part of the package deal. They come as a pair."

"Tarot cards are cool, I guess. Can you read something about me? Maybe tell me how much richer we're going to be after this?"

"Um…" Daniel looked up at Carlos with embarrassment. "I didn't actually bring my cards with me."

"Oh?…. That's cool, I guess."

Nicole turned the car onto a street and began to slow down.

"What about you?" Daniel asked. "What do you do?"

"This."

Carlos smiled and opened the car door. With the car still in motion, he slipped out and rolled into the street. Nicole didn't pause to see if he was okay. The door hadn't closed behind him, so the sound of the passing road invaded the car. Daniel turned his body into an awkward position, looking out the back window to see if Carlos was alright. A silhouette slipped between some bushes and out of sight.

"What is he?" Junior asked. "The unbreakable man?"

Nicole patted his leg and made a left turn, not bothering to answer the question. They circled the block for a few rounds before she turned off her lights and pulled into a driveway. Carlos stood inside a garage, the garage door open, and waited for Nicole to fit the car inside.

Daniel waited until the garage door was back down before exiting the car.

"Was that smooth or what?" Carlos asked. "You impressed?"

"It looked like it should've hurt," Daniel said.

"Nah. It's all in how you tuck and roll. You gotta relax your body and keep your head protected. If you tense up, then you break bones."

"Where are we?"

"This is the job site," Nicole said. "Carlos?"

Carlos nodded and turned the knob to enter the house. He approached an alarm panel blinking furiously on the wall and opened the panel, tapping in a sequence of numbers on the green-lit dial. The panel stopped blinking.

"Am I good or what?"

Nicole smiled and patted him on the cheek. "Tell Anthony he did a good job."

"Come on. You could've at least let them think I was responsible for getting the alarm code."

"Junior, let's sweep the house and make sure there's not anybody like a maid or unwanted houseguest that needs to be put to sleep. Carlos, you and Daniel check down here, and we'll look upstairs."

Carlos beckoned for Daniel to follow and turned the flashlight on his cellphone. They started in the foyer. Carlos opened a closet door and peeked inside.

"Nobody in there."

"Should we be doing this a little bit more quietly?" Daniel asked.

"Nah, we're good. Nobody's home. My information is always solid. The homeowners are away for a few weeks in Europe, and the housekeepers don't live on the premises."

"Where do you get your information?"

"Mostly informants," Carlos walked into the living room and looked under the table, making the action look as silly as possible. "I got eyes and ears everywhere, from the car wash to the steakhouse. I mainly use the servants that rich people tend to ignore. You'd be surprised how much of their calendar and appointments are listed on their phones that they leave in the car for the valet to park."

Daniel nodded and looked around the dark formal dining area. Using the dull light from his cell phone screen, he peered under the table. After checking three more bedrooms and a study, he returned to the living area to find Carlos lounging on the couch, rubbing the furniture fabric with a look of amazement on his face.

"You know," Carlos said. "I can't wait until I steal enough money to live like this. It seems like all these houses are the same. Big furniture and fancy decorations. Lavish artwork that you would normally see in a museum."

"How much money have you stolen so far?"

"Wow, you have no etiquette at all. Asking somebody how much they stole is like asking your coworker how much they make an hour." Carlos shook his finger at Daniel. "With that kind of disrespect, I'm guessing your next question is gonna be how many houses have I robbed. Which is like asking me how many women I've slept with. I exaggerate my answer on both of those, by the way."

"Sorry, I didn't know."

"You might be new to this, but there is a little bit of honor amongst thieves. We have an unwritten code." Carlos got up from the couch to admire the large television mounted on the wall. He traced his finger along the edge in amazement. "The answer is 12, by the way."

"12 what? Houses?"

"Yep. And a little over 800 thousand dollars."

"Wow."

"These jobs are a game of high risk. Eventually, everybody gets caught. You have to get in and get out before the shoe drops. Remember that. You can get addicted to this life and forget that what you're doing is risky. Unless those tarot cards can do more than you say?"

Carlos looked at Daniel, waiting for a response. Daniel shrugged.

"It doesn't take this long to check to make sure the house is empty," Daniel said, looking at the stairs leading to Junior and Nicole.

"Yeah, they didn't go upstairs to check rooms. I thought you would've caught on to that."

"Then why…"

"A lot of people in the game like to take souvenirs from each job. A trinket to remember the heist by. Nicole prefers to leave her mark behind. She screws somebody at every job."

"Oh. So that's Elvira's keepsake? Sex on the scene."

Carlos laughed. "That's funny. I would *not* have expected that reference from you. How old are you?"

"I watch a lot of horror movies."

Daniel thought back to their last job with Nicole and remembered Tiffany taking the laptop and Greg taking a picture of the safe. They were keeping both as trophies.

"I'm well rounded though," Carlos said. "I don't need souvenirs. Just give me my money and let's move on to the next job."

"I would ask how long you've been doing this, but I have a feeling that's like asking when you lost your virginity."

"You're learning. You hungry?"

Daniel shrugged and followed Carlos into the kitchen. They almost collided when Carlos came to sudden halt.

A man, shadowed from the headlights passing the window of the kitchen, stood staring at the duo. Daniel's breath caught in his throat as he realized they hadn't checked the kitchen.

"Anthony?" Carlos said. "How did you get in here?"

"I didn't get to tell you where the address was. I didn't want us to miss this chance," the man said.

Daniel watched Carlos move towards the guy and grab his shoulders.

"You shouldn't be here."

"I didn't get to tell you. So I came myself. I need the money."

"No, you gave me the address. I'm here. You need to leave." Carlos turned to look back into the living room.

"We're both here. We can get all their shit and split it. That way we can both be rich and not just you. I want some of the money too."

Daniel stayed where he was and watched the scene unfold. He realized Anthony was the informant that Carlos had mentioned in the car. He had shown up at the job. From

the mannerisms and random body twitches, Daniel
determined that Anthony was on some form of drugs.

Carlos turned to Daniel. "Watch the stairs. Nicole can't
know he's here."

Daniel nodded and positioned himself where he could
see both the stairs and the kitchen, ready to give a signal. But a
faint sound from outside caught his attention, and he
struggled to focus on the stairs. Something was wrong. He
had a feeling that he wasn't focusing his attention on the right
issue.

"You can't be here," Carlos said. "You gotta go. I'll
give you your share like we talked about, but if you stay here,
then neither one of us will get paid."

"No!" Anthony yelled. "I don't trust her. You're
lying."

"Lower your voice."

"You shouldn't trust her. She's bad for..."

"Sshh"

Daniel took a step back into the living room and
turned his head towards the foyer. That noise he had heard
earlier had been a car door shutting. And the lights that had
beamed behind Anthony when Daniel and Carlos first entered
the kitchen had been from a car turning into the driveway.
The realization kicked him in the gut at the same moment as
the sound of the lock on the front door clicked.

"They're home." He whispered with a fierce intensity.
"They're here. Get down."

Daniel took three large steps and ducked down behind
the kitchen island, out of view from the living room. Carlos
wrestled Anthony to the floor and tried to cover his mouth.
Anthony muffled through the cupped hand, his eyes wide
with anger.

A voice drifted from the foyer commenting on how
somebody had forgotten to set the security alarm. Carlos
turned Anthony's face towards him and glared into his eyes.
Anthony paused for a moment, whatever unspoken signal
that passed between the pair was lost on Daniel. Then the

scuffle started again, louder than before, and Daniel knew there was no way the owner didn't hear this.

Carlos' hand slipped from Anthony's mouth for a brief second during their struggle. Anthony's yelp echoed across the kitchen.

Daniel reacted, pulling from *The Grey* and blanketing it around Anthony. He felt his power encase the irate man, but his power didn't react as it should have. Something inside of Anthony, something that was missing, a void, responded to Daniel's attempts to quiet him. Gaps surrounding Anthony pulled at *The Grey* and drank the power like a liquid. It was quick, so Daniel didn't get a chance to observe what was happening. The *Grey Matter* he had intended to use to push Anthony into a soothing reality disappeared.

Footsteps in the living area, approaching the kitchen, divided his attention. Daniel laid flat on the floor and peered around the island, matching his view to the kitchen entrance to see the feet as soon as they entered. Hopefully choosing an angle that prevented him from being seen.

A man's shoes, blue and gray tennis shoes, and a woman's sandals paused in the doorway. Daniel touched them with his senses, being visually guided by their location, and wrapped them in *Grey*. The noise in the kitchen had been the fridge. It needed to be fixed and the repairman hadn't been called yet. There weren't three strangers lying on the floor in a failed robbery attempt.

The kitchen lights flared to life, and Daniel closed his eyes against the sudden blinding light.

"Damn," the man said. "They still haven't gotten this noisy thing fixed yet."

"Scared the crap out of me." The woman laughed.

"You want something to drink? I can't promise that it'll be cold. This thing has been acting up for a while now."

"Yeah, I'll take a water."

"Sparkling or clear?"

"Sparkling."

Footsteps as the man moved to the fridge. Daniel heard the woman plop up on the island. He looked over at Carlos, who had his body weight on a now calm Anthony.

Carlos signaled to Daniel that they should make a run for it, but Daniel shook his head and waved his hand in front of his eyes hoping that was enough to let Carlos know the couple couldn't see them.

Carlos shook his head furiously, his hand signals becoming more intense. Daniel was going to have to show him.

Daniel stood up and turned around. Looking at the man and woman. His blanket of *Grey* shrouded the couple and prevented them from seeing anything that he didn't want them to see. It was an idea he had gotten from Junior about becoming invisible but had never tested.

Everything in the couple's reality was normal and as it should be. No burglars lurking in the kitchen. No additional strangers in the house.

Daniel signaled to Carlos again that the couple couldn't see them.

Carlos gaped at him with his mouth open. Anthony smiled, pushed Carlos off of him and stood.

The man handed the woman a glass bottle, after taking the top off. She took a sip, and the man laughed. Daniel, standing behind her, couldn't see what had caused his reaction.

"I take it that's your first taste of sparkling water."

"Yes. I wanted to look fancy."

"You don't have to do that for me. I'm just as new to this as you are. The only time I even get to ask if somebody wants sparkling water is when I bring them here."

"How long are your aunt and uncle going to be in Italy?"

"They said they'd be back at the end of the month."

Carlos stood up, confused. He waved his hands at the couple. They didn't react.

"I've always wanted to go to Europe," the guy said. "You ever been out of the country?"

"Yeah, been to Canada and some Caribbean islands for Spring Break. Not overseas though."

Daniel shaped their reality again. The television - they had turned it on before hearing the noise in the kitchen - switched from commercial to the woman's favorite movie.

"You have got to be kidding me," she said, noticing the blank television screen. "This is my favorite movie."

She jumped down from the counter and pulled the man into the other room.

Carlos followed them to the kitchen doorway then turned to Daniel.

"They couldn't see us," Carlos said.

"I know. Weird, right?" Daniel responded.

"Are we invisible?"

"Why are you asking me?"

"You're not going to tell me how you did it?" Carlos didn't believe Daniel's feigned ignorance.

Daniel shook his head.

"I should go," Anthony said.

Carlos looked at his brother, having forgotten for a moment that he was there. "You shouldn't have come."

"I know. I'm sorry. It's the... I needed money *now,* and you didn't come get the address. At least, I think you didn't come get the address. I don't remember. It's blurry."

"I tried to get through to you, but it's so hard to get through the drugs. You're not yourself."

"It's been a long time since I've been myself."

Carlos approached his brother and stared into his eyes, searching for something. "But this is the real you? Not the addict that came in here a few minutes ago?"

"Yes." Anthony was just as amazed at the clarity in mental state. "I don't know what happened. I think it had something to do with *him.*"

Anthony pointed at Daniel. Carlos nodded.

"You should go," Carlos said. "If Nicole sees you here, she won't be happy about it."

"I don't have anywhere to go. If I go back to where I came from…"

Carlos pulled some cash out of his pocket and handed it to Anthony. "Go to the hotel off Walnut Hill. I'll come get you when we leave here."

Anthony nodded, leaving the kitchen, walking slowly past the couple quietly seated on the couch watching a blank TV screen. Daniel didn't bother to tell him that they wouldn't have been able to hear him even if he screamed.

"Thank you," Carlos said.

"It was nothing," Daniel said.

"It was a lot. For a while, I thought this was going to be my last job."

"We should have remained hidden until Junior came down. He could've knocked them out."

"They would have spotted us before that happened." Carlos stared in the living room.

"Well, we're okay now."

"Let me show you something."

Carlos led Daniel into the living room. He stopped in front of the guy and leaned down to look into his eyes. Waving his hand in front of him didn't receive a reaction.

"Where are they right now?" Carlos asked.

"They're here with us. Just enjoying the movie and each other's company."

Carlos turned to the blank television and shook his head. "I need you to let him look in my eyes. Can you let go of just him?"

Daniel nodded.

Carlos leaned down again until his eyes were locked with the man, their faces less than a foot apart. "Go."

Daniel released the man from the false reality, and the man tensed, shifting back from the sudden close appearance of Carlos. Then he paused and relaxed, his body posture shifting into a more slumped position.

182

"Who are you?" Carlos asked.

"Timothy Lester." The man's voice was dreamlike. It reminded Daniel of the night he had questioned Fatima.

"Why are you here?"

"Housesitting for my aunt and uncle."

"And this is your girlfriend?"

"No."

"Who is she?"

"My girlfriend's best friend."

"Well, that's just messy. Why did you bring her here?"

"We couldn't go to my house because my girlfriend is there."

"So you came here to tarnish your aunt and uncle's fancy home?"

The man didn't respond.

"Look. When I snap my finger, you're going to go to sleep. You will wake up in the morning, and remember a lovely evening watching TV with this young woman. I want to tell you that this will be the last night you try to get into her skirt or that you will make a decision to either be faithful to the woman you have at home or break up with her. I want to, but I don't meddle in people's lives like that. So I'm going to ignore what's going on here. Just remember that nobody deserves to be cheated on. Relationships are sacred."

Daniel frowned. Whatever Carlos was doing to hypnotize the man didn't involve *The Grey*.

He snapped his finger, and the man's head dropped forward, eyes closed.

"I need to do the same to her," Carlos said.

He glared into the woman's eyes and gave her the same scenario of watching TV all night with a subtle hint to be a better friend to Timothy's girlfriend.

"I'm not sure how much time we have," Carlos said, his voice dropping to a whisper "I don't know how long your friend usually goes for in the bedroom."

Daniel knew. The hand mirror knew.

"*This* is my power." Carlos shrugged. "I can give people instructions or get information from them. In the car, I hypnotized the both of you. Junior was easy, he doesn't have much of a defense. You, on the other hand, I couldn't get much from you."

"What do you mean?"

"You wouldn't answer her questions. She suspects that you do more than tarot reading. She had questions about your power. But you wouldn't tell. Usually, the only time I have issues getting answers is when there's a chemical barrier like drugs or if the person is a hypnotist like me." He raised his eyebrows with an unspoken question.

"I'm not on drugs." Daniel held back on revealing any additional information on his powers. "What exactly did she ask?"

"She wanted to know Junior's strengths and weaknesses. She needs a failsafe for all of her employees. There were questions about your most valuable possessions and who is the most important person in your life. Junior told us about his money that he had gained from the robberies. And that his daughters were important to him. He told us that he plans on learning how to do what we do then branching out on his own. She wasn't excited about hearing that."

"And what did I say?"

"You wouldn't tell us your strengths and weaknesses, no matter how hard I pushed. Junior told us you're a witch and you cast spells. She found that hard to believe but had me keep going. Your most valuable item is a mirror that you hide in your suitcase. She figured it must be sentimental value since you put it above the cash you had stashed." Carlos stopped.

"And the person most important to me?"

"Junior."

Daniel closed his eyes and took a deep breath. Subconsciously, he had to have known this if it was his answer under hypnosis. But to hear it aloud and have to face the answer was more than he wanted to process at the moment.

"Look," Carlos said, his voice hurried and hushed. "You're different. You have this aura about you that anybody close to you can pick up on. Nicole definitely sees it. She's trying to determine if you are a threat or not. Knowing how much Junior means to you, she will use him against you."

"Why are you telling me this?"

"You helped my brother. I haven't seen him… the *real* him in so long I didn't even recognize it at first. Just that alone has done more for me that she's ever done. Earlier, I told you that there was honor amongst…"

The sound of footsteps descending down the stairs interrupted him. They looked up as Nicole walked down the steps with layers of jewelry around her neck, rings on every finger and bracelets around both arms.

"Jackpot!" she said.

"What happened?" Junior asked. "Who are they?"

"Housesitters," Nicole responded. The surprise on Daniel's face caught her attention. "I can see into the future, remember? I'm surprised you didn't see it in the cards. We got all the jewelry. Left everything spotless so let's see how long before they notice."

"Are they dead?" Junior asked.

"Sleep," Carlos said. "I took care of them."

Nicole rummaged through the sleeping man's pockets, and stopped to admire the girl's necklace. Surprisingly, she didn't take it. They followed her out of the living room and into the garage, not bothering to set the alarm again. But when Carlos opened the garage door, they found Timothy's car parked behind them, blocking them in.

"Damn," Carlos said. "I'll go get his keys."

"Don't bother," Nicole said, dangling a set of keys from her finger. "I already got them. Looks like we get expensive jewelry *and* a Jeep."

CHAPTER SIX

Daniel didn't have an opportunity to tell Junior about the information he had learned from Carlos. Junior and Nicole had decided sitting around the apartment staring at a satchel full of jewelry was boring. Giving Daniel a half-hearted invite, which he had declined, they had spent most of the night out celebrating. Daniel had tried to stay awake so he could have a talk with Junior about the situation, at times wondering if he should text him, but the chance that Nicole might see the text kept him from trying. Daniel was half asleep when they both stumbled back into the apartment, sloppy drunk and shushing each other so as not to disturb Daniel.

Daniel didn't see either Nicole nor Junior leave the room the next day. He didn't expect them to be up for breakfast, and it didn't surprise him when Junior's bedroom door remained close through the afternoon. He waited as long as he could for Nicole to leave but eventually gave up.

He left with a hazy feeling of disappointment and headed for his scheduled meeting. The drive gave him time to think of the things Carlos had mentioned, as if it hadn't been on his mind since he had awaken.

Daniel wondered why Nicole chose to rob houses instead of using her seer powers for a quick come-up that was less likely to lead to jail time. Why didn't she look into the future and seize the winning lottery numbers which currently sat at 203 million? Why didn't she invest in stock that would be worth millions tomorrow? What game was she playing?

His mind was wandering the list of possible scenarios in which he could achieve riches with her power when he found himself parked at his destination, The W, a luxury hotel north of downtown.

The W was the most extravagant hotel Daniel had ever seen, including his adventure to The Bellagio in Las Vegas. His multiple attempts at not looking so astounded by the atmosphere failed. The downtown hotel was constructed with marble floors and sculpted fountains in the lobby. The ceiling reached heights he hadn't expected.

With direction from a staff member, he found the bar lounge with its stairway string chandeliers and high back leather chairs. Through his wonderment, a sense of discomfort descended as he realized how out of place he probably looked. His attention settled from taking in the decor to watching for looks from the residents or hotel staff.

He chose a seat at the bar, making sure to place himself so that he was facing the entrance, ordered a Rum & Coke and waited.

A woman a few seats away took a strong swallow from the almost empty glass in front of her. She cupped the front of her face with both hands, letting her hair fall forward to hide whatever emotion she was trying to keep the other patrons from seeing. The bartender cut her a quick glance from the corner of his eye but didn't interrupt the counting of inventory he was committed to completing on the stock of liquor behind the bar.

A soft melodic piano tune floated through the buzz of conversation, and Daniel could feel a tinge of anxiousness tickle the back of his spine. He closed his eyes for a brief moment and took a deep breath but didn't keep them closed long since he knew he shouldn't let his guard down. His awareness of his surroundings was crucial. With Nicole still in the apartment when he left, he hadn't been able to tell Junior where he was going. Daniel wasn't sure if he wanted Junior to know where he was on the slim chance this meeting turned fatal or if he wanted Junior to volunteer to accompany him. He wouldn't have allowed Junior to come, but the offer would have felt nice.

Not knowing how long he was going to be away from the apartment, Daniel had tucked the hand mirror away behind the toolbox in the laundry room. He felt it best not to leave it in his suitcase since that was where Nicole was told it would be. But having it sitting in the apartment at all was a little worrisome. Bringing it to this meeting was out of the question because it was too big for his pockets, and his new companions might think it weird. The only safe place that would alleviate his worries would be a bank lock box.

Daniel perked up and snapped to attention as two men entered the bar. He studied the gentlemen, taking in their clothes and demeanor, but as they approached, he realized they were not the duo he was expecting. The pair was soon joined by another pair of businessmen, and they sat at a lounge table, signaling the bartender for a round of drinks.

He sighed and took a small sip from his glass, making sure not to drink too much, not because he wanted to be clear headed and sober, but because the drink was expensive, and he didn't want to have to buy another one. Some habits die hard.

The bartender, finally having enough of the depressed woman crying into her glass, walked over and asked her if everything was okay. She nodded her head, pushed her glass forward and asked for a refill. Daniel got a better look at her when she looked up at the bartender and noticed she was older than he had initially thought. She was in her mid fifties, her face taut with the appearance of a woman who relies on a plastic surgeon to help her look youthful. A courtesy smile and nod was thrown Daniel's way when she noticed him staring. Daniel returned it.

Forcing his eyes back to the entry so as not to stare, Daniel wondered what about her life could be so bad that she would need to drown it in alcohol. She was dressed in expensive evening wear, of which Daniel couldn't estimate the cost. He assumed she was a guest of the hotel, so she had to be relatively wealthy. Maybe a cheating husband had finally surrendered to the inevitable end of their marriage and left her for a younger, more vibrant woman.

Daniel's mind created a story. *The she-devil he had left her for was 30 years her junior and still had the perky breasts that the drunken woman had to pay her doctor for. While this depressed lady was a lawyer, having graduated not quite top of her class, the floozy he had left her for was a dumb blonde, nothing more than a stewardess, traveling the various states and disrupting the lives of other not-so-happy marriages. Using her looks and travel opportunities to find the smallest of marital crevices and prying her way inside and letting any and everybody pry inside of her.*

Daniel frowned at the negative scenario his imagination had assigned the woman. For all he knew, she could just be an ordinary alcoholic, albeit a rich one. Or maybe she was forced to listen to her crush have sex with her arch-nemesis in the other room while she gazed into a mirror and asked 'Who's the fairest of them all?' To which the mirror would respond 'Not you, bitch, but I'll throw you a bone if you want one'.

"Damn," Daniel said. "That's a little close to home."

The bartender looked up and gestured if Daniel was ready for another drink. Daniel waved his hand and turned his attention back to the entrance, pushing his barstool neighbor from his mind.

Daniel could feel their approach before he saw them. Although there wasn't a visual alert, it felt like the sun had slipped behind a cloud. The atmosphere changed almost as if he had switched to another plane. A cluster of *voleur*, rounded the doorway, clawing their way up the walls. It was not only the fact he couldn't hear them calling to serve him that made him realize they didn't belong to him, but it was also their size. His *voleur* were smaller in stature and didn't move so aggressively.

Oscar and Alexandre entered the lounge area, their clothing denoting they were not from here. Although not flamboyant or unusual, the style didn't fit the American aesthetic. Their fashion sense was more in line with a European model.

They spotted Daniel immediately and approached without pause. Daniel straightened up and squared his shoulders, determined to look like the prince he was claiming to be. They stopped at his corner of the bar; Oscar with an aggressive smile, and Alexandre with a sly smirk.

"So," Oscar said. "What did Katrine call you? *Mon fils prodigue?* How nice it is to meet you in person. And so much power. It is even more brilliant in person, almost blinding."

"It is a shock to me," Alexandre said. "I knew you were young but not this young. You are a baby. Not to say this with disrespect. I could see youth in your essence when you visited *The Grey* but seeing this in person..."

"I think Alexandre is more accustomed to serving women older than him. He has the face that all the cougars love."

"I do not discriminate a woman's age. I love them young or old. Take for example this precious *donna* here beside us." He turned to the elegant lady bent over her near empty glass of alcohol. "Why are you sad, madame? Is it the pain of a lover lost? The ache of betrayal? I am the healer of the heart. It is no trouble if you choose to lay your desolation on me to bear. What troubles you?"

The lady frowned, not sure of Alexandre's intentions. She tossed the drink so fast into her mouth, Daniel could swear he heard it hit the back of her throat, then got up and left, scurrying away and not bothering to look back at Alexandre.

"Not all prizes can be won," Oscar said.

"I was not playing to win. I was trying to give us some privacy. She was too close."

Daniel doubted that.

"So, my Prince of Veils," Alexandre said. "We have come. What is the next step?"

The pair watched him, waiting for something. They wanted to be assured they had made the right move in coming here to join him.

A Life Seen (1992). A man is plagued with the feeling that he is constantly being watched. The feeling invades his mind and makes him think strangers are waiting for him to do something. Eventually, he goes crazy and suicides in order to evade the ever-watching eyes. It is later revealed he was being watched on a candid camera reality show. A social experiment seen every day by millions.

Alexandre waved down the bartender and ordered a glass of whatever Daniel was drinking. Oscar shook his head when the bartender asked if he wanted anything.

"How did Madame Comtois take the news of you joining me?" Daniel asked, getting straight to the point.

"We will find out soon, I think. We did not tell her directly. We just left."

"If you didn't tell her then how will she find out?"

"Her spies will tell her. How do you think she finds out everything else? About your bank heist? Or your power?"

"I have a mole?"

"You have thousands of moles. They were her gift to you. I think she was a little more than slightly upset with the number of spirits you took from her. A testament to your power and also a threat to her hold on the leadership."

"The *voleur*? I was worried that I would become addicted to using them, but I guess the real power play…"

"They are her eyes and ears."

"So they are going to inform her that you both came here to meet me? That's your way of letting her know that you changed sides."

"They will inform her that we are here. Yes." Alexandre nodded.

"But," Oscar said, "They won't have details about this conversation. We have our own spirits here to help give us some privacy."

Daniel noticed that he only saw Oscar and Alexandre's *voleur*. He had become so accustomed to seeing his *voleur* everywhere that he couldn't remember a time when he didn't see them. So she knew everything he didn't want her to know.

"We can help you build a defense against her spying," Alexandre took a sip from his glass, staring at Daniel over the rim. "We should do this tonight."

"It is something you will need to have a strong stomach for." Oscar's smile had an undertone of apology. "One of the negatives of working with certain spirits is the sacrifice. Katrine had noticed that you did not like to give to the *voleur*."

"It definitely wasn't my favorite," Daniel said.

"It will not get any better, but it will be easier over time," Alexandre said.

"All a part of becoming the Prince of Veils, I guess."

"There is no *becoming* the Prince of Veils," Alexandre said. "You *are* him. We did not come to all the way to America to help you obtain a title. The name is a marker for your strength."

"I'm of the mindset that knowledge is power. From what everybody around me says, I have a lot of power, but I do not feel very knowledgeable. I want you both to help me gain some knowledge. I'm not sure how that works since you left a lot of that knowledge behind with Madame Comtois."

"We keep much knowledge up here." Alexandre tapped the side of his head. "We can give you all the knowledge your young mind can hold. And we did not leave behind everything. We have tomes and books to teach you the ways of spiritualism."

"This isn't the only aspect I plan on learning. I want to learn everything I can… so I'm enlisting the help of other voodoo masters."

Oscar and Alexandre exchanged glances.

"Learning spirit communication is time-consuming," Oscar said. "When will you find time for learning everything else?"

"I'll make time."

"Then let me explain the process of turning off your spiritual wiretap," Oscar said.

● ● ● ● ●

Daniel was glad that he hadn't eaten. His gag reflex had activated a couple of times while Oscar and Alexandre explained what he would need to do to cut off information from reaching Madame Comtois. They had followed him in their own car because although he saw truth in their eyes and trusted they wouldn't betray him, he had ridden with too many new acquaintances lately. Having strangers dictate his path made him feel as if he wasn't in control. And he was determined to take the reins of his kingdom by his own free will.

Alexandre had used the *voleur*, his own, to get a spare key for the door while Oscar called his spirits to find the security camera tapes. Unlike the failed bank heist, this business relied on analog methods of recording. It wasn't often that a pet store was robbed.

The barking that had assaulted their senses when they first entered had dimmed. The animals were alert to the presence of strangers, but most were accustomed to unfamiliar smells. This was a temporary home, so what was there to guard? New people, animals and inventory were shifted around daily. The entrance of patrons made the animals bark with excitement as opposed to a sense of threat. Especially at this time of night when there was normally a long stretch of time before the animals saw another human.

But Daniel knew they didn't have anything to be excited about. Oscar and Alexandre stood watching, giving

Daniel time to adjust to the thought of what he was about to do. Daniel didn't want to show weakness, so he didn't allow himself a moment to reconcile his emotions. Instead, he took a breath and internalized his senses, searching for his many, many *voleur*.

It took more than a simple call to get them to respond. He had to press them with his need or desire for something. And he needed to call as many as possible, so it had to be a big desire. Nothing simple like the red book or a quarter from Fatima's purse. Daniel was going for quantity.

Focusing on their failed bank heist, Daniel thought about all the money Junior thought they were going to walk away with but hadn't. The money locked in the vault, each individual bill stacked into countable stacks. Denominations of ones, fives, tens, twenties, hundreds. He could picture clear cases of stacked bills, similar to what he had seen in movies, locked away, protected by thick walls of metal, and he began to almost salivate from the image.

And their voices came. Their voices carried on the sound of a dog scratching, and a car passing from the street outside, and a bird flapping its wings within a cage.

"We are here to serve."

"We are yours to command."

"Let us provide."

And Daniel began to picture more than just money. Tennis shoes at the mall, designer sunglasses from a swanky shop, diamond earrings from a jeweler.

Their voices cascaded upon the store like an avalanche of dissonance.

"We want to please you."

"We can serve."

"We can provide."

The barking in the store intensified, and a small thought invaded Daniel's brain. What if the noise attracted attention from outside, and somebody came to investigate? He didn't linger too long on the thought though. He knew that anybody who showed up could be handled. Not to mention

Oscar and Alexandre were watching his back. He pushed harder, calling as many of the *voleur* as he could.

The noise was almost intolerable, the sound of animals screeching and spirits pleading. He opened his eyes and a wave of fear clutched his stomach. So many *voleur* in such a tight space. They crawled and squirmed around the walls and shelving and cages like a disturbed beehive. Their eyes shifting wildly but always returning to him. Oscar and Alexandre stared in amazement at the first glimpse of his blinding power. His strength in the arts was unmatched even if it was untrained. And even with so much exposed power, he felt he could call more of the *voleur* if he wanted to. He could call them all. But this was enough to get started, probably too many.

Their voices, although great in volume due to the quantity, still didn't resonate through him the way the spirit at the cathedral had. Daniel could still taste the vibration the eyeless gargoyle had emitted, a sweet nectar he would never forget. It was the free taste of cocaine that he would always yearn for. The shouting whispers of the *voleur* would never compare. But hopefully, he could get damn close.

Daniel held up his hand, and the spirits stopped pleading. He wasn't sure how he knew this gesture would work, but he was glad it had. The store was a bomb of sound from the barking, chirping and screeching still.

Little Shop of Horrors (1987). With the promise of obtaining the love of his life, an orphaned nerd agrees to feed a man-eating plant. What starts off as a sacrifice of the nerd's own blood evolves into the accidental murder of the man who his crush has been dating. During feeding time, the plant requests that the nerd chop up the body and feed it to him.

The resistance from the gravity of his actions made his stomach turn with anxiety. Before he could linger on second guessing himself, Daniel dropped his hand and spoke.

One word.

"Feast."

If he had thought the store couldn't have gotten any louder, he was wrong. It's one thing for a dog or cat to howl in fear or excitement, but the pitch and volume change when they are in pain. The *voleur* descended on the animals with a ferocity that Daniel didn't expect. Legions of the pocket size spirits clumping down on each animal and writhing with hunger as they tore their tongues into flesh and drained the blood.

Daniel flinched, wanting to close his eyes, but he knew that Oscar and Alexandre were observing him, taking note of his reaction. And so he watched the death of these canines and felines with a neutral face, keeping his mournful screams of sympathy internal. Fighting any waves of nausea and knowing that he just needed to make it through this night, he kept the thought of the Prince of Veils title firm in his mind.

The sounds of the dismay dropped within seconds. With so many *voleur*, it didn't take long for the pets to be drained.

A pitiful whimper from the biggest dog in the bunch and all was silent. Daniel could see no animal was left untouched. The mice husks lined their bedded cages. Deflated fish floated to the top of aquariums. Birds lay flat in cages, a depression of feathers.

Like the nature shows on TV, when lions were satiated after a meal of wildebeast, the *voleur's* movement had slowed to a crawl. Though they still moved like an entangled beetle mound, it was slower. The pattern of their scaled skin was almost hypnotic.

"What now?" Daniel asked.

"We clean up the mess," Oscar said. "Dispose of the evidence and move on to the next buffet."

Daniel caught himself from gagging at the Spaniard's reference to a buffet. He still had more *voleur* to feed. This was only a portion of his total legion.

"You did good." Alexandre clapped him on the back and smiled with sympathy in his eyes. "My first time, I did not handle it so well. And I did not have the same number of *voleur* as you have. You are truly a powerful one. If there was any doubt in my mind about you being the Prince of Veils…"

"They feel… *different*," Daniel said. "They are quiet and slower. And heavier, if that's possible."

"I'm sure that's true. I do not have experience with this number of them so I cannot explain what you are feeling. But now they are loyal to you. You have provided, and they will serve. They are no longer starved and willing to be commanded by anybody that will feed them."

"I have to keep feeding them? Like forever?"

Daniel looked at Alexandre, his eyes begging him not to respond with the answer he dreaded.

But Alexandre nodded his head, eyes downcast and turned away.

•   •   •   •   •

Daniel sat in a coffee house situated in the middle of a busy shopping center. The shop's windows were angled for a perfect view of passing patrons. It was the ideal location for customers who liked to relax and sip their cappuccinos and lattes while people watching. The shopping center, located in an eastern suburb of the city, housed a range of stores that catered from the middle-class to the wealthy. This expansive price range brought people from all corners of the city to shop. So it wasn't unusual to see customers browsing while wearing plain jeans paired with old faded shirts and then the next moment, see a woman walk past wearing a Hermes blouse and Louis Vuitton shoes, a her teacup Yorkie tucked into a traveling bag hoisted on her shoulder.

Sitting in the coffee shop reminded Daniel of the days in college when he would pass time in the student center or the courtyard and watch the mix of stressed students among carefree ones. College was a time when he started to find himself. It was where he discovered his love for neo-soul music. It was where he had his first sexual experience with a guy. It was where he had his first puff of marijuana, first pill of ecstasy, and first (and last) bump of cocaine.

Thinking back on these experiences, he knew he didn't explore new and exciting things because he wanted to or because he was curious. He experimented in areas outside of his comfort zone because of whatever guy he was enamored with at the time. Daniel enjoyed seeing the surprise on their face when they realized the nice guy had a bad side. It was their reactions that satisfied his need for inclusion and pushed him to do things that he would never have done. It was a temporary evolution of his overzealously responsible nature.

But a sampling of drugs or underage drinking was nothing compared to the things he had done recently. This wasn't college. The crimes he now had committed were serious and could have consequences.

Daniel shifted in his seat, his change in mood apparent in his demeanor. He sighed and took a sip of coffee, trying to move back to thinking of happy things and not what life would be like in prison.

Earlier that day, Carlos had texted him and wanted to meet up to discuss things that he hadn't been able to talk about the night of the jewelry heist. Daniel wasn't sure how Carlos had gotten his number. Curiosity overcame his brief moment of wariness, and he had agreed. Oscar and Alexandre were scheduled to give him another lesson on spirits, but he had postponed their meeting to later. At first, he was worried about inconveniencing them by delaying, but he was their prince. If they wanted to serve him, then they would serve him in the capacity that he wanted and schedule he preferred.

His thoughts were interrupted as he spotted Carlos walk past the window, unaware that he was within Daniel's view. Daniel waved to him, getting his attention, and watched as he approached.

A few of the *voleur* were perched in various areas of the coffee shop. Daniel had noticed he saw more of them now, their demeanor more melancholy and relaxed. It had taken a few days for him to not get nauseous from the thought of their gorge fest. But he had pushed through, focusing on other things, and eventually he didn't think on it as much, the images fading in his memory. But he doubted he would ever be able to completely forget.

"Thanks for meeting me," Carlos said.

"No problem."

"I don't think I had a chance to thank you for what you did for my brother. I haven't seen him this coherent in a long time."

Daniel wanted to admit to Carlos that any help he provided was accidental but would a prince admit something like that? "Don't mention it."

"I feel like I owe you for your help. Like you've scratched my back, and now I should scratch yours."

"Did you have more secrets on Nicole?"

"I know a few things. What do you want to know?"

"I want to know everything about her that she tried to learn about me. Let me get this situation on equal footing. You said she wanted to know about our powers. What do you know about hers?"

"Well... You're in luck. I hypnotized her once and got the same information that she gets from everybody she auditions. She can see in the future. You already know that. But she doesn't have infinite sight. She can only see seven minutes into the future. And only in areas where she will be present. So she can't see what will happen in China tomorrow."

"That explains why she doesn't just hit the lottery and be done with all this."

"I think even if she could use her power to win the lottery, she would still be doing this. She enjoys being a thief."

"Her and Junior were made for each other," Daniel said.

"The limit on her seer powers was seven minutes when I met her. That was two years ago. She could be stronger now."

"I'll keep that in mind. What other weaknesses should I know about? If I throw water on her will she melt?"

"She can't see into the future while she's sleep. If you're going to decapitate Medusa, that's the time to do it."

"I'm not going to kill her. What kinda person do you think I am?"

"Judging by the crowd you run with?"

"So seven minutes or more of future vision and she's blind when asleep? I can work with that. Seven minutes of *The Grey* and she won't know..." Daniel trailed off, realizing he had said more than he intended within Carlos' hearing.

"Not sure if this will be of any value. She is also afraid of a guy named Smitty."

"Smitty?"

"That's all she could give me. She has him locked away really tight in her mind. Wouldn't tell me what he does or how she knows him."

"Hmm." Daniel filed the name away for later. "What about possessions? She asked us what our most prized possessions were, right?"

"She doesn't have any. I'm assuming she got rid of most valuable things before she started this. Doesn't want a way to get caught up or pressured. No family. No friends. History was vague."

"How do you not have a history?"

"She was a foster kid. Grew up in the system and struck out on her own early."

"How did she discover her power? Did she have a teacher?"

"I'm not sure. Didn't think to ask that."

Daniel took a sip of his drink and let the information roll around for a moment. Carlos could see the wheels turning and allowed the silence to linger.

"Thanks for the information," Daniel said. "I think this was helpful."

"When you take over, do I have a spot on your team?"

"Despite how this might look, me asking you these questions, I have no intention of taking her business."

"But we've been sidelined."

"What?"

"Well, I guess maybe I should say *I've* been sidelined. Junior's power eclipses mine because he can incapacitate multiple people more quickly than I can. So I've been replaced. You, on the other hand, never made it past the audition process."

"You're trying to convince me to commit a hostile takeover because Nicole doesn't wanna use me for her jobs? I already kinda knew that."

"Do you know that they have a job tonight? Her, Junior, Tiff and Greg?"

"Yeah." Daniel lied.

"I'm a bench player now, and it doesn't really sit well with me. I assumed you wanted to have a bigger part in the company and maybe would be more upset about the situation."

"To be honest, I have more things going on right now besides this heist business. It was obvious from the beginning me and Nicole weren't gonna happen."

"You have other ways to make money?"

Daniel paused. He didn't have a steady source of income, but he had money left over from the bank robbery and home invasions. That would be sufficient to last him until he got on his feet, at least a year or two. The money he had was a temporary patch on a shitty situation. Daniel knew he could manage.

Carlos took Daniel's silence as an affirmative to his question. "I had a whole conversation planned in my head about telling you if you informed Nicole about what you could really do, that you're more than just a deck of tarot cards, then I'm more than positive you could get back on her team. But it looks like you don't even need her. So why were you even doing this in the first place?"

Daniel knew the answer was Junior but chose a different response. "I needed something. Junior said I needed the experience, but the real reason is I needed recruits. As much as Nicole was interviewing us, I was gathering information, too. I'm setting up my own empire."

"How can I get in on your team? I know I was supposed to be here to help you, but now it looks like I'm begging for a job."

"I don't offer that kind of employment."

"What do you offer?"

"It's hard to explain."

"Try me."

"I'm creating…" No, that wasn't the way he wanted to phrase it. "I'm gathering a collection of individuals with abilities like mine. Sort of like a community of voodoo artists."

"Like the X-Men? You want to be Charles Xavier?"

"I was thinking more sovereign than teacher. Right now, I'm in the process of surrounding myself with generals, people I can trust. Individuals with something they can offer me."

"What's the pay rate?"

"There's no pay. You fend for yourself."

Carlos scoffed.

Daniel grinned.

"So a cult?" Carlos asked.

He shook his head trying to think of a better way to explain what he was attempting when he noticed a pair of children walk by wearing matching shirts with black clovers. It made him think of a deck of cards which sparked in his brain the memory of the tarot cards that started this avalanche of events.

The Five Death Cards.

Was the shirt a sign, shown to him from his power of coincidence or was this just pure chance?

"I know a way you can repay me," Daniel said. "That thing you do, the hypnosis. Teach me."

"Teach you how to stop other people from hypnotizing you? I think you already have a pretty strong defense against that."

"No, teach me how to do it. I'm trying to learn all aspects, and I think I met you for a reason."

"I'm not sure it's something that anybody off the street can learn."

"Fortunately, I'm not anybody off the street. I'm the Prince of Veils."

"The what?"

"Do this for me, and I'll see what I can do to get you back on Nicole's roster."

"Learning hypnotism is that important to you?"

"No, but it wouldn't hurt to know how, right? Plus, this will help you get your source of income back."

Carlos stared for a moment, and Daniel tried to push a sense of empathy into his eyes to portray his sincerity.

"Okay. Deal."

Daniel took a sip of coffee and smiled.

●　●　●　●　●

There wasn't an official training curriculum for voodoo. Javier's method of teaching was similar to an apprenticeship. Daniel would tag along whenever he wanted, ask questions when something didn't make sense and imitate whatever he saw Javier do. It wasn't the most efficient method of learning, but since Daniel already had to suffer through 8 hours a day of schooling in the real world, he wasn't too enthusiastic about more structured lessons.

Javier's knowledge of voodoo focused on *The Grey*. Manipulating *The Grey* in both itself and the real world. Daniel was a natural at mystical arts. It didn't take much effort for him to learn the things Javier had to teach. He was the youngest member in Javier's community of misfits, only later finding out that he was the strongest of the bunch. His inner conduit allowed him the ability to accomplish things that were impossible for others.

On one occasion, Daniel was home simulating a family dinner with his mother. His father, a DEA agent, worked late nights, and it was common for Daniel to go days without seeing him. Keeping a regular schedule of voodoo training, Daniel invited his mother to the dinner table and placed a scenario in her mind that his father was joining them. Whatever Daniel wanted her to see, she experienced. It was what Javier called 'covering someone with *The Grey*'. One could transform the substance of *The Grey* into a form of reality.

"So," *The Grey* version of his father said, "Charles wants to lay low on the arrest of the Dominican player because he thinks there's a bigger fish we can catch. I'm trying my best to get it through his skull that this is a big bust, and we should jump on this opportunity. But he has his eyes on that department head position. All he can think about is how good this is going to look on his skill sheet – Pass me the mashed potatoes, Daniel."

"But wait," his mom said, "I thought Charles had given up hope of getting promoted. Gail told me he could barely handle the stress of the job he has now."

"He *says* he's not competing for it, but actions speak louder than words. And his *actions* are saying he isn't looking at getting drugs off the street. He's trying to get a big arrest to make him look good."

"Hmm. Well, I'll be glad when y'all wrap this up. That way you can be home more. I hate not having you around the house as much."

Calvin reached over and grabbed Loraine's hand. Daniel wanted his mother to feel his dad's touch. So she did. With *The Grey*, the false reality was real. He knew that she would feel the texture of skin his dad's hand pressed into her palm and a sense of comfort would flush through her.

Any form of sadness she had carried through the week from having an absent husband vanished. The crushing pressure of worry that stalked her subconscious thoughts evaporated. The daytime fear that her husband would not return home from work due to a violent drug arrest melted away.

Seeing his mother happy made Daniel happy. This simulated reality wasn't just for her. It also gave him a sense of family and togetherness.

"I've been going on and on about work," Mr. Leonard said. "Tell me how you all's day went."

"Ugh. I don't even want to get started on that. I'm not at work, and I don't want to think about work until tomorrow. Johnathon's been stomping around the office on his high horse and getting on my last damn nerve."

"Daniel, what about you? How was your day?"

"Fine," Daniel said.

"Fine? That's all? Nothing interesting?"

Daniel shook his head.

"Teenagers." Calvin and Loraine exchanged glances.

Daniel was never sure why he let the situations make him out to be a brooding young adult. Maybe it was just to invoke a sense of realism and authenticity.

The moment was interrupted by the doorbell. Daniel frowned. His dad froze with his fork halfway to his mouth.

"I wonder who that could be," she said.

"We should ignore it," Calvin said.

"Yeah, right. We're not going to be rude." Loraine rose from the table, walking out of the formal dining area and into the living room, out of sight.

Daniel heard the door open and broke out into a cold sweat. A moment later he heard the voices of his mom's two sisters, Dee and Sheryl, echo through the door. If they were here, then their three children would be also. Daniel became more nervous.

His Aunt Dee mentioned to his mom that tonight was the night for their weekly Spades game. Loraine replied that she had forgotten due to the excitement of Calvin making it home in time for dinner tonight.

"Calvin? Here and not working like he always does?" Aunt Dee said. "Where is he at? I have to see this with my own eyes."

The group swarmed into the dining room, and Daniel panicked. A warmth spread through his spine and traveled to his head. He could feel the pounding of his heart and a headache blossom into existence. He rose from his seat, knowing that the recently arrived guests wouldn't be able to see his dad and scrambling for an excuse for why his dad wasn't at the table when he felt *The Grey* expand.

Aunt Dee looked around, her eyes sweeping over the spot where Daniel had Calvin seated. *The Grey* enveloped her and suddenly Calvin was visible.

"Well, you still look the same," she said. "But it's been so long since I've seen you that I'm surprised I remember what you look like."

Daniel stared, stunned and unable to respond. His Aunt Dee was experiencing the false reality in tandem with his mom.

He didn't know how to mold the experience to make it realistic for Aunt Dee. He didn't know the relationship his aunt had with his dad, so Daniel didn't have a clue what Calvin's response should be.

The sense of shock was still present when his other aunt, Serena, entered the dining room, her eyes dancing from the food on the table to the empty chair where Calvin should be then back to the food. *The Grey* expanded again and included the additional participant. And Daniel knew that when her eyes shifted back to the seat, she would see Daniel's version of his dad.

As each member of Daniel's extended family passed through the doorway, they saw what Daniel wanted them to see. Daniel was not confined to using his ability on one individual like Javier had told him. He could use it on at least six people.

Daniel shared a look with the shadow of imagination posing as his father. His dad's response was a sly smirk directed at his son.

Daniel was beyond excited and could hardly wait to tell Javier about this revelation.

"Six people?" Javier's tone was sprinkled with disbelief.

"I felt it grow as I needed it. I'm not sure if it was the adrenaline from the situation or…" Daniel said. "It just… It was… It came through me in waves, and they didn't even realize that they had been covered. I don't know how to explain it."

"I know how to explain it. Try 'impossible.'"

"It's possible."

Javier snorted.

"So what does this mean? Did I discover something new?"

"No, you discovered that you got a little more strength with *The Grey* than most do. We already knew you were a quick learner."

"I gotta find my limit. I need to know how many people I can mold *The Grey* around."

"Don't exert yourself."

Daniel ignored the fact that he was more excited about this revelation than Javier. And yet his excitement didn't get a chance to blossom into the range of abilities that he dreamed.

Months later, he was reading the tarot cards on his dad, a weekly pastime that helped expand his experience with voodoo and also helped him reconcile the fact his father worked a dangerous job. He had been given a few lessons on reading tarot from Keith, one of Javier's followers. Daniel didn't know what he would have done if he ever saw a possibility that his father wouldn't be coming home, but he kept a mystical eye on his well-being anyway.

When his mom, Lorraine, walked through his bedroom door, Daniel's first instinct was to cover the cards spread out on his desk with his body, as if to shield her from reading them herself. Javier had urged him to keep his talents a secret even from his own family. He failed to predict the reactions he would receive from anybody he loved on his abilities.

Upon seeing Daniel jump to attention, Loraine stepped back, not completely sure what she had walked in on. The smile on her face dropped into a tense grimace as her eyes soaked up everything that was in front of her.

"I was coming to get your laundry," she said.

She paused, taking note of the cards scattered across the desk, and her son hurrying to scoop them into a pile.

"What is this?" she asked.

The look on Daniel's face, although he didn't verbally respond, was enough to let her know that it was something she needed to investigate further. She approached the desk, her eyes squinted and lips tense, plucking a card off the desk.

"Is this pornography?"

"No."

"What is this?" The tone in her voice funneling towards anger.

"Nothing."

"This isn't nothing. Tell me what it is."

"Tarot cards."

"Tarot cards? Why do you... *why* do you have tarot cards?"

"It's just something I do."

"Tarot cards? You brought... Not in *my* house you didn't. What the hell is wrong with you? I will not have this... *evilness* in my house."

She shoved him off the cards and started sweeping them off the desk, tossing them into the clothes basket she carried in her arm. A few she picked up and ripped in half.

"How dare you bring something so demonic into this house. Where did you get these? What would possess you to do this? Are you crazy?"

She bombarded him with more questions than he could answer, not caring to hear a response. He watched with sadness as something he loved in secret was stripped away.

"Look at me," she yelled, turning his head up towards her as she stood over him. "We are a God-fearing household. You will not bring demons in here, do you hear me? You don't know anything about what you are playing with. If you ever feel like playing with anything like this again, then first you find yourself a new place to live. I won't have it, not under my roof. Do you understand me?"

"Yes, ma'am."

"Is there anything more? Do you have a Ouija board under the bed?"

"No."

Lorraine got down on her hands and knees and checked anyway, pulling out shoes, a textbook and any other random item that had been kicked beneath the bed.

"There's nothing there."

"There better not be nothing there. I can't believe you would bring… Don't you ever let me find something like this in my house again, do you hear me? No more of this."

"Yes, ma'am."

"I can't hear you."

"Yes, ma'am."

The next day, Lorraine assembled with her sisters, Dee and Serena, to pray over his room and sprinkle it with holy water, quelling any demonic presences he might have summoned from participating in something they didn't understand. Daniel felt the weight of embarrassment from his aunt's side glances and snarky remarks. He found out later his mom had burned the cards.

Daniel vowed to hold to his word and not practice voodoo in her house. As a result, the number of family dinners where his dad was present decreased dramatically. This satisfied his need to inflict a form of punishment on his mother for handing down judgment on something he loved.

Later, Daniel would reflect and wonder if she hadn't reacted so vehemently or prohibited him from reading tarot, he would have foreseen her death and possibly prevented it.

• • • • •

"I do not understand," Alexandre said. "How is he *too* important?"

"Because he gives me insight into what's going on over there," Daniel said.

The music on the radio blended into the background and mingled with the sound of traffic as they whizzed down the semi-crowded roadways. Daniel was driving since he wasn't sure Alexandre was allowed to drive in the US, while trying to fill Alexandre in on the conversation with Carlos. The Italian didn't like the thought of turning away potential members to the newly formed group.

"So he is on our side but as a... spy?"

"More like a mole. He's really loyalty driven. I can tell that about him. So while he won't technically be a part of our group, he'll still have a sense of loyalty to me. I need more information from him on Nicole. I'm not sure I can completely depend on Junior to tell me everything. He didn't even tell me that they were going on another job."

"A friend you cannot depend on? I do not think that is a friendship. It appears to me- and I am only viewing this relationship from the outside- It appears to me that your friendship is only on your side. It does not hold the same weight from both of you."

"Isn't that how all friendships go?"

"No." The sadness in Alexandre's voice carried a flint of sympathy. "Me and Oscar, we are friends. We look out for each other. The benefits of our friendship are the same on both sides."

"Junior had my back when my mom died. He's been there for me when I needed a place to stay. Otherwise, I would have been homeless... or worse, I would've had to move back home. Me and Junior's friendship is mutually beneficial."

"First it was how all friendships go, and now it is mutual friends with benefits."

"You're using that phrase wrong."

"You sacrifice for him. From what you say, you have committed to a life of crime. That is not equal to allowing somebody to sleep on your couch. What do you lose by letting somebody have a place to rest? In towns in Italy, people open their homes to strangers. It is a sign of compassion, not loyalty."

"I think we just have a different definition because of the culture. This isn't Italy."

Alexandre scoffed and threw up his hands. "You are blind about this friend. Your sense of loyalty is your weakness. I give you the advice that you should work on destroying this weakness or else it can be exploited."

The thought of Nicole passed through Daniel's mind.

"If loyalty is something you consider a weakness, why are you here? That means you're not loyal to me."

"I think you will see that everybody has their own reasons for following you. Just because it is not a reason that *you* would follow somebody does not mean that it is less valid. We are human. If loyalty were the reason I pledged devotion, then I would have stayed with Katrine."

"It makes me think that tomorrow, you'll leave for the next potential source of power."

"Let us also not forget that although you say loyalty is bond to friendship, you betrayed Javier not once… but twice."

Daniel sighed.

"But no," Alexandre said, "I do not want to be the negative person in the bunch. With Katrine, it was always Maxence that had bad things to say. He could never see the sunshine side of the conversation. So dark and cloudy. If I could label his personality, I think overcast with rain would be the perfect description."

"I think you just described me."

"No, you are not overcast. You are a powerful hurricane. You are the imbalanced turbulence before clear skies. I think it is your purpose to shake things up."

"Flattery will get you everywhere."

"Believe me, I know. I do not think there is a person in the world that cannot be flattered with this charm. This is your home, and I dare you to show me a person that can give me a challenge. Back home, the women are just as aggressive as the men. There is no chase. Sometimes it makes me feel like a piece of beef."

"Can't relate."

"But here, the women like to pretend to be innocent. They do not fool me though. It is an act. I have heard it in your songs, 'lady in the streets, freak in the sheets'. And it is true."

"You've been here all of four days, and you already know this?"

Alexandre smiled and thumped his chest with a fist, puffing up like a proud pigeon.

Daniel rolled his eyes and pull the car into a parking lot.

"Where are we?" Alexandre asked. "This does not look like a safe neighborhood."

"We are here to talk to some psychics."

"But for why? If you needed cheap parlour tricks and magic shows, we could've flown to Vegas and seen something much more entertaining."

"Okay, let me stop you before you finish that insult. Katrine Comtois said the same thing about my abilities with *The Grey*. I didn't like it then, and I don't like it now. One thing I don't tolerate is disrespect for somebody's culture."

"I do not mean it as disrespect."

"Regardless on how you intended it, you are insulting somebody's beliefs and practices. You have this superiority complex about your avenue of voodoo, but I do not think any aspect is greater than another. What I wanna build is a community where everybody is free to learn any aspect that they want. We can't do that if someone in my leadership is looking down their nose at choices others may make."

"I understand."

"I don't think you do, but we're here. We'll discuss it more later." Daniel turned off the car. "I'm tempted to make this our headquarters to teach you a lesson."

"No, I do understand. I have once again turned to being the Maxence of the conversation. I will be more positive." He plastered a grin on his face and spoke through his teeth. "I cannot wait to learn how to read palms and tarot cards."

"I can't tell if you're being a smartass or not. Get out. Let's go."

Daniel looked up at the Psychic Readings neon sign and remembered the last time he had been here. The older gentleman had read his tarot, but Daniel had felt the psychic had been withholding information. It was obvious now the man knew Daniel was the Prince of Veils but didn't want to reveal too much too soon.

Inside, they were greeted by the friendly smile of the man's daughter, Regina. Her smile faded with the recognition and memory from Daniel's last visit.

"Can I help you?" Her tone said she would have preferred not to.

"I don't know if you remember me…" Daniel said.

"Yeah, I remember."

"I was wondering if maybe I could speak with your uncle. Mr Toussaint?"

"We knew that you'd be coming back." She placed her hand on her hip and squinted her eyes. "So, I'm not surprised. The question is who did you bring with you? *The Lover, The Sword,* or *The Poison?*"

"I don't know how to answer that."

"We see many possibilities. There's a different future depending on who you bring. So, I'm trying to figure out who he is to you."

"Well," Alexandre said, "Although I am a lover of many, I am not *his* lover. I think the best guess, if I must pick one, is *The Sword*."

"I was going to say *Poison*," Daniel said.

"Either way, I'll go tell him that you're here and let him figure it out. He's taking a nap right now, but he would be pissed if I didn't wake him up. He's been thinking this is pretty important. Y'all wait here." She looked Alexandre up and down, sizing him up. Then turned her eyes to Daniel. "Don't *steal* anything."

Burn.

"Poison?" Alexandre questioned as soon as she left.

"It was a joke. Don't look too much into it."

"You left an impression on these people if they remember you and have been trying to see what your future holds."

"Mr. Toussaint recognized me for who I was before even *I* knew."

"If you learn this new aspect, what will you do with it? How will you use it? You will check to see if you get caught before you go rob a bank?"

"My bank heist and home invasion days are over. I don't need that. I want knowledge."

"You are smart. Knowledge can be a powerful tool. If you master all parts of voodoo, who can stand against you?"

"Not all power has to be used as a weapon."

"I say this so you can change your mind about me being *The Poison*. If I say voodoo is a weapon then, obviously, I am *The Sword*."

Regina peeked her head into the front of the store and beckoned them to join her in the back. Alexandre followed Daniel, shutting the door behind him. Clyde sat at the table covered with patterned cloth and a crystal ball in the center, the decor familiar to Daniel.

"Mr. Toussaint," Daniel said with a nod.

"I knew you would be back. The cards rarely lie. Especially the cards we used to read you with. They sing like a chorus." Clyde nodded at Alexandre before returning his attention to Daniel. "My question is how much have you learned about yourself?"

"I would like to think I've learned a lot. But I would like to learn more."

"Do you know who you are yet?"

"I am Daniel Leonard… Prince of Veils."

"Hmm. That answer alone tells me this is not *The Lover* with you."

"I am *The Sword*," Alexandre said.

"We'll see." Clyde Toussaint leaned back in his chair, the wood in the legs groaning with age. "What is the Prince of Veils in this instance? Revenge or Seduction?"

"Neither," Daniel said. "I wanna gather us, anybody like us, and share knowledge."

There was a pause. The elderly man stared at Daniel. The gaze was intense, and Daniel willed himself not to sweat. He was being assessed and didn't want to fail whatever test was being performed.

"Well…" Clyde finally said. "I still do not think you know who you are. I will let you ask what you came to ask. I've become more patient in my old age. I can wait still."

"I need to learn. Will you teach me tarot reading?"

"Regina!" Clyde called out. She returned to the room with her hands on her hips. "Grab the tarot cards. You know, the ones from last time. We're going to give the Prince of Veils his first lesson."

CHAPTER SEVEN

Daniel believed himself to be an observant person. But when he got home from his first lesson with Clyde, it took him more than a second to notice the changes to the environment. The boldness of the decor slammed him with a delayed feeling of shock.

He was mentally disoriented and had difficulty realizing the living room was not the one he had left three days ago. Everything was new and expensive looking. Junior's apartment had been converted into the type of home Nicole's Company would have been charged with robbing.

The musty couch and run down coffee table had been replaced with a plush sectional and glass table. The TV had evolved into a device twice the size as the old model and looked ridiculous in the tiny apartment. A new bookcase, a new dining room table, new lamps, a rug.

Daniel couldn't believe his eyes; Junior had gone on a spending spree in Daniel's absence.

It was three hours before Junior came home. Three hours for Daniel to sit and stew in his confusion and frustration. He played a mock conversation in his head to determine the best way to approach what he was sure was going to be an argument. But when Junior walked through the door, any script that had been mentally prepared was forgotten.

"What the hell?" Daniel said.

"Where have you been? I thought you had run away to Mexico or something."

"What's with all the new furniture?"

"Oh yeah. This is your first time seeing the changes I made around here. How do you like it? I promise you that couch is going to be more comfortable than the last one."

"How much did all this cost? I thought we were gonna try to avoid drawing attention to ourselves."

"How much? I never spend and tell. But I'll give you a hint. It was a lot."

"Junior, we agreed to be more responsible than this."

"Calm down. Calm down. I didn't spend enough to attract any attention. I made sure I purchased from different stores or whatever. I know what I'm doing. I'm a pro at this now."

"You're not a pro. We've been doing this less than a month. What happened to us laundering the money we earned?"

"If we're being honest, we didn't *earn* this money. And I still plan on cleaning the money. But I'm tired of sleeping on a mattress full of cash. What's the point of jeopardizing our freedom if we don't get to reap the awards?"

"What's the point of getting away with a burglary if you're just going to get caught by spending the money so quickly?"

Junior grabbed Daniel's shoulders and looked him in the eyes. "I think you're overreacting. But I could be wrong. There's a chance you could be a lot more upset right now."

"I'm not overreacting."

"Then walk with me to the window and take a look outside for me." Junior guided Daniel to the patio window and waited.

Daniel's eyes drifted from the window of the third-floor apartment and lingered on the glossy sedan sitting in the parking lot with chrome rims. Next to the flashy, bright blue and yellow car stood Nicole. It took a moment for Daniel to realize it was Junior's car but with some expensive improvements. Three days ago, he hadn't had rims. And the car had been a different color. Nicole waved at them. Daniel didn't bother to return the gesture.

"What did you do?" Daniel asked. "You went and fucking tricked out your car? There's no way you can tell me that didn't cost an arm and a leg."

"I was right. You could get more upset."

"Did you do this to impress *her*?"

"How have you been able to sit on your money this whole time?" Junior said, "This money isn't burning a hole in your pocket? You're not anxious to spend it?"

"The most expensive thing I've purchased is a few days at a nice hotel. I just wanted to play this safe."

"Don't look so depressed about it. You should be happy that one of us is enjoying this income. Look, the furniture I paid for with cash and bought from different stores. I didn't spend more than three thousand at any particular store so there shouldn't be any alarms there."

"And the car?"

"I know a guy that knows a guy. It was all handled by some back-alley mechanic. Only takes cash so he's probably not reporting it on his taxes. Nothing to worry about there."

Daniel shook his head and moved to the couch, taking a seat. The desire to chastise Junior screamed like constant static in his mind, but Daniel's heart wasn't in it. He didn't care if Junior spent all his money and got caught. Daniel wasn't invested in the crime sprees and bank heists anymore. He had a more important goal to focus on now. "You know what? If you wanna spend recklessly and attract attention, I'm not gonna stop you. I don't care."

"That was easy." Junior frowned. "*Too* easy. I'm scared to mention the private jet I have parked out back."

"I'm not my brother's keeper. Do what you want. I have more important things to focus on. We haven't had a chance to talk since the jewelry heist."

"Yeah, things have been a little crazy with the hits Nicole has lined up. Quitting my job freed up some time though."

"That guy from the jewelry heist, Carlos, he's a hypnotist. He hypnotized us."

"No fucking way."

"You can't trust Nicole. She had him question us about our powers and motives. She knows that you want to go rogue and start coordinating your own robberies."

"Am I going to cluck like a chicken every time I hear a doorbell?"

"You just need to be careful around her. I think it would be best if you had somebody there to watch your back... since I don't think I made the cut for her teams."

"If you really want to be a part of this, I can persuade her to come around. I think it would help if you would let me tell her about your power though."

"I don't want this. Take Carlos instead."

"The guy that hypnotized us?" Junior looked unsure. "Is he blackmailing you? Blink twice if you're being held against your will."

"He's loyal. He didn't have to tell me what she was doing. I helped him out in a bind, and he came clean about it."

"Just because he's loyal to you doesn't mean he'll be watching out for me."

"He'll be loyal to you if you get him back on the team. You probably didn't notice that you're the reason he was handed the pink slip."

"Now that you mention it..."

"He bases his loyalty off favors. So, if you do him a favor then he'll be indebted to you."

"What are you getting out of this?"

Daniel paused, not sure how to answer without revealing too much. "I need him to help me with some connections. My meeting at The W went really well. We're building an empire. Carlos has something I need to help me build."

"An empire?"

"Nicole has her Company. I have my Empire. Like I said, I have important things to focus on."

"Oh."

"Yep."

The room turned silent as Daniel massaged his palm not sure how to handle the awkwardness.

"Junior, just be careful. I have this feeling that she's just as bad as the guys that your dad was dealing with." Daniel watched Junior's expression change. "Being on her team is just the same as being involved with a mafia. Do you know what you've signed up for by working for her?"

"How do you know about the guys my dad was dealing with?"

"What?"

"*How* do you know about the guys that my dad was dealing with?" There was something in his tone that made Daniel tense with worry.

"You told me."

"No, I didn't."

"Yes, you did. Back when you were…" *sketching in your notebook and I was watching over your shoulder after we had sex…* Daniel had been about to say but stopped. That hadn't happened here. That was Mirror Junior, not Real World Junior.

"I never told you that. I never told anybody that. So how did *you* find out?"

"I…" Daniel couldn't think of a lie.

Junior chuckled, shaking his head with a look of disbelief. "You used your power on me?"

"No, it wasn't… I didn't mean to… Wait."

"You're a hypocrite. You talk all this shit about how we should trust each other, but you go behind my back and use your voodoo on me? Where's the fucking boundary?"

220

"I'm sorry. It was *not* intentional."

"But I shouldn't trust Nicole, huh? I shouldn't trust her because she used power on me to find out shit about me the same way you did?"

"The way I got my information was different. It wasn't intentional."

"How did you do it then?"

By seducing you in an alternate plane that I'm not sure is real or not. Daniel held his tongue.

"It's probably best that you've found something else to do. Whereever you've been the last few days, you should probably go back there."

"You're kicking me out?"

"You were leaving anyway, right? We've reached different paths in the road. You go hang with your coven, I'll go hang with my band of thieves."

Daniel stared at Junior, their eyes locked in a staredown. Neither wanted to break the silence. The thought of using his new hypnotism ability tip-toed through his mind. Daniel's line of sight into Junior's eyes was the perfect access to flip the 'hypnosis switch' that Carlos had taught him about. But how would that be any different than the betrayal that got him in this situation in the first place?

Finally, Junior turned away, making Daniel's decision for him. Daniel nodded with a sigh and started to gather his things, pushing loose clothing into already overstuffed bags.

With a duffle bag hanging from each shoulder, one filled with cash, and a suitcase in his hand, he turned to look back at Junior, hoping to resolve this before he walked out. But he couldn't think of anything to say. He had broken the one rule they had set from the beginning.

He opened the door to find Nicole standing on the other side, her gloating smile almost sending him into a violent rant.

"I heard you were leaving," she said, a reference to her seer powers. "I hate to see it end like this. If there's anything I can do…"

Not knowing how much she knew about the conversation he had just had with Junior, Daniel pushed past her choosing not to say anything. He struggled to carry everything but didn't want her to offer any help.

"Oh, Daniel," she said. "I think this is yours. Sorry, I picked it up by mistake the other night."

He turned, ready to let the first profane statement that he could think of flow from his lips when he saw the object she was holding. The mirror decorated in gaudy jewels, worth more to him than the cash in his bag. The link line he had to Mirror Junior was in the palm of her hand, teetering on the tips of her fingers and sending a wave of fear through Daniel's stomach from the thought that she might accidentally drop and break it. Or that she might intentionally drop it because she knew what it was.

He looked her in the eyes, her gaze even more boisterous than her grin. Daniel couldn't decide if it was from the fact she had the drop on him, having taken something he wanted to remain hidden, or if she had seen what was in the mirror. Did she know about Mirror Junior?

Silently, with his eyes, he pleaded with her. For what? He didn't know. Don't drop it. Don't reveal anything you've seen. Don't do anything to make the situation worse.

"You shouldn't leave anything this valuable just lying around," she said. "You never know who could walk through the front door and take it."

•　•　•　•　•

Learning new aspects of voodoo was more tedious than difficult. Daniel found that his Prince of Veils status gave him volumes of strength in both spiritual communication and hypnotism. With the spirits, there was an overbearing amount of information to learn. Oscar and Alexandre constantly emphasized that it could take years to even reach an intermediate level and a lifetime to master. After hearing about his encounter with the spirit at Madame Comtois' cathedral, they had reacted in horror, equating his experience to jumping into the ocean without knowing how to swim.

He had accepted their claims of his inexperience and promised caution, but he knew sooner or later he would explore further. The call of the beast was heavy in his heart and not knowing the fate of his friendship with Junior made him yearn for a distraction. So he moved to fill his days with anything to keep him occupied.

"You're not listening," Oscar said.

Daniel looked away from the high-rise view from his hotel window, sighing deeply. His constant need to fill his lungs in an exaggerated huff had become a new mannerism in the week since he had stopped speaking to Junior.

"You said the bank accounts are set up, and I can begin depositing money," Daniel said.

"And?"

"And I should vary the deposit amounts each day. It'll look suspicious if I'm depositing the same amount each day."

"Keep going."

Daniel paused, not sure what else Oscar had said. "I might have missed the next part."

"Do not just make deposits. You need to write checks from the account. You will get noticed if the only thing you do with the accounts is make deposits."

"Oh, yeah. That makes sense."

"Are you sure we cannot hire a helper for you? Somebody to handle this for you? Even I have somebody to take care of doing this for me."

"No, I can handle it. I don't need a personal assistant."

Alexandre, unusually silent, got up from his chair and sat on the bed next to Daniel. His eyebrows furrowed in confusion and the slight resemblance turned Daniel's thoughts back to Junior.

"What is wrong, *mio fratello*?" Alexandre asked. "You are quiet more than what you normally are."

"Nothing is wrong."

"There is something. Your aura has changed. Both of us can see it. We try to ignore it and let you have some space, but it is distracting you."

"I'm sorry. I guess it's trying to juggle everything. Learning and meeting my new followers..."

Word was traveling about Daniel's status, and followers were trickling in every day. Some were interested in joining him, others just curious to see the Prince of Veils. He had used his hypnotism on the hotel manager to clear out the rooms on the floor so everybody would have a place to stay. Hypnotism was more effective than *The Grey* in this instance because it was permanent. He didn't have to keep a cloud of reality cast over the staff to keep the floor clear. For all everybody knew, this floor was under construction and would not be booked.

"That is not it," Alexandre said. "I know what it is, but I do not want to overstep. It is a lover, no?"

"Not at all." Daniel glanced at the nightstand where he had hidden the hand mirror, untouched since the fallout.

"I am not ever wrong about these things. But I can see you don't want to admit it. You trust us, but you do not look at us as family yet."

Oscar shook his head. "I think it is best we do not pry."

"You cannot fully hold his attention when teaching, so it is either get a resolution to his problem or wait until he has resolved it himself. Therefore, we need to pry." Alexandre turned back to Daniel. "I have had many lovers in my lifetime..."

"And you have this habit of telling us every chance you get." Oscar laughed.

"Because it is true. I do not do it to brag. There is value in having this information."

"How so?"

Alexandre waved away Oscar's question. "When I was younger, I fell in love so easily. Any young woman that gave me food and attention had my heart. I have seen women come and go. It is a part of life to experience pain as the end result of love. And as a person looking from the outside of your situation, I can see this lover is no good for you. He is… He changes you but not in a good way."

"Not to say we are the angels of heavenly morality," Oscar said. "We are not here to chide you on what actions you take that are good or evil."

"Yes, of course. We are not hypocrites. But the things you do are not… they do not move us forward. You risk a lot by participating in those endeavors with him. Your feelings for him blinds you and steers you away from what you are building here." Alexandre sighed. "When I was ascending the ranks of Madame Comtois, I met a woman who also blinded me. It was an accidental love because when I met her, there was nothing extraordinary about her. She was not beautiful, simply average. Her power was less than mine. She didn't have the desire to be greater than she was. But we had attraction and chemistry. We loved hard and fast.

"She was toxic. We argued and fought. And that poison seeped into my heart and fed what I thought was love. During our brief time together, I lost myself. The burning love made me unrecognizable, and I became obsessed with keeping her. It took a friend to show me I wasn't myself."

"A conversation and a physical altercation can really help clear the mind," Oscar smiled.

"But let's not discuss that now. We are here for Daniel," Alexandre snapped before placing his hand on Daniel's shoulder. "Tell us what the problem is."

Daniel shook his head, not knowing where to start. He wanted to tell them about the situation but didn't know how he could do so while omitting the parts regarding the mirror. They would be disappointed, maybe even angry if they found out he had made a deal with a spirit. They might even confiscate the hand mirror, and he wasn't willing to sacrifice the only link he currently had to Junior. Even if it were a fake version of his friend.

"I messed up," Daniel said. "I took advantage of my power and misplaced Junior's trust. I didn't..."

"Junior is the one that you make the bank robberies with?"

"Yeah. I don't think this is gonna be easy to mend. It's ironic how a few weeks ago, I was damn near bragging about my loyalty and how I would do anything for my friends... and now I've lost Javier and Junior and Veronica and... I don't know who else I have now."

"Well, we are here."

"That's not the same. You both follow me because I am the Prince of Veils. If anybody else ascends into this title, then your allegiance moves with them. Y'all are followers, not friends."

Alexandre looked to Oscar. Neither knew what to say.

"I've been thinking," Daniel continued. "If this is what it means to be... if the trade-off to becoming the Prince of Veils is to lose everybody who means something to me..."

A knock on the door didn't allow him to finish. He got up from the bed, happy for the interruption, leaving Alexandre and Oscar trying to find words of solace.

He opened the door to find Clyde and Regina. They greeted him, early for their tarot training. Regina sashayed past him, the smell of her perfume lighting the room with a feminine fragrance.

"If this is a bad time, we can come back," Clyde said.

"No, this is good," Daniel said. "Oscar and Alexandre were just leaving."

The pair had declined to try to learn tarot reading despite saying how open they were to expanding their knowledge. It appeared their biases would take time to overcome.

"Do not forget that we have dinner with the new members tonight," Oscar said to Daniel before turning to the psychics. "You are both invited to join us. We can have the full leadership here to greet them. It would make a great welcoming party."

"I don't know if we came dressed for a party at this place." Regina smoothed her hands over her dress. "This place is a little bit more high class than I'm used to."

"It's not as haughty as you think," Oscar said. "You look fine."

She smiled.

Alexandre leaned in close to Daniel, choosing the semi-private moment while Oscar showered Regina with compliments and Clyde set up the tarot table.

"Everything will be okay," Alexandre said. "Everybody has insecurities. We would be worried if you did not have them because it would mean you are too confident. Ego can be even the greatest of kings' downfall."

Daniel nodded, looking away embarrassed. Alexandre provided parting words to Clyde and Regina then followed Oscar out of the room.

Regina and Clyde babbled in the background with small talk as Daniel positioned himself across the table from Regina. Their lessons consisted of Regina demonstrating while Clyde narrated and explained. Daniel straightened his back, pushing the feelings of sadness away and focusing on the lesson. But it turned out this lesson didn't follow their normal routine. Regina pushed the tarot deck across the table and told Daniel to read her tarot.

"Trying to read your own tarot cards is like being a deer in headlights," Regina said, "Blinded by the oncoming future until it is too late. The most efficient way to read your own future is by reading the future of those close to you. Somebody who is close enough to be affected by your actions. What do you see when you read my future?"

"I see love."

"What else?"

"I see something that needs to be handled carefully." Daniel flipped the cards and scanned the spread. "It'll be a major turning point in your life. But it's not something you can control. You're just going to be a leaf in the river."

"Good. You're learning."

"I see... sadness. Loss. Tragedy."

"Can you see why?"

"No, I can't."

But it had something to do with *The Lover*, *The Sword*, and *The Poison*. There was a decision to be made.

"Keep looking," Clyde said.

Daniel couldn't decipher the pattern and frowned. He could see Junior in the cards but didn't want to admit the distraction was affecting his reading. He could feel the mirror in the nightstand buzzing like a cell phone on vibrate.

"Does this have something to do with me?" Daniel asked.

"I don't know," Regina said. "Does it?"

"I'm the river. I'm the reason you're going to be sad later." Daniel flipped more cards into the pattern, struggling to see what she wanted him to see. "A confrontation. An escape. But you both already knew this before you came here."

"Something is going to challenge you and change everything. We need you to see that your decision will affect us."

"What do I need to do?"

"Don't run. You'll have to make a choice. I can't tell you what the other one will be, but if you run..." A look of sorrow shaded her face.

"I'm here to stay. I'm not going anywhere."

She reached across the table and placed her hand over his. "You may have all the good intentions in the world, but that won't save your decision from hurting those around you. Just be wise and remember this reading."

Daniel nodded, somber. "I promise."

Regina and Clyde glanced at each other before they moved on with the lesson.

The look said they didn't believe him.

● ● ● ● ●

"What is she doing here?" Daniel asked.

Mirror Junior looked up from the couch, surprised to see Daniel in the mirror reality.

Daniel had tried to avoid the mirror, accepting his part in what it represented, but the addiction... the need to talk to Junior had overcome his willpower. He had stepped into the mirror, promising that this would be the last time, but subconsciously compromising that he would make short, infrequent visits.

What he found when he entered the mirror was a shock to say the least. Junior stared up at him. Daniel would have expected a bigger look of guilt from him.

Beside Junior, a blonde version of Nicole sat, nestled in his arms, her eyes fluttering open with a sleepy gaze. From Daniel's point of view, it looked like she had fallen asleep while watching a movie. The coffee table held a bowl of popcorn, three empty beer bottles and a half-empty glass of wine. This was a romantic evening.

"What do you mean?" Junior asked.

"Why is she here in the mirror? She shouldn't be here."

Daniel noticed everything in the house shouldn't be there. The furniture was different. The carpet was different. Things had changed since his last visit. This was not the same house. This was not the same mirror.

"Nicole lives here. What are you talking about, bro?"

Bro?

"She changed it," Daniel said in disbelief. "She took the hand mirror and changed it."

The duo exchanged glances and shifted their positions on the couch, uncomfortable with Daniel's rising voice.

"I can't believe this. Junior, please, I can't lose you too. I need you here if I can't have you out there. She can't have you in both places."

Junior got up from the couch, a look of concern on his face. "Daniel, are you okay? You're not making any sense."

Daniel opened his eyes and looked around the hotel room.
The hand mirror was face down on the floor. He closed his eyes and
fell back into the unfamiliar house.

Daniel brushed past Junior, walking through the
unfamiliar hallway. Entering the bathroom, he grabbed a bar
of soap and scribbled the necessary symbols on the mirror. His
hands were shaking with such intensity, the markings were
barely legible, and he worried if the summoning would work.

But the bathroom mirror dimmed. He didn't have to
worry for long.

The figure appeared.

"What did she change?" Daniel asked. "Why is it
different? Did she give you something to make this change?"

The figure didn't answer. Instead it began to solidify,
taking more than its normal shadow blur.

"Hey, dude." Junior appeared at the door to the
bathroom. "Are you okay? You're acting a little weird."

Even the way Junior spoke now was different. His
New York accent gone, replaced with something more West
Coast.

Daniel shut the door in his face, not bothering to
answer and turned back to the mirror. The face of Ghiy-
āthu'd-Dīn stared back at him, clearer than he had ever seen
before. Was this what the shadowy figure looked like or was
this an illusion? The mirror fogged with steam and words
began to appear as if written with an unseen finger.

Smitty, it read.

"Answer me," Daniel said. "I don't need cryptic
messages."

The figure continued to stare through the haze of the
steamed mirror, and Daniel became irritated. Of course the
spirit wouldn't respond to him.

Daniel punched the mirror, thinking he could hit it
hard enough for it to shatter but not hurt himself, since this
wasn't real. The man stepped back and looked around as if
startled by something unseen. Daniel scoffed and stepped out
of the restroom.

Daniel sat up, sweat dusted across his forehead. He picked up the mirror and placed it back in the nightstand, next to the remote control for the television. A face stared back at him, - Ghiyāthu'd-Dīn's - from the bathroom mirror. Daniel struggled to keep his eyes open.

Junior stood at the end of the hallway holding Nicole and comforting her. Daniel walked back into the living room, feeling the weight of defeat dragging at his shoes.

"Why?" Daniel asked to nobody in particular.

"Why what?" Junior said.

"I know karma is a real thing. What goes around comes around. What goes up must come down. But I didn't put anything out in the universe to deserve this. I'm not a bad person. I started doing this stealing shit for you..."

Nicole looked up from Junior's shoulder, pushing her hair out of her face. "Don't you think that's kind of sad? Going against your upbringing and moral compass for a man?"

"I didn't do it for a *man*. I did it for a friend."

"Everybody can see it. Why keep lying to yourself?"

"You don't care about him like I do. You're only around to have somebody to play with when y'all go on jobs. You're new. I have been here for years. I've told him about my power, my strengths and weaknesses. I've given him an ear to listen when he was going through things with girlfriends and his kids. When Amanda's mom wanted to move out of state, and he was depressed about losing his daughter, I was there. You haven't been there. You're new."

"And yet... he still chose me." She shrugged.

Never had Daniel felt such a strong urge to harm anyone before. He could feel *The Grey* calling him.

"I don't think this is helping," Junior said. "Maybe we should take a breath and calm down. Talk this out like adults."

"Good idea, babe. I know what will calm us down. Daniel, would you like anything to drink?" Her demeanor changed, and she stared at Daniel as if he were a close friend, her eyes sparkled with excitement to match her smile.

Daniel didn't respond, just taking a moment to try to work out in his mind what he did to deserve this. If he was being honest, he wasn't the angel he tried to portray. He had robbed a bank, in the process putting the lives of two innocent college students in jeopardy. He had taken money from a drug dealer and participated in a jewelry heist. Not to mention using the mirror to partake in a reality he knew was a fantasy. And even after the crack in the friendship that he wasn't sure would mend, caused by information received from this reality, he still came back. He was using the key that had opened the door to his broken friendship.

Daniel ignored the question, using his eyes in a silent plea with Junior. She shrugged and left the room, giving Daniel a chance to speak with Junior alone.

He jerked his eyes open and looked around the room. Everything was sharp, as if he were still in the mirror. The walls too bright, the pictures too clear. He wanted to close his eyes and shake his head, but closing his eyes was dangerous. Daniel needed to get out. He stood up, intending to race for the door.

The front door to the house in the mirror stood open. The view that should have been the perfectly manicured lawns in the always sunny atmosphere was replaced with the dark, TV lit hotel room with the high-rise view.

"Do you remember anything we had here? The things we shared?" Daniel turned from the door to Junior and watched for a spark of remembrance in those hazel eyes. "I told you about what I wanted to do with my community, what I wanted to build. You told me about your family and your dad... everything..."

"This house is safe. You're safe. I think you're the type to look for security, you want protection. But I can't protect you out there."

"So this is punishment because I leave the mirror? I can't stay in here forever. This is a fantasy. I can't live in a fantasy."

"But... you already do. You don't have to leave. Stay here with us."

Nicole came back and handed Daniel the glass of something dark. Daniel looked down at the floating ice cubes and sighed.

"As tempting as it is, I have people that depend on me. I started something and I need to finish it."

"What about after you finish it?"

"Regina told me that I can't run from this. It makes sense now."

Nicole took Junior's hand and led him away to sit on the couch. Nicole, sat on his left, legs folded on the cushion and her head on Junior's chest.

Junior turned to Daniel and patted the cushion on his right, an invitation to join them. A non-verbal lure similar to the first time Daniel had entered the mirror.

Daniel knew the longer he stayed in the mirror, the more tempting it would be to join the two. He turned and walked out the front door.

Daniel opened his eyes. He was lying on the floor, slumped in an uncomfortable position. The mirror was in his hand. He looked and saw a reflection of Mirror Junior and dark-haired Nicole. Junior mowing the lawn. Nicole cooking dinner for Izzy and the faceless child. He put the mirror in the nightstand drawer and closed it.

• • • • •

"I just didn't feel like Political Science was the right fit for me. So I changed my major to Economics, which at the time seemed perfect, but now I'm starting to reconsider."

Daniel watched the mindless chatter of one of his newest recruits. She was more than eager to share information about herself. So much of her life story had poured from her lips that Daniel had forgotten her name. Crystal? Caitlyn? Catharsis? He had no idea. Appetizers had been served, and the waiter was walking around the table refilling glasses.

Alexandre was seated to his right, his mask of interest in the girl's story plastered to his face. An occasional nod and 'hmm' kept the illusion that he was paying attention. Daniel had attempted to follow Alexandre's lead, but his interest soon waned, and he wasn't sure Cassandra had even noticed how the expressions of everybody at the table had fallen to boredom.

Oscar had become sick that afternoon, the greasy American food too much for his stomach, and skipped the meal.

This was the sixth wave of new recruits to Daniel's kingdom. Every other day brought a new group of individuals ready to acknowledge his reign. Some had been curious, wanting to know what the Prince of Veils could do. Daniel had given them a display of his power, choosing to show them his gifts with *The Grey* and how he used it on the hotel staff. And he had shown them the numerous *voleur* he had in his possession. Even without showing them half his legion of spirits, they had been impressed and ready to commit. A quick lesson with *The Grey* enabled a few of them to perform the same stunts he had with the hotel staff. This freed up some of his time from having to keep the 19th floor reserved for his followers.

After pledging alliance and the introductory dinner, new members would be free to leave as they wished. Daniel did not require them to stay. If they needed anything, they could report back to this location in *The Grey*. The W Hotel had become Daniel's version of Javier's run down opera house.

"I've never really thought about grad school, but my friends tell me that Bachelor degrees aren't as valued as they used to be. So I'm considering at least a Masters. My scholarships are only four years so I would need to find a new way to finance..." The motor-mouthed young lady droned on.

Dinner arrived and was served. Daniel looked down at the salmon and rice with disdain. He would force himself to eat, but he hadn't had much of an appetite since his last visit to the mirror. He had resolved that Nicole, whether intentional or not, had affected the mirror. He wondered if the mirror had enveloped her the same as it did him. Had she seen the secret life he kept inside? Would she tell Junior, giving him more reason hold a grudge against Daniel?

As much as Daniel tried to occupy his time, his mind couldn't stop wandering back to his friendship lost. A few times he had typed out a text message, a pitiful explanation and apology to Junior, but he never hit send. He couldn't say what kept him from reaching out - the fear of rejection or having to accept their friendship was gone. He hoped that Junior just needed time and nothing would happen to him in the meantime.

Daniel jumped out of his self-loathing and turned his attention to the one-sided conversation at the table. Something said sparked his interest.

"Did you say necromancy?" Daniel asked.

"Hmm?" She stared at him, apparently not expecting to be interrupted with a question. She knew she was boring everybody. "Yes, I can talk to the dead. And once or twice I've talked to demons, but that's not something I recommend."

Daniel considered the things he could do with that aspect of voodoo. He could learn from voodoo masters long gone. Or even speak to his mother.

"How did you learn to do that?"

"It just kind of happened. I don't think I really knew I was doing it until I knew I was doing it. If that makes sense. There's no visual form that I can testify to seeing though. I'm not talking to ghosts or nothing."

"How do you know it's not a spirit?"

"I don't think I know the difference between the two to answer that." Carol shrugged. "I had never seen a spirit until you showed us your *voleur*."

"I think I would like you to show me this one day. I'm interested in investigating this more."

The other four recruits perked up, seeing Daniel's interest, and tried to gather where the conversation had moved since they had stopped paying attention. Daniel took advantage of the interruption to move to the next person in the line of introductions, a tall, slender guy with locs that grew past his shoulders.

"I'm Jason," he said. "I don't really have much to tell about myself. I think what everybody is most interested in is our power…"

A woman at the entrance to the dining hall caught Daniel's attention, a familiar face that distracted him from hearing anything else Jason had to say.

"I'm sorry," Daniel said. "I see somebody that I know that I need to speak with. I'll be back."

He rose from the table, feeling the eyes of the group following him to see who was important enough to catch his interest. Daniel stared in disbelief and approached with caution, stopping a short distance away and frowning.

"Hey," he said.

"I expected a more excited greeting than that," Veronica said.

"Sorry. It's good to see you." He leaned in for a hug and held it, taking in her slim, model frame and long hair. "What are you doing here?"

"Well, you don't come to *The Grey* anymore, so I had to find some way to contact you."

Daniel's face dropped. "Is everything okay? Did something happen? Don't let it be Javier."

"No, nothing is wrong."

A moment of silence as Daniel waited for her to continue.

"Okay?" he asked.

"I've come to join you."

"But…"

"What you're doing here is awesome. Word travels fast, and from what I gather, I won't be the only one of Javier's followers that he loses."

"Veronica, no. He can't lose us both. This would be too much on him."

"He knew he never had you to begin with. It was only a matter of time. Otherwise, he would have tried to manipulate you into serving under him. I know it hurt him to see you go… again… but he knew that day was coming. It sucks it happened so soon."

"I never doubted his intentions. It hurt when he told me we weren't friends anymore."

"That was the pain talking. You give him time. He'll come around."

"Seems like all I'm doing right now is giving people time to come around."

She gave him a smile of empathy and took his hand, the feeling of her affection in real life was a little off-putting.

Daniel's phone buzzed in his pocket. He took it out and glanced at the text message from Junior. His pulse quickened.

"I gotta go," he said.

• • • • •

Daniel parked his car and took a deep breath. Anxiousness had sat in his stomach since he left the hotel. The phone call from Junior was enough to put him on edge. On the drive from the hotel, Daniel had rehearsed conversations in his head on how to handle apologizing to Junior. He figured if Junior was willing to meet then there was an opening for some form of apology.

A thump of footsteps answered his knock, and he fixed his face to look sorrowful. He wanted the full remorse of his actions to be evident in his mannerisms and facial expressions.

The door opened, and Daniel took a step back. Nicole greeted him in the doorway, a sly grin on her face. But it wasn't her presence that almost made him gasp. It was her newly dyed hair. Blonde. Same as Mirror Nicole.

"Took you long enough," she said.

"Where's Junior?"

She stepped aside. Daniel entered, still unaccustomed to the newly decorated apartment. Nicole's employees sat around the living room, watching as he came in. Greg sat next to Tiffany. Carlos stood behind Junior.

"Hey, everybody?" Daniel's voice lifted as more of a question than a greeting.

"Glad you're here," Junior said. He rose from the loveseat and guided Daniel to the table. "We're planning our next job. Or should I say, *I'm* planning our next job."

"That's why you called me over?" Daniel was unable to hide his disappointment.

"Yes, I couldn't leave you out since it's your intel that got us this far."

Daniel looked at the coffee table. Various sketches and documents were scattered in view, vaguely familiar. Everything visible displayed his handwriting. He leaned forward to get a better look, remembering the bank blueprints that Ghiy-āthu'd-Dīn had provided during its first contact.

"If I had known you could get this kind of information," Nicole said, "I wouldn't have brushed you off as a crazy psychic."

"Sorry," Junior said, "I had to tell them what you could do. I know. I know. You didn't want to have all your business out there, but this is for the good of the team. We can walk out of this with the biggest haul any of us have ever seen."

"He doesn't look excited yet. Daniel, why don't you look excited?" Nicole's falsely cheerful tone irritated Daniel.

"I think I know what will get him excited. I haven't told him the prize amount yet. Daniel, we're talking two million to three million dollars. Between the six of us, that's over five hundred thousand dollars each... *tax-free*." There was an eager and rushed blanket of emotions in Junior's presentation.

"Junior," Daniel said with a sigh, "I told you I was done with that. I'm not trying to rob any more banks. Y'all have what y'all need so..."

"No, we *need* you. You are a part of this plan. Look, let me explain it to you. Look. Just look. Everybody has a part to play in this game. We need all hands on deck."

Nicole placed her arm around Daniel. "You're an important part on the game board."

Daniel was tired of all the analogies.

"Let me explain," Junior said. "We have the schematics for the bank. We have Tiffany to cover the security cams and alarm system. Thanks to you, she also has the algorithm for the vault security token."

"And not just the bank downtown," Tiffany said, "But all their bank branches in Texas. We can do some serious damage with this. Fuck you for sitting on it this whole time."

"And Greg here," Junior continued, "He's our muscle. With the amount of money we need to haul, we need some serious weight behind us. Nicole is making sure we have enough time to escape. Nobody can surprise us with anything as long as she sees what's coming. And you wanted me to include Carlos, so he's here. He can cover us in case we need a distraction or memories erased. For me, I'm the backup plan in case we need to incapacitate anybody..."

"And me?" Daniel asked.

"That's the major piece. You're our camouflage. That might not be the right word. You're our invisibility cloak. You can make it so that nobody can see us. Carlos told us about your trick at the jewelry heist."

Daniel looked at Carlos. Carlos was staring at his hands, avoiding Daniel's eyes. That hadn't been his information to give.

"We need you if we want to make this work." Junior stood. "We can pull this off, and nobody would even know."

"Do you mind if we talk privately for a minute?" Daniel asked.

The group exchanged glances, not confident in where this was going.

Junior nodded and led Daniel into the bedroom, closing the door. Daniel rolled his eyes at the new bed that was too large for the small room, cramped next to boxes of new shoes, electronics and other valuables.

"I thought you called me over here to talk about what happened before I left. I didn't know you were dragging me to a sales pitch."

"That's in the past. We can forget about that."

"No, I owe you an apology. I never should have used my power for information like that. I'm sorry."

"Don't worry about it. Thinking back on it, I probably overreacted."

"I understand why you would though."

"I haven't thought about it since that night, to be honest."

"Then why haven't you texted me or called me? I thought you were pissed and needed time to cool down."

"I don't know. I been busy. As you can see, I've been planning something big here. Something that we need your help with."

"Yeah, well, I have something big going on too. I don't think I have time to be doing shit like this anymore."

"Come on. We need you."

"Y'all will manage. I mean, I have followers now and generals and... I'm creating something that I'm proud of, and this isn't in the cards for me anymore."

"Look, you found out something about me that I never tell anybody. It was something I kept to myself because I didn't want to be judged or have to answer questions about. But it was a relief to finally have a friend that knows about it. I didn't even know how much tension I had built up inside just keeping that to myself. I don't think you understand what that's like because you're so open about everything."

"Not everything."

"I'm coming to you as a friend," Junior stared at Daniel, letting a moment of silence emphasize the importance of his words. "I need you to help me pull this off. This is my chance to prove that I can lead. With the success of this heist under my belt, I can prove to Nicole that I can carry my own team. I can branch out and have my own employees. Or have my own followers. Just this last bank robbery, and I won't ask you for anything else."

Daniel stared at Junior and could feel the pleading pull. Only in the mirror did he get to gaze this long into Junior's hazel eyes.

Taking a deep breath, Daniel nodded his head. "Fine, I'll help you."

Junior embraced him in a tight hug.

"But," Daniel pulled away, "this is the last one. I'm done after this. This is going to be my final heist."

"Well, let's make it a good one then." Junior placed a hand on Daniel's shoulder.

They exited the room, and Junior told everybody the good news. Greg, Tiffany and Carlos shrugged at the announcement. Apparently, Nicole had already told them.

● ● ● ● ●

"This is not loyalty," Alexandre said. "This is blind devotion. All week you sulk and walk around without seeing what is in front of you. We think you begin to turn back to your normal self and you step back into the life that is not for you."

Daniel sat on the bed, frustrated, wishing he hadn't even brought up Junior's next bank heist. The hotel room was starting to make him restless since it only had a bed, a bathroom and a sitting area. He thought maybe he should have pushed for the luxury suite, but he knew this was just a temporary headquarters. He had invited Alexandre down to talk hoping that company and conversation would settle his nerves.

It hadn't.

"This argument is moving in a circle." Daniel sighed. "My friend asked me for a favor, and I'm gonna help him."

"A couple of days ago, you did not even know that you still had a friend. He is a user. He calls on you when he needs to use you. You are a tool that he needs to complete... whatever analogy fits this scenario."

"Our friendship has mutual benefits."

"You can't see it." Alexandre's voice pitched toward an empathetic sadness that made Daniel stop. "You love him. That's the only thing that could make somebody act this blindly."

"Yes, I love my friends. That's why they're my friends."

"How can English be labeled so complicated but be inadequate at the same time. You understand me."

Daniel's phone buzzed. A message from Junior that they were downstairs.

"I have to go," Daniel said. "We can talk about it later. Maybe by then you won't be overreacting as much."

"Does he love you back? Is your affection returned?"

Daniel didn't answer as he started towards the door.

"Seigneurs have served in many capacities for their Head. There was a time when I had to provide sex to Madame Comtois. I am willing to do the same now if it keeps you from doing this stupid thing."

"As tempting as that sounds, I'll pass."

"Why do you pass? What is it about your friend that keeps you from moving on? He is better looking? Better body? I know he is not richer because I do not need to rob banks for money."

Daniel pressed the button for the elevator and tried to find an answer to Alexandre's questions. Junior was not better looking. Alexandre was definitely more charismatic. But whatever attraction Daniel had to Junior was non-existent for

Alexandre. And although he didn't want to admit it, deep down inside, Daniel knew why he would never take Alexandre up on his offer.

"Because I love him," Daniel finally admitted.

The words were painful. Daniel blinked furiously to hold back the floodgate that threatened to open from his eyes. He hadn't cried since the night his mother died. He vowed that his tears were his final gift to her and wouldn't be shed for anybody else.

"He knows that, and he exploits it. I predict that he will be the stone that keeps you from making what you are trying to build here into something great. If you cannot see how he affects you, then how can you see how you affect us?"

The tears got heavier. Daniel remained silent, staring ahead at the falling numbers on the elevator display.

"Have you thought about your followers? The many men and women who have come from everywhere to join you. They have paused their lives to follow you, putting trust in what you are trying to build. Why endanger it for love? A love that will not be reciprocated?"

"I can't run from this. Regina read my tarot, and it said I have to stop running if I want to be successful."

"And you think she meant don't run from a bank robbery? You are not that daft."

The elevator dinged, and they stepped off, moving toward the lobby.

"I've watched Madame Comtois over the years," Alexandre said. "She never tried to find love. Of course, she has sex and yearns for affection sometimes. She feels the void of not having companionship, but she fills that hole with her true purpose. Gaining followers and growing in power is her focus. I've always thought that was a miserable way to live, but it works for her. To each their own. I do not say this to say that you have to live like her. I believe there is somebody out there for everybody. I really think there are multiple people out there for everybody. But this guy, Junior, he is not for you. And I think you know that. Refusing to accept it is going to hurt more than you at this point. Is it that you need to hear him say it?"

Daniel halted and turned, causing Alexandre to almost collide with him. "Alexandre, stop. Please."

Alexandre peered over Daniel's shoulder and didn't respond. Daniel turned to find Clyde entering the hotel doors.

"Shit," Daniel said. "Mr. Toussaint, I forgot about our lesson for today. I am so sorry."

Clyde nodded but didn't say anything, assessing Daniel's water-heavy eyes and Alexandre's frowning face.

"We can pick up tomorrow if that is okay?" Daniel asked.

"Yes, that's fine," Clyde said. "Is everything okay?"

"As good as it can be."

"If you will not accept reason," Alexandre said, "Then I will go with you."

"No. This is not... I don't need you involved."

"You do not want your seigneur with you? We are here for you, but you reject my advice, advances and offers. So then why are we here? Why bring me and Oscar from across the world to come meet with you? Just so you could see if we were lying? To force us into exile from everything we've worked for with Katrine?"

Patrons of the hotel walked past the group, staring at the obvious heated conversation being conducted in lowered voices. Alexandre's body language was becoming hostile.

"I brought you here to help me build..."

"To build a community that you refuse to make your top priority. A community that you will eventually bring down by chasing after somebody who will never love you."

Daniel bit his lip and stared at the anger in Alexandre's eyes. Nodding his head, he turned and walked out the lobby doors. He could feel Alexandre following behind him.

Greg's SUV was parked at the entrance beside a line of taxis. Without looking back, Daniel climbed into the car. Greg was in the driver's seat with Junior on the passenger side and Nicole in the back. As Daniel reached for the door, a hand stopped it from closing. Alexandre stared at Daniel, his frustrated gaze begging Daniel to step out of the car. His eyes conveying a message that it was not too late to turn back and accept everything that Alexandre had said in the last five minutes.

Daniel could see out of the corner of his eye Greg start to respond. A hand motion from Nicole stopped him. They allowed the standoff for a few seconds before Alexandre released the door. Daniel closed it, watching Alexandre stare as the SUV drove away.

"Friend of yours?" Nicole asked.

"One of my followers," Daniel said.

But Daniel wasn't sure Alexandre would still be here when he got back.

CHAPTER EIGHT

"It's such a nice day for a bank robbery," Junior said.

"The only thing that would make it better would be tea and crumpets," Daniel said. "I hear that's what the Dutchess of Gladenstein partakes in before any bank jobs."

"I should've took a shot of tequila and a snort of cocaine."

"You want to be Scarface so bad."

"Scarface was rich. So yes, I want to be Scarface."

Junior and Daniel sat on a park bench across the street from the bank. It was the same park they used to scope out this bank weeks ago. To Daniel it seemed like a lifetime past.

Tiffany and Carlos had entered the bank half an hour earlier with plans to disrupt the security camera system. Dressed as security technicians, they had introduced themselves to the interim bank manager. Carlos had implanted the idea in the manager's head that they were there to upgrade the security system, seeing as how the system had failed some weeks earlier during a crucial time when the bank was robbed. From that point it was up to Tiffany to disable the system and let the team know when it was safe to enter.

Greg was stationed nearby waiting for their signal to enter through the back while Nicole was waiting with the van.

"Are you nervous?" Junior asked.

"Surprisingly, no. I think we've done this more than enough times for me to not have butterflies anymore."

"You've really come a long way. When we did this the first time, you didn't even want to sit here and run surveillance."

"I think I'm proud to say that under your positive influence, I have become the supervillain you wanted me to be."

"This confidence looks good on you." Junior smiled. "I think everybody has noticed it. Did you see the way Nicole looked at you?"

"I think we both know that Nicole is more your type than mine. Plus, I wouldn't trust her as far as I could see her."

"Okay, if not Nicole, then Carlos. He owes you for finding a way to keep his job."

"Still not my type…"

Junior had never asked Daniel what his type was. And the more Daniel thought about it, the more grateful he was that the topic wasn't explored further.

"The guy at the hotel, the one that didn't want you to get in the car…" Junior said. "What's his deal?"

"Alexandre? I told you. He's one of my followers."

"Does he know about what you're about to do?"

"Yeah, he knows. He was trying to stop me." Daniel paused and took a deep sigh. A cloud passed in front of the sun and covered the block in shade. The smell of heat on concrete pressed on the duo as the sound of dogs barking in the background filled the silence. "He… *mentioned* a few things about where I'm headed with my voodoo community, the things I'm building, and I think he's right. I really don't think bank jobs are for me."

"So what are you saying?"

"What I said yesterday. This will be my last job. I got other things I need to focus on."

Junior nodded his head and looked Daniel in his eyes. "I can understand that. To be honest, I knew it was a long shot when I asked you to come work this heist with us. After the way we fell out last week..."

"Listen, Junior, about that..."

Their phones buzzed in unison; a message from Tiffany that her part was complete.

"Water under the bridge," Junior said. "Time to get to work."

They rose from the bench, looked both ways before crossing the street, leaving the green park behind. Daniel opened himself to the familiarity of *The Grey* and began pulling massive waves of *Grey Matter* into the street. The flood of his magic washed around him and created the tranquil and comforting atmosphere of thick fog that he knew only he could see. And even with the haze more dense than any amount he had ever pulled before, he continued to pull even more. He had a bank to fill.

Greg joined them at the entrance, and Daniel entered first, letting *The Grey* spill into the doorway like a broken dam. It cascaded across the room with a rushed intensity, covering everything and everybody in its path.

The usual method was to cover, but now, Daniel used it to bathe the customers and bank tellers. He molded a reality for the bank patrons of a busy bank with long lines, and irritated customers. They were given the option to either wait to speak with a bank teller or leave and come back later.

Damn lunch rush.

The tellers, on the opposing end of Daniel's scenario, would see a long line of angry, irritated customers who couldn't wait to gripe at the first employee they came across.

Can't wait until five o'clock.

Daniel smiled, impressed with his power. It was a lot to hold, and he felt pinpricks of sweat across his forehead, but he knew he hadn't reached his limit. The amount of *Grey* he held was more than enough, so he let it do what he needed it to do at the volume it was at.

Junior and Greg slipped through the doorway behind him, looking around cautiously, unable to see his work.

"Is it okay?" Greg asked.

Daniel peered from the side of his eye before raising his arms and yelling. "Everybody on the floor, now. This is a stickup."

Greg and Junior flinched, ready to bolt out the door. But they quickly realized nobody in the bank had moved. None of the customers or employees had reacted.

"You're an asshole," Junior said.

"Am I a pretty asshole?"

"Let's get started." Junior nodded to Greg. "You got what you need?"

Greg pulled out his phone and waved the screen at Junior. "Tiffany sent the vault code right on time."

Daniel watched the pair walk away, Greg towards the back vault, Junior headed to the loading dock to let Nicole in. The feeling of so much *Grey* in his grasp made Daniel lose a sense of focus for a moment as he let himself get caught in the pressure of the magic substance. Although he was sure he was standing still, he could feel his body swaying as if on a large boat.

He embraced it for what he assumed was only a moment, but the sound of his name interrupted his reverie. Nicole and Junior were staring at him, asking if he were alright. How long had they been standing there?

"Yeah," Daniel said. "I got it. It's just a lot. More than I've ever tried to do before."

Nicole waved her hand in front of a customer's face as if checking to see if he was awake. "I wish I had known about this sooner. Ms. Cleo has more layers than a cake."

"You're lucky I'm preoccupied right now, so I can't give you the comeback you deserve."

"Let's make off with this haul, and you can give me whatever you want."

"Wrong tree, Courtney Love."

Daniel saw a smirk on her face before she turned to head to the back.

Where had Junior gone? He was here a second ago, right?

"They're like mannequins."

It sounded like Junior, but Daniel turned to find Carlos mesmerized by the frozen customers.

"Where did Junior go?"

"Probably helping Greg. So are they hypnotized? Can you use your power to hypnotize them all at once?"

As Daniel wondered how to respond, he felt the *Grey* conform in response to the question. It started to condense and compact, pulling even more into the room. The burden of carrying so much power got heavier. It took an effort to stop it from growing.

"I think it's hungry." Daniel said.

"What?"

"Nothing. How much longer?"

"I'm not sure." Carlos came to stand beside Daniel, taking a look around awkwardly. "I don't know if I got a chance to thank you for getting me back on the team. Junior told me that it was because of you."

"No problem." Daniel's voice was strained. Did Carlos notice?

"You might think it's nothing, but it really is. Without these jobs... I can't go back to working after making money like this. No job would ever pay me this much for easy work."

Daniel nodded, choosing not to speak. *The Grey* had started to move in a slow, circular current around the room, washing in and out of offices and back rooms. He had to focus to keep Junior and the others from being enveloped in it.

"And I know that you've provided me with favor after favor. It seems like I'm asking you to do things for me or whatever... What I'm trying to say... I guess... I need one more favor. I know it feels like I'm being needy, but it's something that I can't do myself. Believe me, I tried."

Daniel thought he said something pushing Carlos to continue, but he wasn't sure.

"My brother, you helped him a lot. And he was sane for a few weeks. I was glad to have him back. Even those two weeks mean everything to me. I'll never know another way I could repay you for that. But he's starting to drift back to where he was before. I was wondering if there was a way for you to pull him back to himself… permanently?"

A mind muddled with holding so much *Grey* struggled to understand what Carlos was asking. Daniel could cure his brother every couple of weeks if he wanted. But that would get tiresome.

"I could make it permanent that way I did my high school bully. Use so much *Grey* that it makes him sane."

More *Grey* than he was using now?

No, it wouldn't take this much, would it?

"I would really appreciate that," Carlos said. "You don't know how much he means to me. He's the only family I have left. And if there's anything I can do for you in return…"

"Watch after Junior."

"Okay."

Daniel heard somebody in the bank yell that the vault was open.

"This is my last job," Daniel said, "so I won't be around to watch his back. You can do that for me. Make sure he stays safe and doesn't turn into some mob boss with his powers. And make sure he doesn't get too greedy. He needs to know when enough is enough."

Carlos stared at Daniel for a moment before nodding his head. "He's lucky to have a friend like you."

The front door to the bank opened, allowing two customers to walk in, their body washed with *Grey* before their eyes could process the real world. Seeing the long line from the reality Daniel had created, they were given a choice to stay and wait or to leave.

They both chose to leave.

Greg turned the corner pulling a rolling pallet. On the pallet was a plastic cube filled with stacked bills. Daniel stared at the money stacked neatly in the clear, four-foot by four-foot container.

"We could use some help here," Greg said to Carlos.

Junior followed behind Greg pulling an identical cube. "Are you okay? You holding up?"

Daniel wasn't sure if he responded or not. Junior nodded and turned the corner out of sight, taking the money to the loading area at the bank of the bank where Nicole had parked the van.

One patron in line became tired of waiting and turned to leave. Daniel let her go.

Tiffany passed, toting a bag of money. Daniel kept a path open from the vault to the back, but the amount of *Grey* cascading through the bank was a lot to try to control. He was sure the team was seeing flashes of what the customers saw as they hauled the cash to the van. They didn't react, so he didn't worry too much about it.

Another customer entered the bank.

This feeling of power was hypnotic. It reminded him of the gargoyle spirit in Katrine's headquarters. He imagined this is what it would probably feel like to communicate fully with that spirit.

"We're almost done." Daniel wasn't sure who said that. It was a male voice so Junior, Carlos or Greg.

Probably Junior, trying to direct everything and show he was a leader.

Something tugged at Daniel's attention. The customer that had entered hadn't left, but the waves of *Grey* flowed around him like water around an oil slick. Daniel peered through half cracked eyelids, not remembering when he had closed them, and saw a familiar face standing at the door.

Where had he seen this kid before?

He opened his eyes fully. Greg and Carlos hauling more cash in his peripheral vision. The kid, college age, stared at the scene, eyes frowned.

Daniel recognized him. It was the guy from his first heist, the one that was immune to his reality bending. But he had seen him somewhere else too. In *The Grey* with Javier. Was he a spy? What was he doing here?

The young guys eyes widened with the realization with what was going on. A robbery in progress. He locked eyes with Daniel.

Daniel wasn't sure if the guy recognized him yet, but he could see panic in the young man's eyes. The decision the kid faced was fight or flight.

Shaking his head in warning, Daniel tried to sway the kid from choosing flight.

Junior must have noticed something in Daniel's demeanor. He asked "What's wrong?"

Daniel could see the kid choose to flee and tried to act quickly. Using the eye contact they still held, Daniel reached into the kid's mind and tried to find the hypnotism switch that Carlos had taught him about. But he wasn't quick enough. He didn't have the skill or the experience to hypnotize as quickly as Carlos.

The kid turned, slipping to the floor in his rush, and yelped.

"No." Somebody yelled. Was it Daniel?

The kid looked back over his shoulder, running towards the door. The fear in his eyes too intense to penetrate with hypnotism. This must be what it felt like when Junior tried to control somebody that was feeling an extreme emotion.

A loud bang sounded through the lobby and the sound carried ripples through the ocean of *Grey* filling the room.

Daniel watched the kid fall. The patrons looking around not sure how to interpret the blend of reality caused by the disruption in *Grey Matter*.

What was happening?

Daniel approached the guy, strengthening his hold on his power to keep the customers calm. A pool of red expanded from the spot where the kid had fallen.

The sound had been a gun.

He turned. He spotted the shooter.

Nicole stood braced, legs apart, arms pointed forward, a gun in her hand.

She had fired the gun.

The Belko Experiment, 2016. Employees trapped in their place of employment by an excessive but cinematically necessary security system are given instructions to kill their coworkers if they want to be released. What starts as one murder by an unsuspecting peer explodes into full chaos as each coworker is maimed and dismembered in explosive scenes of violence.

"No," Daniel said.

There wasn't supposed to be any guns involved.

Greg, Carlos and Tiffany rushed from the back to find out the source of the gunshot. They assessed the scene in shock.

"What did you do?" Daniel asked.

"I made sure we didn't get caught," Nicole said.

Daniel squatted down and placed a hand on the guy's chest. There was a rattling noise with each breath and the guy looked around wildly for an explanation as to why he was lying on the floor. Did he realize what had happened? Did he know this was his last moments?

The dying boy sputtered a gasp of blood and began to choke. His blood-filled lungs sounding worse with each breath.

"I'm so sorry," Daniel said. "I'm…"

The pool of blood was getting bigger. It was on Daniel's hands and clothes.

"This wasn't supposed to happen."

"Daniel," A hand on his shoulder.

"I'm so sorry." His voice now a whisper.

"We gotta go," Junior or Carlos was shaking Daniel's shoulder, trying to pull him away from the boy.

Daniel watched the guy's eyes close and the wheezing stop. Something inside Daniel pulled him away from the situation. He rose from the guy's corpse and followed the team out to the van. He climbed into the back next to Carlos with the cubes of stacked bills. Junior in the driver seat, Nicole in the passenger. As planned, Greg and Tiffany would be taking a separate car and meeting the group at the predesignated location. As they drove away, Daniel's hold on the flood of *Grey* within the bank slipped away. He knew that within a few minutes, the scene he had crafted would dissipate, and the customer's would find the recently deceased.

There wouldn't be any record of how the boy had died. No camera footage or witnesses. Others would think the kid had been wounded outside the bank, before he entered.

Junior was controlling Daniel's body or else Daniel would have still been kneeling over a dead body.

"I'm so sorry," he whispered.

Carlos looked at him with concerned.

Daniel was still holding on to a pool of *Grey*, the haze of his power simmering in the van. The group had been sitting outside their predetermined rendezvous, a boarded-up shop, formally an ice cream parlor, for a few minutes, but the only person in the van that didn't realize that they weren't still driving was Daniel. Nicole rotated her hands around the wheel, making a wide left turn.

The van sat unmoving.

Daniel waited seven minutes. He got out of the van and moved around to the driver's door, opening it.

Nicole and the team were visualizing themselves at a red light, anxious and not talking because Daniel was acting weird in the back. Was he traumatized?

Daniel stared into Nicole's eyes and felt for the switch like Carlos had taught him. It was a fumbling effort, but it accomplished the goal he wanted. *The Grey* reacted weirdly to his probing into her mind, but he ignored it. He felt her conscious move into a state of hypnotism before she slumped forward into a hunched position. He repeated the process with Junior and made the pair exit the vehicle.

Carlos would not slip so easily.

Daniel dropped *The Grey* and released the misty haze from around Carlos.

"Where are we?" Carlos asked.

It took him a minute to realize where they were. He assessed the situation after seeing Nicole and Junior standing outside the car, not reacting.

"Get out," Daniel said.

"What are you doing?"

Daniel watched Carlos exit and close the back door. Daniel slid into the driver's seat and rolled down the window.

"Go inside and wait," Daniel said. "Wake up when Carlos says the word popcorn."

Nicole and Junior turned, zombie-like movements, and headed towards the building. Greg and Tiffany would be here soon; the plan called for them to ditch their car.

"You have a choice, Carlos. You can hypnotize them, make them forget this robbery even happened. Or you can tell them I took the money, and you can all come after me."

"Why are you doing this? I didn't think you would be the one to betray us. Seems more like a Nicole thing to do."

"I'm not betraying you. This is blood money. One of my own died today for this money. Y'all don't deserve it."

"Why leave me to witness it? You could've taken this money and erased all our memories."

"I can't hypnotize you. So it's your burden too."

Carlos shook his head, not sure what to do.

"Greg and Tiffany will be here soon," Daniel said. "They are just as complicit in that guy's murder as the rest of us. Make them sleep until you make a decision."

Carlos ran his hands through his hair and looked at the shop door where Nicole and Junior had disappeared. Then he looked back at Daniel.

"What about my brother?" Carlos asked.

Daniel nodded, not sure what he was answering and drove off.

Leprechaun, 1994. When a group of teenagers steal loot from an evil leprechaun, the robbed sprite follows and tracks each member down, exacting revenge in deliciously gory ways on each thief until his pot of gold is recovered.

Daniel didn't look back.

•　•　•　•　•

Daniel had completely disassociated himself from the dilemma. It was as if he were watching a suspenseful thriller at the movies. A bank robber has betrayed his teammates and taken the money. But like all good thrillers, the backstabber failed to eliminate the people involved in the heist. It wouldn't make for a good story if the antagonists were killed so early in the movie. There needs to be a chase.

One hour into the drive, he had turned off his phone, worried that Tiffany, with her tech-savvy talents, would be able to track him by his phone signal. A few minutes later, he had removed the battery and the SIM card. He remembered hearing somewhere that turning off the phone wasn't enough.

With his body on autopilot, he maintained a comfortable speed limit so as not to attract attention from police in the small Texas towns. He had no idea where he was going. He was just driving in a direction, looking to escape from the dying eyes of the young man shot and killed. The scene continued to replay in his mind like a child's favorite movie. Daniel wanted it to stop, but refused to make any effort to make it stop. It was a punishment that he deserved.

Two and a half hours into the drive, he passed through Abilene, his hometown. The thought of stopping to see his dad was fleeting, and he didn't entertain the notion.

When the sun had set, Daniel flicked on his headlights and continued driving, stopping only once for gas, not daring to use his debit card.

The van's gas tank had taken all the cash he had on him. The next stop he would have to dive into the plastic cubes for a withdrawal.

Would the gas attendants be able to tell it was blood money? Would they know the guilt on Daniel's face was from the pain of watching a man whom Daniel was supposed to protetc die? The kid was one of Javier's followers and therefore had the potential to maybe one day depart from Javier and join Daniel. Veronica had done it, so why not?

Long past midnight he reached El Paso, the last town in Texas. Daniel knew this was a fork in the road where he would have to decide where his destination was. Driving blindly through Texas could last you twelve hours because the state was so big. But once he crossed state lines, he needed to have an end goal.

He could break south and cross the border into Mexico. Having never been outside of the country, this seemed more daunting than it should have. Or he could continue on the interstate and make his way to California, maybe detour through Phoenix.

The opposing options played a game of tug-of-war in his mind, and he knew his characteristic flaw of indecisiveness had reared its head and happily married his mental weariness. It was late, and he was tired. He needed to find a hotel for the night. Without cash, he would have to use his power to 'persuade' the clerk to give him a room.

Next thing Daniel remembered was opening his eyes to sunshine. He hadn't made it to the hotel.

The van was parked in an empty parking lot of a church. The city's morning activities had commenced, and a flutter of passersby wandered past via the sidewalk.

He rubbed his eyes and rolled down the window, allowing some of the stale air out and a fresh breeze to help cool the hot interior of the vehicle. On the other side of the parking lot was a charity center with the logo for Abraham's Children and next to that a recreational center. From what Daniel remembered, Abraham's Children was a charity organization run by nuns and priests dedicated to providing services to the community. It was similar to the Salvation Army or the American Red Cross.

Daniel wondered if this were coincidence that he was here. This would definitely be a way for him to atone for yesterday's sin.

As if on standby, the face of the slain kid flashed through his mind.

He started the engine. He couldn't help but notice the gas tank was below a quarter. Reversing the van into the alley behind the building, he looked around to see if he was noticed. Nobody paid him any attention. A school bus passed, and a mother waved at a child peering from its window.

Exiting the van, he opened the back door to give him room to push the money-filled plastic cubes from the van. The rollers on the bottom of each cube made them easy to roll out. The loud bang as each one hit the pavement seemed to echo against the building wall. They should be safe here until somebody from Abraham's Children found them. Or maybe somebody in the city would find them and think they hit the lottery. Daniel didn't care.

After pushing two or three cubes out of the van, Daniel realized he would have to push them away from the van to make room for the others. None of them landed on the rollers so the sound of friction created from the plastic scraping against concrete grated against his ears. The task was tedious… and loud.

With one cube left in the van, the squeal of a door hinge in the alley caught his attention and by reflex, he weaved a spool of *Grey* through the alley to change his appearance.

It was a woman in a religious tunic, her hair veiled in matching cloth.

"Good morning," she said.

Daniel nodded and pulled more *Grey* to cover the van. But she had already noticed it, her eyes peering at the open van doors and trailing along the scattered cubes on the ground, two of them cracked from the fall.

"Making an anonymous drop-off?" She smiled.

He nodded again, not sure how much she had seen. "I didn't want…" He wasn't sure how to explain.

"I understand. My name is Fernanda."

"Sister Fernanda. I'm… Sebastian."

"Just Fernanda. Do you want to come inside?"

"No." His tone harsher than he intended.

Daniel dropped the illusion around the cubes on the ground and allowed her the full scope of what he was hiding.

Her face maintained a mask of non-reaction which surprised him more than anything. She took a step forward to get a better look before pasting the smile back on her face.

"That's a lot of money. Dollars or pesos?"

"You don't seem too surprised."

"We can't hide this for you if that's what you're looking to accomplish. We're not that kind of organization."

"I'm not trying to stash it. It's stained… and I think the only way to clean it is if it goes to something good."

"Are you also stained?"

"Yes."

"Would you like to come inside? Maybe we can pray. Brother Antonio wakes early so I'm sure he's available…"

"No, I can't stay."

She took a step forward and brushed her fingers across Daniel's cheek. "Everything will be okay. The fact that you still feel guilt means you have a soul worth saving. Don't ever stop listening to that guilt. When you stop listening, that's when your soul dies."

Daniel took a step back, his chest heaving in anguish. He stared in her eyes in disbelief. The desire to ask how she knew he was hurting played on his tongue. But the look in her eyes told him everything he needed to know. She was taking in the scenario, the van and the cubes of money, and knew that he had to be in some sort of trouble.

This time, quicker than his effort with the murdered boy in the bank, he reached into her eyes. He found the switch within a moment and turned it on, slipping her consciousness into a state of suggestiveness. *Grey Matter* was used to hide the present but hypnotism could be used to hide the past. He needed her to forget he was ever there. And also wanted to make sure the money was used for something good. He couldn't risk her turning it over to the police.

But in that moment, something happened that he hadn't intended. Her eyes drank in the scene he had created with *Grey*, similar to how Carlos' brother had absorbed his power. The pool of *Grey* he had been holding snapped into a single line of focus and tethered her to him.

She looked confused for a second, then the smile reappeared and she curtsied.

"My Prince," she said.

His hold on the *Grey* was gone, but somehow Daniel knew she saw something different than what was actually there. The line between them, a black thread entwined with silver, fed her the image he wanted her to see, the reality he wanted her to experience.

He was her Prince of Veils, this woman of a religious order.

"Fernanda?"

"I can make sure the money is taken care of. We will put it to good use. We've received large donations before, not this big, but still large."

"And you don't turn it in to the police?"

"If we were to turn in every donation that we suspected to be crime revenue, we would be bankrupt within a year. We don't turn away what the Lord has chosen to provide."

"That's… good to know."

"I will need to call some of the other sisters to help me bring it inside."

Their new connection changed her. He could not only see the change in her, he could feel it. He could feel her.

She was malleable. She was willing. She was eager to please him.

"Yeah, they're really heavy," Daniel said. "Sorry to just dump them like this."

Fernanda placed her hand on his arm and looked up. "I'm telling you about the sisters so you know you should leave if you do not want to be seen. I know you wanted to do this anonymously, My Prince."

She was his servant.

Daniel nodded, understanding. After closing the van doors, the one cube of money still perched in the back, he climbed back in the van and looked at Fernanda through his side view mirror. Her smile lessened a little but the genuineness in her eyes remained as she allowed her gaze to gather all the cubes strewn along the ground. He leaned out of the window and craned his neck around to speak.

"Can you make sure that the ladies send a prayer up for somebody I recently lost?"

"Yes, what was their name?"

Daniel remembered the nerdy college kid introducing himself to the distracted jock before their FoodHub delivery.

"Eric."

●   ●   ●   ●   ●

"Cousin Daniel, it's about time you got here."

Daniel stared at the enthusiastic man and let his newly discovered power do what he needed it to do.

The Hispanic man ushered Daniel inside the house and pulled him into the kitchen. "Look who's here."

A plump woman and two kids looked up from their activities in confusion, labeling Daniel as a stranger. Individually, Daniel covered them in a wash of *Grey* and pulled a tug of hypnotism. The result was instantaneous as a sense of recognition snapped into their eyes. They were connected to him now, just as Sister Fernanda was. He controlled them.

The woman, most likely the man's wife, rushed over and hugged Daniel, her arms squeezing him in a motherly manner. She looked up at him and smiled. "We are glad you're here. Hector has been talking all week about you coming to town."

"How long has it been since we've seen you?" Hector asked. "Wait until you see how big the kids have gotten. Kids, come say hello to your cousin Daniel."

Daniel wasn't in the mood to play pretend just for a place to sleep. All he wanted was to be shown a bed and find some solitude.

"No, Hector, Daniel is probably tired," the wife said. "I should get the guest room ready so he can rest. I'm so embarrassed that I didn't do that sooner. You would think we haven't been expecting him for weeks. I need to change the sheets and…"

"You don't have to do all that," Daniel said, his voice dry. "Just show me to the room, and I'll be good."

"Did you have any luggage? Is the truck outside waiting to be paid?"

The guy outside was a stranger Daniel had used to hitchhike the four and a half hours to Tucson after ditching the van in El Paso. Daniel hadn't consciously made the guy wait, but the truck driver had known what Daniel had subconsciously wanted.

Daniel didn't have any luggage, but the case of money was in the back of the stranger's truck. The drive through the mountainous region had been silent, per Daniel's mental request, so they hadn't even exchanged names.

"I can get the luggage," Hector said.

Hector would see the cube of money as a trunk of luggage. The stranger would assist, making sure Hector would store the money somewhere safe and away from prying eyes. With everything situated and Daniel settled, the stranger could return to El Paso or where ever it was he was heading when he picked Daniel up.

On the short tour through the house, Daniel could see how expensive some of the decor was and knew he had chosen a good place to rest. It would have been a house that Nicole would choose for a job.

Lying on the bed, Daniel took his phone and SIM card out of his pocket and placed them next to him. He wondered if he was being paranoid about Tiffany's phone tracing abilities.

This place would be a temporary visit; he didn't plan on staying more than a day or two. His decision on a more permanent place could come later. With that in mind, he could turn on his phone and make some calls, be gone before anybody could make it to Tucson to find him. But if they found out he was in Tucson, then they would know he was heading west. California would be the obvious destination.

"Throw them off track and head north instead?"

Daniel fell asleep before he made a decision, waking to find the room darker and both the phone and the SIM card on the floor.

He picked it up, placing the card into the slot and powered on the phone. Within a minute, the phone vibrated with the influx of missed texts and voicemails. Everybody was apparently looking for him.

Ignoring the texts, he played the first voicemail. "I dropped the ball." It was Carlos. "I could've made them all forget about the robbery, but I took too long to make a decision. I was questioning what you were really up to. Greg and Tiffany wanted to… I'm still here with them. They kept asking me about what you said. I told them most of it, but I'm not sure what you wanted me to say and what you wanted me to keep secret. Call me back. Let me know how you want me to play this. I want to get my brother back to normal, so I'm on your side or whatever. Loyalty amongst thieves, huh?"

Daniel deleted the message and moved to the next one.

"What the fuck?" It was Junior. "Where are you? Are you crazy? Is this about the guy in the bank or were you planning this the entire time? You need to call-"

Delete.

"Daniel. This is Alexandre. Just checking in on you. You said you wouldn't be gone long, but it's been a few hours.

And the news is talking about a… *death* at one of the banks. Me and Oscar are worried, so call us back and let us know you are okay. Don't forget we have a dinner with the new followers tonight. I think we need to talk about some things afterward…"

Delete.

"Where the fuck are you? If you don't bring that money back we're going to have a big fucking problem, bro."

Delete.

Delete.

Delete.

Daniel got the general idea on what the next few messages from Junior were going to be like.

"Hey, Daniel." It was Veronica. "We missed you at the dinner last night. Alexandre and Oscar left to look for you. We found a way to view the body of the deceased guy at the bank. We were relieved it wasn't you under the sheet. But you still have us a little worried. We're trying to piece together what happened but… Call me back and let me know you're okay. We're worried."

Delete.

"One thing I refuse to be taken for is a fool." It was Nicole. "You played this pretty cool. I was so busy watching Junior with his aspirations of graduating to upper management that I was blind to the weasel in my own company. I have to commend you though; you are a more skillful player than I took you for. I guess that's just a part of the game. But it's not checkmate yet because I know what your weakness is. I know who I can hurt that will also hurt you. I'm going to start there and see if I can flush you out. Bring me the money or he dies. I'm giving you an hour to call me back."

Daniel frowned. She wouldn't hurt Junior, would she? He was one of her most valuable employees. The message was more than 12 hours old, so he continued to the next recording.

"Alexandre is missing." It was Oscar. "I'm not sure if this has anything to do with you being missing too, but we are going to find him. We have voodoo on our side. We know the general location of where he's at. It would be nice if you would help us. It does not look good for one of your seigneurs to go missing, and you do not help us retrieve him. I will only keep everybody from knowing about your absence for so long."

Delete.

"I warned you what would happen if you didn't respond. Your hour is up. I hope you cleared up the disagreement you had with this Italian stallion before you ran off with my money."

Next message.

"Daniel…" It was Veronica. "I'm sorry. We didn't get to Alexandre in time." A long pause and sniffle. "Oscar wanted revenge, but I talked him out of it. He's taking the body back to Italy. He said it's where Alexandre would want…"

There was a muffled few words and a scuffle across the mic. A new voice spoke. "We talked about this. You made it seem like you understood what we were trying to tell you." Regina's voice was loud with anger. Daniel pulled the phone away from his ear. "The tarot said not to run and you ran anyway. Why would you run?"

She sobbed into the phone. Daniel could hear Veronica speaking words to comfort her.

"Daniel, they have Clyde," Veronica said, answered by a long wail in the background that Daniel assumed was Regina. "We need you to come back and fix this before they… before he… call me."

Next message.

"I guess you didn't care too much about your Italian lover. So we've moved on to your mentor, Clyde I think his name is. Maybe hearing him scream will move a little bit more empathy in your heart and have you BRING OUR MONEY BACK."

A cascade of screams from Clyde's torture.

Next message.

266

"You need to bring the money back, dude." It was Junior. "She's not going to stop. Just… tell me where I can meet you and get the money, and I promise you won't get hurt. I'll make sure of it. Just… call me back, please."

Next message.

"We're relocating to a different location. We need to decide what to do." It was Veronica. "I didn't plan on assuming a leadership role but with you gone and Oscar gone and Alexandre… We need to do something because we have power and we need to use it. Let me know if you plan on fighting for this or if you've given up. Because I don't want to fight for something that you are never coming back to. We can count our loses now, but some of your followers can't go back to where they came from."

Delete.

"Hey, this is Carlos." It was Carlos. "My brother is getting pretty bad. I need your help… Look, I did everything you wanted me to do. I think I've proven that I'm with you. What more do you want?…" A short silence, Daniel could hear sirens in the background. "Please, just help me out. I don't care about the money or what beef you have with Nicole… All I care about is Antonio… I wasn't involved with anything that they did to your friends. I've walked away. I didn't sign up for this. Nicole is mad, and she's on a rampage about that money."

There was a long pause. Daniel could hear a soft sigh on the other end.

"Don't forget about what I told you about her weakness. Find out who Smitty is."

Delete.

Daniel didn't want to hear any more. He pushed past the text notifications and additional voicemails, tossing the cell phone on the bed.

Alexandre was dead. Clyde was most likely dead too.

It was all his fault.

He closed his eyes, shutting out everything and trying to focus on what he could do. People who had chosen to follow him were in danger, something he should have considered. What kind of leader was he if he put himself before everybody else?

Daniel felt the answer to his call roll across the city like thunder. The walls vibrated and the sky hummed. The pressure of the rumbling mental rush was familiar. He knew this spirit. He had communed with it before.

Domza'in.

He could feel its presence approaching from somewhere beyond and knew that it was moving within *The Grey* also. And if he could feel it in the real world then what did it feel like there?

Domza'in, the dark stone creature with the insect face.

Daniel stepped out of the bedroom and faced the empty hallway. There was a light from a television beaming from underneath a door, the rest of the upstairs was silent.

He pushed his desire to remain undisturbed through the tether connections and raced down the stairs. He reached the entrance to the house and flung the door open, expecting to see a torrent of rain or a wave of rolling clouds. The atmosphere felt tornadic, and the building tension made his head ache.

Dusk had settled on Tucson, the glaze of purple and orange hues painting a romantic view in the cloudless sky.

The tension continued to build. Daniel had called it, and he didn't know how to stop it. Secretly, he didn't want to stop it. Daniel could recall the addictive power he had tasted in Madame Comtois' cathedral. He wanted to savor it again.

The rumbling grew heavier. The taste of buzzing air coated the back of his throat.

The headache sharpened and felt like it was piercing his eyes. He fell to the floor and cupped his hands over his ears. That didn't help.

He could feel the dissonance in his bones.

The sound and sense of movement coalesced and stopped. The sudden silence caused Daniel to rise and stumble backward through the door. He stopped as silent lightning flashed outside, silhouetting the shadowed figure.

The winged gargoyle statue with the stone skin that drank light stood towering over him in the doorway.

Domza'in was here.

• • • • •

Daniel stared at the gargoyle statue in awe. He had called it, and it had answered. He could feel the vibration of its power humming through the tile on the floor, buzzing through the walls and drizzling from the ceiling.

Domza'in. That was its name.

It was more powerful than Ghiy-āthu'd-Dīn, definitely stronger than the *voleur*. Daniel felt fear but couldn't stop himself from being fascinated. It had felt his desire and came. It didn't speak to him the way the *voleur* did, but he knew it was calling to him, offering to help him.

Daniel wanted to avenge the death of his follower, Alexandre, and Domza'in had answered. All Daniel needed to do was accept.

Contrary to his character, Daniel didn't take a moment to consider what he was accepting or what Domza'in was offering. He embraced the offer and gave himself to the black stone creature.

Its mind enveloped him, pulling him downward in a rush of mental confusion. Its power held a familiar taste, and Daniel savored it, his previous fear gone. The delicious flow of liquid stone didn't give Daniel time to be fearful. It was overwhelming.

Daniel's senses expanded, riding the awareness of Domza'in, and he felt his mind explode into a million pieces. Each piece assembled into individual sparks and developed senses of their own. Together the pieces formed a collective unit that worked as single entity that imitated a network of nerves.

Damza'in called to the scattered pieces, and they turned to him, aware of his command. They were a hive network of bees. There were bumblebees, honey bees, carpenter bees, and more. Daniel opened his mouth to speak, to ask a question to Damza'in, but either the hive ignored him, or the words never left. Instead, a signal sent, an image from Daniel's mind that vibrated through the network and instructed the hive to search. Daniel felt a moment of confusion, but within moments, the object was located.

Nicole had been found.

A new command: Swarm and gather.

The bees obeyed. It was an appendage that Daniel could physically feel. Domza'in wanted to close its fist, and as a result, the bees coalesced into a central place. They condensed into the area where Nicole was.

Daniel skimmed down the network, moving his awareness down the connection the bees had with Domza'in. It was similar to the network he had formed with the family he was staying with, a parasitic connection that could be used.

He stored this information away for later as he settled into the mind of an insect. He could see Nicole. She was in front of a building. The receptors in the bee weren't enough to distinguish where they were, but the image became clearer as more bees gathered in the area, each one contributing to the collective image. Their antennae collecting smells and vibrations to enhance the image, catching information that Daniel would not have been able to gather from sight. The colors were different, not the normal visual range that Daniel's mind could interpret.

The swarm was gathering, taking to dark corners and alleys. They were compiling an army before attacking.

Daniel stood with them, determined to get revenge. His mind flickered to Alexandre, and the image floated along the hive network. The memory of Alexandre's lifeless body being pulled from a river was passed from bee to bee. They had seen him.

This made Daniel more furious, a sense of sadness swallowed by anger.

The swarm buzzed in response, and Nicole looked up. There was enough of them that she could hear them. They numbered in the hundreds if not thousands. Passersby watched in awe.

There wasn't any time to wait for more bees from the network to gather, Nicole had been alerted to the forthcoming danger. The swarm was waiting for a bigger gathering, but Nicole had her seer powers on her side.

Daniel's thoughts on the situation were communicated along the network. If Daniel knew, then the bees knew, and Damza'in knew. Damza'in attacked, sending the swarm of bees as a mighty fist towards Nicole. But she was already fleeing, her body moving away from the danger.

Thousands of legs detached from walls and trees. They focused on the target, ignoring the screaming onlookers who fled in terror from the sudden explosion of insects.

Nicole disappeared inside a building. The swarm collided with a clear barrier. A glass door stood between Daniel and his revenge.

She had escaped the swarm. Daniel thought about possible entrances. The air ducts or an open door. Parts of the swarm peeled away to check other possible entrances.

A thought of vague familiarity traveled up the network. It plagued the bees and caused them to shiver in response. Damza'in turned to Daniel, even trapped in the network he could feel the statue turn its attention to him. A stray thought wiggled from Daniel's memory, and the sense of recognition blossomed within the system of insects.

The individuals Nicole had been talking to were recognized. They were also a part of the problem. If Domza'in could not get revenge *on* Nicole, he would get it *from* her.

By Domza'in's command, the swarm turned. Two individuals, male and female stood staring at the building

Nicole had entered. As if they could sense the change in wind, they turned to flee.

No, Daniel urged, *Not them.*

No acknowledgment came from Domza'in. It was hungry, and the bees answered only to it.

The swarm caught the first target within seconds, the weaker individual, a female. The first aggressive stings biting into her flesh as she swatted in pain, her sprinting legs not faltering. More bees followed, planting their legs against her skin and inserting stinger to inject venom, then tearing away their abdomen to leave behind the injector pulsing on her body. The sound of her screams touched their antennae. Members of the swarm that had stung her flew away to their deaths; job accomplished.

No, she isn't a part of this. Please, leave her alone, Daniel begged.

They engulfed her, overtaking her feeble attempt to evade Domza'in's punishment.

She stumbled, using more energy to try to swipe the swarm off her than in running away.

Her companion, the fleeing male, received his first bite of Daniel's vengeance. The swarm had reached him.

Daniel tried to disconnect from the swarm, move back into his body. But he was locked in. While not an individual member of the hive, his awareness was entangled with theirs, locked like fibers in a blanket. The time and ability it would take to unravel the thread of his mind from theirs were beyond him.

The woman, covered in bees, screamed in agony. Each bee in the flood delivered their venom and flew away one by one, only to be replaced by another bee, ready to deliver more poison. They interpreted her open mouth as an invitation and swarmed into her throat, delivering pinpricks of pain.

The man flung his arms at the bees, his body releasing pulses of fear pheromones. But the bees could see movement better than they could see stillness. The target couldn't hit them and was wasting energy. More bees caught up to him and began the same process as Domza'in had commanded with the female.

Daniel pulled his mind, willing to accept insanity from a ripped mental state than to have to watch more of this. He could feel the pulse as a wave of satisfaction flowed up the network to Domza'in. The female had been killed. The death fed Domza'in.

With a feeling of helplessness, Daniel wrestled for control of the hive. The swarm was starting to cover the male, his screams just as loud as the female's.

The crowd of onlookers reacted differently from the audience that had surrounded the female. Instead of gawking in horror, they tried to help, taking swats at the swarm with clothing and articles.

The bees twitched, using outlier members to retaliate against the strangers.

The hive was unmanageable. Daniel couldn't control them. Domza'in was in command. They wouldn't respond to Daniel's pleas.

He wept internally and reached for the male.

The male tossed on the ground in pain. The bees swarmed into his mouth, traveling down the moist interior before stinging.

Daniel felt the man die.

Domza'in swallowed the bees' gift and turned its attention on Daniel.

The focus of the gargoyle made Daniel nervous. The bees, located in Dallas, turned their attention to the West, slightly North, a line of sight to Tucson, Arizona. Daniel felt the hum of the stone statue, which he now understood to be the buzz of bees.

It stared back at him, unmoving.

He was back in the foyer, staring at the marble gargoyle. Daniel had fallen onto his back and from his viewpoint on the floor, the stone statue looked even bigger than before.

Greg and Tiffany were dead.

Feeling the gorge rising, he slid away, and heaved, his hands pressed against the cold tile floor. He hadn't eaten, so it was with dry heaves that his body tried to purge itself of the experience in the hive network.

The stone statue smirked and licked its lips.

• • • • •

Daniel wasn't sure when he finally fell asleep. His body was tired, but his mind wouldn't stop replaying the scene of Tiffany and Greg being killed by the bee swarm. The feeling of depression regarding the murder at the bank was multiplied with the grief from Nicole's employees. They were not his intended target for revenge. But Damza'in had taken it into his own hands on how to delve out punishment.

The thought of the stone statue sitting in the lobby made Daniel open his eyes. The large window in the bedroom allowed the sunlight to brighten the room with a cheerful glow.

He hadn't wanted to be disturbed, and the parasitic connection with the members of the house made everyone aware of his wants. It didn't create any alternative reality to push this information. Subconsciously, they knew. And so, Daniel could hear them shuffling and gathering personal items to leave the house. Their excuse would be they had errands to run or people to visit.

A barrage of missed calls and texts informed Daniel his actions weren't secret. There was small news coverage of the bee attack, and it didn't take much for Veronica to figure out this wasn't ordinary.

Daniel sighed and pressed the call button.

The phone rang.

Junior answered but didn't say anything.

Daniel waited. He could hear voices in the background. None of them sounded like Nicole.

"They didn't deserve that," Junior said.

"Neither did Alexandre and Clyde."

"I didn't have anything to do with that. I tried to call and warn you what you did wasn't cool."

"It might not have been your finger on the trigger, but you had just as much a hand in their death as Nicole. If you sat and watched, then you are complicit in their murders."

"If that's true, then what responsibility do you take with the guy at the bank? You were there. I don't see you turning yourself in?"

"His death is the reason nobody has the haul from the job. None of you deserve that money. None of *us* deserve to reap those rewards. That was an innocent man."

"Where is the money, Daniel?"

"You'll never see it. Especially since you can't accept responsibility for your actions. Have you thought about the consequences for the things that you do? It's like you don't ever think about how your actions affect other people."

"If you called to lecture me on how to be an adult then this conversation is over. I just need to know where the money is. This can all stop here."

"The money is gone. I burned it."

"I don't believe you."

"Then go find out for yourself. The van is probably still smoking outside the city limits of Clovis, New Mexico."

"Is that where you are? New Mexico?"

"No, I'm in Tucson. But I'll be gone by the time you get here," Daniel said.

"You talk about me not accepting responsibility. Have you looked at the fact that you run from your problems? If you really wanted to show some maturity, you would come back and face the situation. It isn't going to stop. Nicole isn't going to just let this go. You stole money from her, and now you *killed* two of her employees."

"I'm not scared of Nicole."

Junior sighed, the noise in the background had faded. He was somewhere private now.

"Look," Junior said. "We were friends. I don't know if we'll ever get back to that place, but I still have enough compassion for you to try to help make this right. I don't want to see anybody else get hurt. To be honest, I really don't see the point in dragging this out. I mean, why? I'm trying to act as a liaison here and find a way to mediate between you both. I understand it was an eye for an eye, so let's say the score is tied and everybody is even. Bring us the money, we can split Tiffany and Greg's share..."

"Junior, there is no money."

"I don't believe you. Nobody takes millions of dollars to the desert and burns it. You want me to believe you burned it all?"

Daniel thought about the single case of money sitting downstairs. Probably about four hundred thousand dollars.

"How does this end?" Daniel asked.

"This ends with either you bringing us the money or more of your friends ending up dead."

"Leave them out of this. Let's keep this between me and you. If you want the money then you'll have to kill me."

"Name the time and place."

"I can be back in Dallas by tonight. I'll bring the cash, and we can fight for it. Winner take all."

"Fight? You really want to fight the son of a professional boxer?"

"I'm not talking about a fight with our hands, Junior. I'm talking about a show of power... just me and you. I'll show up with my *tarot cards* and my *dolls* and my *bees* and my ability to warp your reality. And you'll show up and try to stop my heart or collapse my lungs before I get a chance to use these things to kill you."

The phone was silent.

Daniel pictured Junior thinking about the way Greg and Tiffany had died. He was weighing his options and deciding what his chances were that he could win a fight against the Prince of Veils. Daniel could imagine that a power-driven fight two months ago would be advantageous for

Junior, but now they both had a glimpse of the things Daniel could do. But there was also the added bonus of Nicole and her seer sense. She could tip the scales in Junior's favor.

"When and where?" Junior asked.

"Klyde Warren Park. Midnight."

"I'll be there."

Daniel ended the call. He popped his head out the door to catch the teenage son before he vacated the house as everyone else had previously done.

"Can you drive?" Daniel asked.

"Yes."

"Do you have a credit card?"

"Yes."

"Good. I need you to take me to the airport. Look for any non-stop flight to Dallas that can arrive by this afternoon."

Daniel left the boy to his task and went back into guest bedroom to handle one more task. The plastic cube of money would stay here. Whether he lived or died, he refused to let Junior and Nicole have that money. Leaving it here ensured they would never find it.

He placed his hand on the dresser mirror and took a deep breath, his mind still heavy with grief over the deaths of so many people.

A dark smudge lingering in the reflection coalesced into a shadowed form.

"You're stronger," it said.

Daniel nodded. "I need contact information for a guy named Smitty."

CHAPTER NINE

Daniel spent the two-and-a-half hours flight from Tucson to Dallas planning how to end this battle with Junior and Nicole. As much as he didn't want any more deaths on his hands, he knew it would be the only way to survive. Junior was determined to reclaim the money. Their friendship had been dismantled over money and the blood of an innocent man.

While waiting for his flight to board, Daniel had a conversation with the man named Smitty who had been very interested to learn that Nicole was in Dallas. He agreed to help Daniel put a stop to her crime spree. Especially since he had been looking for her for quite some time.

Smitty could handle Nicole, and Daniel could handle Junior. It was the best course of action to ensure Daniel's followers weren't caught in the crossfire. Daniel told Smitty, who had been located in St. Louis, the time and the place Junior had agreed to meet. Daniel was more than positive that Nicole would show up to help Junior reclaim the money. If by small chance she didn't, Daniel could find her. He wasn't worried about that.

He was worried if he had the courage and determination to kill Junior.

Landing in Dallas, he found a house on the west side of downtown to rest for a bit, using the same method of manipulation he had in Tucson.

Even without untethering himself from the nun El Paso and the family in Arizona, he didn't feel overwhelmed or burdened from the use of his power. While he could feel his connection to the members of his web, at this distance, he couldn't tell more than in what general direction they were positioned.

Hours before their scheduled battle, Daniel took a bus to the designated meeting point. He wanted to clear the park of any innocent bystanders before things got too extreme. The confrontation needed to be between him and Junior, nobody else. It wasn't hard to imagine Junior and Nicole using innocent people to distract Daniel.

After clearing the park, Daniel planned on calling on as much *Grey* as he could possibly manage. The volume of *Grey* at their last bank heist was more than he had ever held, but he knew that wasn't his limit.

Tonight, he would explore what a fully realized Prince of Veils could do.

With enough *Grey Matter*, Daniel could warp the minds of both Nicole and Junior. He had seen what a pool size amount had done to his high school bully, Chris. Imagine what a lake of it could do to two people.

The bus was crowded with passengers. Daniel had chosen the wrong time to try to commute downtown. He figured there must be a special event going on to explain the crowds. That would hopefully make clearing the park easier, if everybody was already headed somewhere else more special. He hoped the event wasn't at the park.

Daniel stared out the window and watched the stream of people, hoping the bus didn't get crowded to the point where he would have to give up his seat for a woman or elderly person. The bus braked at a corner stop to allow some people to get off and some to get on.

In a state of reverie and planning, an odd sense of familiarity washed through Daniel as a pair of eyes outside the bus window latched on to his. A single passerby, standing on the street waiting to cross, glanced at Daniel. The realization took a second, but then it dawned on Daniel who was staring back at him from outside the window. The recognition blossomed in Junior's hazel eyes at the same moment. There was a pause before either reacted.

Daniel threw himself to the floor, breaking the line of sight. But not before Junior's first wave of attack hit. Daniel felt a wave of dizziness, and a burning tingle sliced up his shoulder.

He pulled from *The Grey* and flooded the bus with it. He didn't have time to draw the passengers into a hypnotic state, choosing instead, with a moment's decision, to make them as fearful of Junior as Daniel was. He gave them the reality that Junior was a terrorist, a active shooter, a mass murderer, whatever scenario they needed to defend the bus.

The bus driver took his foot off the brake, slamming the bus door shut. The bus tires squealed as the vehicle pulled forward a couple of yards before coming back to a stop. The driver put the vehicle in park and opened the door. The patrons yelled in terror, trying to decide how to react to the driver allowing a way for the killer, hijacker, demon to enter the bus.

Junior had control of the bus driver.

Grey Matter flooded the bus and poured into the street and onto the sidewalk. Junior stepped into the bus, scanning the passengers for Daniel's face.

The false reality enveloped Junior, and Daniel used it to his advantage. To Junior, everybody on the bus would look the same. There was no way to tell anybody apart. Every face staring back at him was Daniel's.

This didn't stop Junior. He turned his attention to the approximate area where he had spotted Daniel and lashed out. The man in the seat in front of Daniel clutched his chest and fell to the side. The woman next to the fallen man grabbed her head with both hands and began to scream.

Panic bubbled up amongst the other passengers. A few reacted with hostility and rushed Junior.

Junior's hold on the driver was released. The man took a swing at Junior, his fist connecting with the back of Junior's head.

Daniel crawled forward, keeping the reality that he was invisible, but wanting to escape the area where Junior had seen him seated.

The *voleur* called out to Daniel. Asking for instructions or directions.

Junior turned again to the driver. The man slumped to the floor, his head hitting a metal rail on the way down.

More *Grey* washed through the bus. Daniel used it to shut down Junior's sense of sight and hearing.

Two passengers reached Junior and grabbed his arms, taking him to the floor.

But in less of a second, Junior stood up. The pair of passengers remained down.

People screamed in fury, seeing their fellow passengers killed. A new determination to fight against Junior rose through their emotions.

A younger man, standing over Daniel, dropped to the floor, his torso landing on Daniel. The dead weight kept him from moving any closer to Junior. The man's eyes were wide with pain as he screamed from the torture.

Even without sight, Junior was killing people. He could still use his power.

More *voleur* called to Daniel. Their cries loud with a desire to be used.

Daniel couldn't process the situation and fight at the same time.

More passengers dropped before they could reach Junior. And Daniel felt the slow burn of pain enter his body.

His left side became numb. The pain in his shoulder faded away. He couldn't move his arm, and his left eyelid slid close.

Junior had unknowingly found him.

Daniel pushed more power into the cramped bus, past the fallen strangers. He mentally scrambled for anything that would help. But with the numbness from the attack also came an inability to concentrate and think.

He was trapped. The last passenger dropped at Junior's feet, weakly batting his arm in a last desperate attempt to fight. Daniel tried to speak, but his mouth was unresponsive. It felt loose as if the muscles in his lips were gone.

Daniel refused to give up and decided his option would be to run. His spirit tugged away from his dying body with the intention to enter *The Grey*. The little slice of fight left in him reached towards Junior. Daniel wrapped his senses around Junior like a leash and yanked. He would bring Junior to *The Grey* too.

Junior's body crumpled to the floor.

Daniel's world faded to black.

● ● ● ● ●

Daniel found himself in *The Grey*. His senses were still alert. The adrenaline in his veins was sharp despite the dull atmosphere.

He set out on a mission to find Junior. They were in Daniel's territory now. He didn't have any doubt the scales of this fight were in his favor.

We live to serve.

We're here to please.

We aim to fulfill your desires.

"Find him," Daniel commanded.

The figures raced off in all directions. Daniel shifted himself from one location to another, aiding in the search.

Junior would be lost, confused. It was an advantage Daniel needed.

Unintentionally, Daniel found himself in front of the dilapidated theater house. Veronica stood waiting.

They stared at each other, not speaking.

"You're alive," she said, breaking the silence.

"For now." He approached her, his senses still cast around in hopes of finding Junior. "Is everybody else safe?"

"Everybody is gone."

"I'm sorry that I ran. I…"

"I know."

"I don't think I was ready. Javier tried to tell me that, but…"

"It's okay. The important thing is that you're safe."

"I'm not safe. He's here. I still haven't finished this."

"Who's here?"

"Junior. I pulled him into *The Grey*. Now I have the advantage and…"

"No, he's not here. You can't pull somebody into *The Grey*."

"But,… I pulled him out of his body. I felt him leave it. He has to be here."

"Do you remember the story I told you about my husband?"

Daniel took a moment to think. The dots connecting in his head. "Yes."

She smiled, but sympathy remained in her eyes. Daniel could see the sympathy in her face.

"You can leave him there," she said. "But then you'll be just as imprisoned as he is."

"I'm so tired. I'm so, so tired."

Veronica nodded and opened her arms. Daniel embraced her and sobbed. They weren't real tears; this astral plane didn't allow small quirks like that. But the feeling of release was genuine. With each heaving sigh, Daniel felt a wave of cleansing wash over him.

Embarrassed, but feeling better, Daniel released Veronica. She nodded to him, and he left *The Grey*.

Daniel opened his eyes and looked around the drab room. The cream and olive colored walls reflected the dull sheen of fluorescent lights. He lifted his arm to find an IV sticking from his vein. His head pulsed with a dull ache. The sound of shoes passing by the door made him turn his head. As a result of the sharp movement, pain thundered through his body. His neck was stiff, and his arm bruised.

Where was Junior?

Struggling on weak legs, he rose from the bed, snatching the IV out of his arm, and shuffled towards the door. His personal items were on a table next to his bed. He snatched up his keys, wallet and cell phone, holding them in his hand.

A quick glance out the window notified him it was night time. Daniel wondered how long he had been out. If it was night time then maybe only a few hours. Hopefully, it wasn't days later.

He left the room and approached the nurses' station. A pair of nurses were chuckling over a shared conversation. As they looked up, Daniel's power acted with reflex, snatching them into his web. They responded to his inquiry without him having to speak it aloud.

"Room 475," the male nurse said.

"Take this hallway around the corner, take a left after the elevator bank, and a right at the end of that hallway," the female nurse said.

Daniel didn't bother providing a false quip of gratitude. He dragged his feet along the tile, his hospital robe swaying against each knee, his feet covered in only socks. His left arm and leg were numb and didn't respond to his mental commands as they should have. The journey took incredibly long, multiple nurses passing by him along the way. He used the *Grey* to encourage them to ignore him. They were minor obstacles to his end goal.

He reached Room 475 and turned the door handle with a touch of caution, hoping to be as silent as possible, taking a peek inside.

Inside, Junior slept on the bed, a multitude of tubes and monitors connected to his body. The room was silent despite the fact hospitals on television portrayed a comatose patient as a constant rhythm of heart monitors and EKG machines. A female figure sat in a chair next to the bed. Her head was slumped into Junior's lap. Her eyes were closed.

Daniel closed the door with the same slow stealth in which he had opened it. Junior would not be waking up, but Nicole was still a threat.

He unlocked his phone and selected the intended contact.

The phone rang.

"What happened? Where are you?" The man said.

"There was an incident. Change in plan. I'm at the hospital. Nicole is here too."

"Which hospital?"

Daniel wasn't sure. He stopped a passing nurse.

"Which hospital is this?" A touch of *Grey* helped to not make him look so crazy by asking this.

"Baylor."

"I'm at Baylor," Daniel said, dismissing the nurse with a mental push.

"I can be there in ten minutes."

"Room 475."

Daniel hung up the phone. He took a deep breath and sat on the cold floor, leaning his back against the wall.

He allowed himself to fall into *The Vale*.

It wasn't what he expected. The word 'vale' insinuated green grasslands or blue lagoons. But it was all white. Not a pure white but a bone white. Everything blended together, the floor, the walls, the ceiling. He wasn't sure anybody would be able to visibly see the distinction between a floor and wall, but it was his own personal Hell, so he knew they were there.

In the center, Junior sat, slumped on the ground in the same manner as Daniel in the real world.

Daniel approached, not worrying about Junior being a threat.

Junior looked up, and without warning, reached for his power, attempting to stop Daniel, to hurt Daniel. Everything Junior tried to do, Daniel could see.

Nothing happened.

Junior did not have power here. Junior was here in essence, but it was Daniel who controlled the environment.

The walls dimmed. Junior stood, bracing himself for a physical fight.

But there wouldn't be a fight. Not again.

They stared at each other for a moment, neither saying anything. Daniel allowed the silence. Junior couldn't take it for long.

"What did you do to me? What is this place?"

Daniel didn't respond.

"So you're not gonna answer? I know this is some of your voodoo shit. You're using this to torture me? You think this is going to help me to learn my lesson? Well, do your worst then because I'm ready."

The walls brightened. The lighting in the room was on a cycle as if *The Vale* had a heartbeat.

"What's the worst you can do to me?" Junior glared into Daniel's eyes, waiting for a response. Whatever answer he found in Daniel's eyes made him frown. "No. No way."

Junior took a step back, his face slack and eyes wide.

Daniel remained still.

"You can't be serious. We're friends. We're fucking friends. I was there for you when you needed me. Who had your back when your mom died? I took you out and got you drunk. Helped you forget your grief. And this is what you do to your friend? I was there for you. So I get punished although you're the same as me. You pretend you're innocent, and your hands aren't just as dirty as mine. You can pretend you don't see the blood on your hands, but that doesn't make them any drier than mine. You wanna know why you deserve to be in the same spot I am? Because of Fatima. Yeah, you ruined the life of an innocent woman. She's crazy now. Whatever... voodoo you touched her with made her go crazy. She's obsessed with that damn quarter, the one you used to poison her mind. She can't work. She can't leave the house. She's not the same. She might as well be a shell of herself.

"And here you are judging me. But you're not God. You don't have a right to judge me. Of course, you're not going to look at yourself though. You have this image of yourself that can't be tainted. You can't see..." Junior broke off, his voice shaky. "You can't see yourself for who you really are. You think you're a good person. But you're not. You're just as much a villain as I am. Except you want to have an ethical clause in your sins so that you can try to say you're better than me and Nicole.

"So how do you justify killing Greg and Tiffany? It wasn't you, it was the bees? That's definitely some bullshit. That means Nicole can say it wasn't her that killed that kid at the bank, it was the bullet. We're all fucking guilty for playing this game. You don't get to punish anybody like you're the fucking..."

Daniel took a step towards Junior who flinched and tried to take a step away, bumping into an invisible wall.

"Shit," Junior said. "Look. Nobody... nobody is innocent. If I'm saying you have to look and see what *your* part in this is, then I should be able to do the same. I know it was me that pulled you into this life. I shouldn't have ever asked you to rob that bank with me. I guess I was... I don't know... I saw you as one of my closest friends. I knew with your power and my power, we could accomplish the impossible. If I could take it back, I would. But we can't change the past. What we can do is make all our wrongs into rights. The money isn't even important to me. Whatever you brought with you, let's give it to the guy's family. I know it won't bring him back, but it might be some comfort to his parents or siblings. I know there's still some good in us, and there's no reason to extinguish the little light we have left. Please."

A loud pop echoed through the open area, the sound of Daniel's jaw unhinging from his skull. His mouth dropped down into an extended, muted scream.

"Nicole told me about your secret world, the one in that mirror. You don't think it's a little sick how obsessed you are with me that you created your own virtual world. All those times you sat on my couch and looked into that mirror, you were living a lie of a life. I don't love you. I will never love you. As much as you dream of us being together, you will never be stepmom... or stepdad to my kids. It's just not how this works. But you can have your fantasy. I don't care about that. Just let me go, and we can call this thing over. Go our separate ways and forget we even knew each other."

Daniel's mouth had grown to supernatural proportions. His tongue flickered, the only sign of his anger.

"Please," Junior whispered. "I have... I have to see my kids again. I can't go without seeing my girls. I need to see them. I love them. Please just let me see them one more time. I need to tell them I love them. Daddy loves them. And no matter what, I did this all for them. One thing I've always known about you is you are a compassionate person. You have empathy, and you care about people. You know how much they mean to me. I just have to see their faces one more time. Izzy looks so much like me. She's like a little curious doll, asking questions about everything. She's gonna be smart. Hopefully, smarter than me. I should've been around more for them. I think if given a second chance, I will be around more for them.

"Please don't do this. They need me."

Daniel's jaw continued to lower, his chin creeping past his chest, an open view into his gullet.

"I can help you get rid of Nicole. I can join your group, become a follower. I can do whatever you want... Please."

Daniel stepped forward and wrapped his arms around
Junior. The warmth of Junior's body familiar, a thought of the
hand mirror fluttered through Daniel's memory.

Junior cried. It started as a soft moan and evolved into
a parade of tears and shoulder heaves. Daniel placed his lips
around the top of Juniors head and began to work his mouth
downward. In the background, a chant resounded.

*"Over the lips and through the gums. Over the lips and
through the gums."* It was originating from Daniel's own
thoughts, a memory from his childhood.

Junior's cries continued as Daniel's mouth enveloped
Junior's eyes and nose. But the cries stopped by the time
Daniel had consumed his shoulders. The only sign Junior was
still alive was the slow rise and fall of his chest.

"Can you promise me you'll give them the money?"
Junior's voice was muffled from Daniel's throat. "Not the
bank money but the haul I have saved from the previous jobs.
I haven't spent everything. I said I was going to give them
gifts and take them to see the world, but I didn't get to it. I
was too busy worrying about myself."

Daniel stopped.

*"Over the lips and through the gums. Over the lips and
through the gums."*

"I want my last gift to them to be that money. It will
give them a better life than what I had. That's all I want for
them is a better life than I had, a better dad. Maybe it's best
I'm not there. It's not like I had a good example myself to
show them. I don't see how else I could be a good influence on
them. I'm doing almost the same shit my dad did. This will
break the cycle. So if you can… if you can find it in your
heart… I know you don't owe me anything, but can you make
sure they get the money."

A moment passed. Daniel couldn't speak with a lower
torso and legs hanging from his unhinged mouth. He nodded,
hoping Junior could feel the intention and continued
devouring.

"Over the lips and through the gums. Over the lips and through the gums."

"Thank you."

After that, Junior didn't say anything else.

• • • • •

Daniel opened his eyes to feel the hot tears flowing down his face. He swiped them away, his left arm reacting sluggishly. He hadn't cried this much since his mom died.

Junior was gone.

A man, muscular and tanned, approached with a woman. Daniel tried to avoid eye contact, hoping they wouldn't be the sympathetic types and ask him what was wrong. He was too weak to pull from *The Grey* and make himself invisible. He was exhausted mentally and physically. The fatigue covered him like a blanket and coaxed him to close his eyes and sleep the pain away.

The couple stopped in front of him. Daniel looked up, the annoyance obvious on his face. But recognition sparked in his mind, although slightly slower due to his lack of energy.

The woman was dressed in a green gown, something too expensive for this drab environment. The dress shimmered almost as much as the jewelry that decorated her neck and wrists. Her lips pursed together, and she nodded at Daniel.

"Is she in there?" Even outside *The Grey* her voice sounded irritated.

Daniel nodded. "The guy she's visiting is in a coma. He won't be waking up. Last I checked, she was still sleeping."

She turned to the man. "Smitty, she's all yours."

Smitty cracked the door open, peeked inside, and closed it without entering. He looked back down at Daniel, concern played across his face, the opposite of the woman's mask of indifference. Daniel's appearance, the hospital gown, bruised body and tear-stained face, was enough to warrant concern. Daniel watched the decision on whether or not to approach the subject play across Smitty's face.

"Are you okay, kid?" He asked, sympathy winning out.

"Nothing some alcohol and time can't heal."

The man nodded. An awkward silence followed. Daniel wondered what he was waiting for. Now was the time for him to strike before Nicole awakened.

"It's not going to take long," Smitty said, more to the woman than Daniel.

Daniel closed his eyes and leaned his head back against the wall, numb to what would happen next.

The sound of the door closing made Daniel lift his eyelids a slit. The man had gone inside. He listened, waiting to hear a scream or a scuffle.

"I am sure you are wondering why I am here." The woman said. A chair slid across the floor, the legs creating a groaning sound as they moved across the linoleum. She sat and leaned forward, peering at Daniel.

"How did you know I was here?" Daniel asked.

"Nothing happens in the spiritual world that La Marieé des Espirits does not know. I am all seeing. Ghiy-āthu'd-Dīn... Damza'in... When you talk to them, you are talking to me. When they talk to you, it is only what I want them to tell you. You are a natural master of *The Grey*, but you will never be able to overpower me in anything spiritual."

She paused, and her hand came towards Daniel. He flinched before he realized she was trying to provide comfort. A wash of emotions danced across her face, and she pulled her hand back.

"Are you here to kill me?" Daniel asked.

"You don't have anything left to fight with. You spent everything you had on a lovers' quarrel. I am here to give you the same offer I have presented you with before. And you still have the option to refuse. But if you decline me a third time, then you will become my enemy. And my enemies do not live long."

She pulled a document out of her bag and placed it on the floor in front of Daniel.

"I want you to live, though." She said. "You have power that I can use. I have knowledge that you can use. That's what your goal was anyway, right? Knowledge?"

Daniel stared at the document; his mind too tired to comprehend the words peering back. He took a deep breath and exhaled it slowly through his nose.

He pushed his palm up towards the woman and nodded. She pricked his finger with an instrument Daniel didn't see. The pain was quick and gone before he had a chance to react. He pressed his bleeding finger at the bottom. With his blood signature, Daniel knew he had lost. He was now a follower of Madame Katrine Comtois. She owned him.

She gathered the paper and placed it back in her bag. She stood, and the chair ground its way back down the hallway. "I will be in touch. Do not be in this area when Smitty finishes doing what he does. It is not going to be pretty."

Daniel looked up to see Madame Katrine Comtois walking away. He watched her green gown grow smaller as she got farther away. He didn't have any more grief to spare on any more losses. Eventually, she turned a corner and disappeared, along with the document where he had just renounced his claim to the Prince of Veils' title.

Little Shop of Horror, (1960). After losing the love of his life, Seymour, a simple nerd that has gained fame and fortune, sacrifices his life to the man-eating plant. Later, a bud sprouts on the plant with the sorrowful face of Seymour as it laments 'I didn't mean it'.

Daniel had lost everything.

Prince of Veils

ACKNOWLEDGMENTS

If I could dedicate this book to anybody, it would be one of my best friends, Arrisha. I remember when I first started tossing around the idea of trying to become an author, I enrolled in a creative writing class but didn't tell her. When I finally got up the courage to bring it up, thinking she would laugh or call me a nerd, she surprised me and said it was a good idea since I read so much. That was the boost I needed to take the plunge into letting strangers enter my mind and see the grotesque and abnormal stories that I've been holding inside. While I think jumping the hurdle of sharing my writing dreams with my friends is a small step, it was also the most important for me.

I would like to thank my creative writing teacher, Lee Sneath aka The Captain. It was his great advice to read my work aloud that helped me see how much work it took to write well and how far I was from being as great as I thought I was.

To my writers' circle (who are also my editors and beta readers), I thank you. Wayne Petersen provided me with the structure of a story. Tank Gunner helped me to appreciate description in the smallest details. Melissa's questions pushed me to research the differences between young adult and adult fiction (of which I prefer adult). Many thanks to Daniel, Diane, Joel, Catherine, Randy and anybody else who has suffered through my first drafts and provided critiques.

www.ingramcontent.com/pod-product-compliance
Lightning Source LLC
Chambersburg PA
CBHW031112030726
47496CB00002BA/505